Catherine Ryan Hyde, the author of several highly acclaimed novels, lives in California.

WHEN YOU WERE OLDER

New York, September 11TH 2001. Russell Ammiano is rushing to work when he gets a phone call that saves his life. As the city he loves is hit by unimaginable tragedy, Russell must turn his back and hurry home to his brother in Kansas . . . Kansas, September 15TH 2001. Ben Ammiano is mentally disabled, and a creature of habit. Any change to his routine sends him into a spin. But now his long lost brother has reappeared, and Ben's simple, ordered world has turned upside down.

Books by Catherine Ryan Hyde
Published by The House of Ulverscroft:

WHEN I FOUND YOU
SECOND HAND HEART
DON'T LET ME GO

CATHERINE RYAN HYDE

WHEN YOU WERE OLDER

Complete and Unabridged

CHARNWOOD
Leicester

First published in Great Britain in 2012 by
Doubleday
an imprint of Transworld Publishers
London

First Charnwood Edition
published 2012
by arrangement with
Transworld Publishers
The Random House Group Limited
London

British Library CIP Data

Hyde, Catherine Ryan.
  When you were older.
  1. Kansas- -Fiction.
  2. Large type books.
  I. Title
  813.6–dc23

  ISBN 978–1–4448–1302–9

Published by
F. A. Thorpe (Publishing)
Anstey, Leicestershire

Set by Words & Graphics Ltd.
Anstey, Leicestershire
Printed and bound in Great Britain by
T. J. International Ltd., Padstow, Cornwall

This book is printed on acid-free paper

For Dad and Monika

Part One

Tumbling Down

15 September 2001

It was four days after the towers fell, and I woke in the morning to see a giant standing over my bed. I was all set to scream a very unmanly scream, but it came out silent. I never managed any sound. Good thing, too. Because that would have scared this particular giant right under the bed.

It only took me a second or two to figure out who it was. And, worse yet, where I was.

Then, as I'd done every time I'd wakened from post-9/11 sleep — usually just a vague nap in somebody's moving car — I ran the list in my mind. What was lost, what had changed.

New York is over, the job is gone, Mom is gone, all my friends went down with the towers, all the work I did to leave Kansas behind for ever has come to nothing. I'm back in Nowhere-ville, right where I swore I'd never be again. And I'm stuck.

It was a perfect storm of nightmare scenarios. All was quite effectively lost.

I looked up again at the skinny giant, who was only my brother Ben. Not that I hadn't expected to bump into him, but . . . I'd gotten in late the night before — well, late by Ben standards — and he'd already gone to bed.

3

He still wouldn't look at anybody. But it was nothing like that old business trick of focusing on a spot between the other person's eyebrows. Ben did everything big. He turned his head away and looked off at a forty-five-degree angle, eyes turned down to the floor.

So there it was. Something that hadn't changed.

'Hey, Buddy,' I said.

'You have to take me to work. You have to get up.'

And those were the first words my brother Ben and I had said to each other in over six years.

I sat up in bed, in just my boxer shorts, blinking. That had not been nearly enough sleep. Not even close. My eyes felt sandy, my stomach borderline.

'Do you have a car?' he asked.

I could tell he was nervous about his ride.

'I don't.'

'Then how are you going to take me to work?'

'Mrs Jespers said I should start using Mom's car.'

'Oh.'

'But she didn't know where Mom kept her keys. Do you know?'

'Yeah,' Ben said. 'I know.'

'Will you tell me?'

'Yeah.'

'Now? Or at least now-ish?'

'She keeps them on the hook by the front door.'

'Good,' I said. 'Progress.' I didn't say, Finally. 'So . . . look . . . do you know who I am?'

'Yeah,' Ben said.

'So you remember me?'

'Yeah.'

'So, who am I?'

'My brother.'

'Right. Good. Do you remember my name?'

'Yeah.'

'Why don't you say it?'

'You didn't say I should. Just if I remember it.'

'Actually, I meant, why don't you? Like, how about saying it?'

'Rusty.'

That old identity, so long left behind, sliced me like jagged metal. Jagged and, well . . . rusty.

'I go by Russell now.'

'Why?'

'Because I'm all grown up.'

'I have to get to work. I have to be there by quarter to seven. I can't be late. Mr McCaskill wouldn't like it if I was late.'

'Sure. Fine. Let's get you to work, then. Have you eaten?'

'Yeah.'

'What did you eat?'

'I ate cereal.'

'How long have you been up?'

'I get up at five.'

'I didn't hear an alarm.'

'I don't have an alarm. I don't need an alarm. Every morning I just get up at five.'

★ ★ ★

'Why aren't you getting in?' I asked, raising my voice a little so he'd hear me, but keeping it

5

down for the neighbors' sake at the same time.

Our mom's old Buick was running, warming up. I could feel the vibrations under my butt. It ran rough. I'd opened the driver's side door to lean out and talk to Ben, who was standing by the open garage door, not getting in.

'It's not one of those doors that closes all by itself,' Ben said. Loudly, with no concern for sleeping neighbors. And impatiently. As if I should have known already. As if everybody in the world should be just as informed as Ben figured they should be. 'I wait here by the garage door till Mom pulls the car out. Then I close the garage door. *Then* I get in.'

I sighed, and backed the car carefully out of the garage. I hadn't driven in years. In fact, I no longer had a valid license. But this was hardly the time to address any of that.

Ben jumped into the passenger seat and buckled his shoulder belt. I threw Mom's Buick into reverse again.

'You can't leave the driveway,' he said. Before I could even ask why not, he said, 'You can't leave the driveway till your seat belt is on.'

I nodded a couple of times, and put on the belt. It was the fastest, most stress-free way to settle the issue.

I glanced over at Ben as we drove. Gathering up six years' worth of changes. But as far as I could see, he just looked older. He was over six foot six, which of course I hadn't expected to change. Still lanky and skinny and long, with a looseness in his joints, like the world's weirdest example of a young horse; though Ben himself

6

no longer looked young. His brown hair was longer, shaggy. Probably just a lack of maintenance, but it looked purposeful. It looked like a style someone would wear to seem unconcerned and cool. Girls and young women traditionally found Ben absolutely irresistible. Especially when he was silent and standing still. They thought he was being enigmatic. Fascinatingly reserved. Until he spoke. Then they hurried off to tend to some important business they'd only briefly forgotten.

'Turn here,' Ben said.

'Aren't you forgetting something?'

'No.'

'I think you are.'

'What, then?'

'To tell me which way I should turn.'

'That way,' he said, pointing right.

Every street, every building that rolled by, was a scene straight out of my worst and most common recurring nightmare: suddenly waking up to find myself back in this bizarrely tiny town where I'd been stranded for the first eighteen years of my life. So I tried to experience it that way. As a bad dream. It was easier and less upsetting than accepting it as my actual reality.

Ben's voice startled me. 'You want to know . . . what?'

'What?'

'You want to know . . . something?'

'Oh. That kind of what. OK. Tell me something.'

'In this big city. There are these big buildings.

7

And somebody flew a plane. Into them. I mean, two planes. And they burned up. The buildings, not the planes. Well, both.'

'I know, Buddy. I was there.'

'You were? You're not burned up.'

'I was close enough to see it, but not close enough to get burned up.'

'Oh,' Ben said. 'You want to know . . . something else?'

'Sure,' I said, though it was not entirely true.

'Where'd you go, Buddy?'

I pulled in one long, forced breath and then slowly let it leave again. I knew sooner or later he'd have questions. But I really thought the first one would be about Mom.

'I went away to college. You knew that.'

'Oh. Did you . . . what do you call that? When you finish? School.'

'Graduate.'

'Yeah. Did you?'

'I did.'

'When did you?'

'About two years ago.'

'Oh.'

A block or two rolled by in awkward silence.

'Then I went to New York.'

'New York! That's the name of that big city where the buildings . . . '

'Right, Buddy. I know.'

'You want to know something else?' He didn't wait to hear if I wanted that or not. 'I know a lot about bagging groceries. It's not as easy as it looks. There's a lot to know. You shouldn't put too many glass bottles and jars together cause

8

they can hit against each other and break. And no eggs on the bottom. And no bread on the bottom. You can put some fruit on the bottom, if it's hard like a coconut, but not if it's soft like peaches. And it all has to balance, otherwise it's hard for people to carry. And it can't be so heavy that it breaks right through the bottom of the bag. And I bet you didn't know there was so much to know about it.'

'I guess I didn't,' I said, suddenly thinking I would kill for a cigarette. I hadn't smoked in more than four years. And I had watched the towers fall without ever once craving a smoke.

'I bet I know more about it than you do.'

I couldn't tell if he was feeling petulant or proud. Or both.

'Definitely, you do.'

'I bet you didn't think there was anything I knew better than you.'

'You used to know everything better than me.'

'I did? I don't remember that.'

'Well, you did.'

'But I don't remember. It's there. It's right there. Gerson's Market. Right there on the corner.'

I pulled into the parking lot. Stopped. Waited for him to get out. But he seemed to have lost his sense of rush. I glanced at my watch. He had three whole minutes to spare. He unbuckled his seat belt, but didn't otherwise move.

'Hey, Buddy,' he said. 'Want to know something?'

'Sure,' I said. But I already knew I wouldn't like it.

9

'When's Mom coming back?'

My lungs filled up with air all on their own. Not that they didn't usually. But in this case their capability surprised me. Did we really want to do this at the start of his work day?

'She's not.'

Ben shook his head. 'She always does.'

'And she would now. If she could. But she can't.'

'That doesn't sound right. You don't know Mom like I do. She always comes back. I only wanted to know when.'

He jumped out, slamming the door behind him.

I watched him move the long stilts of his legs toward the door as if they belonged to somebody else entirely. I'd had plenty of time to see that gait before going off to college, but I still hadn't shaken the image of the way he'd used to walk. So self-possessed as to be dangerous. A magnet for girls and trouble. And that was back when the girls never hurried away.

The market was only half-lit inside. Obviously not open. Ben rapped on the automatic sliding door, and in time a woman came and opened it with a key and slid it aside manually. Just enough for Ben to squeeze in.

And I thought, That's my older brother. What can you do?

★　★　★

I was cruising back slowly toward the house . . . I still absolutely refused to call it home

. . . and I saw the kitchen lights on in a little corner bakery. I couldn't tell if the place was open or not.

The bakery was new. Or, at least, less than six years old. I was pretty sure there had used to be a dry cleaner's on that corner.

I pulled up and parked out front. The street felt weirdly empty for nearly seven in the morning. Like one of those old science-fiction movies where you find out you're the only person left alive. Whatever happened to the concept of Kansans getting up early? A lot of work shifts started at seven here, rather than the big-city nine. But if people were awake, they were hidden.

I read the name of the place, carefully stenciled on to one of the front windows. NAZIR'S BAKED GOODS.

So much for the idea that nothing ever changed around here.

The door was unlocked, and I stuck my head inside.

'You open?' I called.

I saw a young woman's head come up in the softly lit kitchen area behind the counter. She had jet-black hair, tied up in back, but not covered with a hairnet or a baker's hat. Her eyes were more black than dark brown, unless it was just the lighting. Her short white tee-shirt sleeves were rolled up almost to her shoulders. She was small. Thin and small.

'Not quite,' she called back. With some kind of accent, but I couldn't place it. 'We open at seven. But . . . what do you want? The Danish are still in the oven, but the donuts are done. You just

11

want coffee and a donut?'

Suddenly I wanted coffee and a donut more than I'd wanted to get out of this town as a kid. More than I'd wanted a cigarette while talking to Ben. It had been days since I'd enjoyed the smallest luxury or felt any pleasure at all. Coffee and a donut suddenly loomed like the promised land. I would be maddeningly incomplete until I reached them.

I wanted to say, You have no idea how much. But I didn't want her to think I was some kind of freak.

'That would be great,' I said.

I closed the door behind me and approached her counter. The display case was not yet filled with donuts. They were still on racks in the back, with her.

'What do you want?' she asked. 'We have glazed, crullers, powdered sugar, cinnamon twists . . . no jelly-filled yet. I haven't had time to fill them.'

Again I struggled with her accent, but it just felt unfamiliar.

'What's good?' I asked, feeling about as adept at conversation as my brother Ben.

'It's all good. But the glazed are still warm. Something special about eating a donut when it's still warm.'

'Glazed, then.'

She pulled a little individual sheet of tissue paper out of a box and used it to pick up a donut without touching it. She placed it on a small paper plate for me, leaving the tissue wrapped around its sides.

12

'Help yourself to coffee. Oh. Do you need me to put out sugar or milk?'

'No. That's fine. Just black. Thanks. What do I owe you?'

'I haven't opened the cash register yet. You can pay on your way out.'

I'd actually intended to take my coffee and donut to go. But, since I couldn't pay for them until after seven, I sat.

I sipped the coffee. It was dark and strong, and made from some kind of good quality imported beans. Definitely not gas-station coffee, which I'd been subsisting on for days. I took a bite of the glazed donut, and my eyes literally tried to roll back in my head, it was that good.

I looked up to see her watching me.

'You've created magic,' I said.

'It's just fresher than you're used to.'

Then I sat in silence for a minute or two, looking out the window. A few cars rolled by, but it didn't seem like enough. I drank and wolfed, treating the food and drink like a lifeline. I consumed them like a dying man who thinks he might still, just barely, be able to save himself.

And then, predictably, they were gone. And I missed them.

I got up and poured myself a coffee refill.

'Another one?' she asked. 'You seem hungry.'

'That would be great.'

'I have some cream-cheese Danish just ready to come out.'

I watched her pull on a long hot-mitt and slide a tray out of the oven. She set the tray on her

13

wooden work table and levered a spatula under the biggest, nicest Danish. I brought her my paper plate, so as not to be wasteful, and she tipped the Danish on to it.

'Careful,' she said. 'Hot.'

I sat back down with it, watching her roll out a big piece of dough and then cut it, with quick motions of a knife, into pieces whose purpose I didn't understand.

I was wondering if she was younger than me — and if so by how much — when she spoke.

'You're new in town,' she said, with the accent that I still hadn't figured out.

'No, I'm old in town. I was born here. I went off to college six years ago and never came back.'

'Until now,' she said, looking up from her work.

'Yes, until now.'

I wasn't going to answer any more questions unless asked.

'Why now?' she asked a moment later.

'My mother died.'

'Oh. I'm so sorry. I should never have asked.'

'No, it's OK. So I promised myself I was done with this place for ever. And I built a whole new life. And now all of a sudden the new life is gone, and I'm back here, and I'm stuck.'

'Why stuck? Why can't you go again, after honoring your mother?'

'Because somebody has to take care of my brother. And nobody else wants the job.'

'Is he much younger, your brother?'

'No. He's older, in fact. I think he just turned thirty. Unless I'm off by a year. No. I'm not. He's

14

six years older. So he just turned thirty. Last month.'

And I hadn't so much as sent him a two-dollar card.

'If he's older, then . . . Oh!' she said suddenly. 'I know who you are. You're Ben's brother.'

Small towns. Gotta love 'em.

'You know Ben?'

'Sure, everybody knows Ben. The bag boy. Over at Gerson's Market. He's very sweet. Everybody likes him. I heard about his mother. Your mother. Very sad. She was very young. I'm sorry for your loss.'

I had no idea what to say. So I said nothing. I watched her load tray after tray of donuts into the display case. But then, when she was done, I decided it didn't look like enough donuts. Not for a thriving bakery on a Saturday morning. Then again, based on the number of customers she had at opening — and it was by then a minute or two after seven — this was hardly a thriving bakery.

'You don't look like Ben,' she said, without looking up from her work. 'He's so tall. And you're . . . '

'Puny?'

'I was going to say, compact.'

'We're only half-brothers. We had different fathers.'

She leaned her bare arms on to the clear glass counter and looked right into my eyes. I looked away. I'm still not sure why.

'I heard a rumor about Ben's brother, but maybe it's one of those things that people say in

15

a small town, and maybe it's not even true.'

'That's all very possible,' I said. 'What did you hear?'

'That you worked on the one-hundred-and-fifth floor of one of the World Trade Center buildings, and so I thought probably Ben's brother is dead.'

'That last part didn't quite pan out.'

'The rest is true?'

'No. I worked on the one-hundred-and-fourth floor.'

'Seriously?'

'It's not the kind of thing people joke about these days.'

'So you weren't at work when it happened.'

'I was trying to be.' I stopped dead for a minute, gauging how much of this I was really prepared to tell. Testing it like an old manual dipstick in a gasoline tank. 'I was doing my best to get out the door. And then the phone rang. And I was late. And so I almost didn't get it. I almost let it go. But then for some reason I did. Get it. And it was my old next-door neighbor. Telling me about my mom. Telling me he had Ben, and he wasn't willing to have him much longer. So I called in to work and started booking a flight. Of course all the flights were grounded before the morning was half-over . . . '

I was careful not to look at her as I spoke. I looked down at my Danish, touched it. It had cooled to eating temperature. I wolfed it down in six bites. It was incredible.

When I finished, and looked up, she was still leaning on the counter watching me.

'So your mother saved your life,' she said.

'Not purposely. But yeah.'

'How do you know not purposely?'

'She couldn't have known.'

'How do you know what people can know? People can do all manner of things if it's important enough. If a mother can lift a car off her son, maybe she can die at just the right time to save him.'

I didn't like talking about my mom. To put it as politely as possible, I hadn't broken through to any kind of acceptance in the last four days. I was still firmly planted in the initial stage of grief: denial. Her death was still something I was dreaming. A bad dream. But a dream, nonetheless.

'You really think that's possible?' I asked, and then slugged down the last of my coffee.

She walked around the counter, and for one awful moment I thought she was coming right at me. That she might touch me, try to comfort me. Some kind of unbearable human interaction like that. Instead, she flipped on the lights in the seating area. I winced, and covered my eyes with one hand.

'Sorry,' she said. 'You never know. In a world like this, you never know what's possible. So I figure, don't say it's possible, because you don't know. But, then again, don't say it's not possible. Because you don't know that, either.'

Suddenly, I couldn't get out of there fast enough.

'What do I owe you for all this?'

'On the house,' she said, walking back to her

own side of the counter.

'Seriously? Why?'

'Because your mother just died, and you came home all the way from New York to take care of your brother, Ben. And so I say the least somebody can do is give you coffee and something to eat.'

I thanked her and ran. Or nearly ran. I wondered if she was as aware as I was of my sudden desperate need to get away.

I looked back through the window and saw her looking out at me. Watching me go.

I read the name of the bakery again. Nazir's. That and the accent came together in my brain. And it answered a question. It explained why nobody else but me had come in for coffee and a donut that morning.

I stuck my head back in the door.

'Where are you from?' I asked.

'Wichita.'

'I meant originally. Not that I care.'

Her black eyes burned right through me.

'You care.'

'Not in a bad way, I don't.'

She turned her eyes back down to her table again. 'Egypt,' she said. 'We are Egyptian. Naturalized. We are not terrorists.'

I didn't ask who the other part of 'we' was.

'I'm sorry. I really wasn't meaning to pry.'

'What did you do there?'

It was too out of context. It sailed right over my head.

'What did I do where?'

'On the one-hundred-and-fourth floor of the

World Trade Center.'

'Oh. That. Advertising. Hatcher, Swift & Dallaire. It's an ad agency. Or . . . I guess it *was* an ad agency. A good one. I was lucky to work there.'

'You're young to be a New York ad man.'

'That's why it was lucky.'

★ ★ ★

I drove home — back — thinking that, in New York, people would get the difference between a terrorist and a naturalized Egyptian. And maybe even care. But this was not New York.

I was guessing Nazir's Baked Goods had been having trouble with cash flow for . . . oh, about four days. Assuming they hadn't been all along.

★ ★ ★

When I got back, I found myself curled in the middle of the living room rug. Literally. I don't remember getting there. I just found myself there. I just came to awareness on my side on the rug, in a fetal position. I don't think I fell, because nothing hurt. I think I climbed down there. But I have no memory.

I shook, and I sweated, and at one point I buried my face against my own knees and let loose a throat-straining scream. One good pull-every-muscle-in-my-body scream.

Call it a delayed reaction.

14 September 2001

It was three days after the towers fell, and I'd been half-walking, half-hitchhiking for about an hour. I mean, since my last ride had dropped me off. Not in total. In total I'd been hitchhiking for most of three days.

Three days ago, when I'd been closer to New York, my thumb and I had been greeted like a civilian survivor of an honorable and justified war. But I was very far from New York by now. In fact, I had only about five miles left to go.

It was also nearly nine o'clock, and dark. People don't like to pick up male hitchhikers after dark. Doesn't let them get a good look at the hitchhiker first.

The car was more like a Jeep or a Land Rover, very old and hulking. I turned when I heard the poorly muffled motor, and stuck my thumb out. The headlights nearly blinded me. I squinted into the light, and watched him roar by without even slowing down. Then, a split second later, the brakes squealed as the monster skidded to a stop. While I was wondering what to make of this, the driver threw into reverse and backed up to where I was standing.

I waited while he leaned over and rolled down the old-fashioned, low-tech crank window.

'Rusty?'

'Oh,' I said. 'It's you. Larry.'

Larry Del Veccio was one of the guys I'd gone to high school with. This may sound like a remarkable coincidence. But in a town with a population of 2,250, not so startling.

'I go by Russell now,' I said. Which so did not matter in that moment.

'Sorry about the headlights. Have to keep 'em on bright because one of the low-beams is burned out. Get in, man. You're going home, right?'

'I'm going . . . yeah. To . . . the house. My mom's house. You know.'

I refused to call it home.

'Get in.'

I observed myself, as if through someone else's eyes, as I got in, levering my huge backpack over the passenger's seat. My lack of sleep was catching up with me big.

'Really sorry about your mom,' he said as he gunned the big beast back out on to the little highway.

'Thanks.'

'So unexpected.'

'It was.'

'She was so young. Or at least she seemed pretty young.'

'She was fifty-four.'

'That's young. I mean, to die.'

'It is.'

Larry pulled a pack of Marlboros out of his shirt pocket, and pressed the dashboard lighter in with a click. I think he was trying to keep busy. I think conversing with me was not soaking up enough of his evening.

'Vince and I went by and saw Ben,' he said, gearing up for another try.

'That was nice of you. How does he seem?'

'I don't know. The same.'

'Does he seem to even get it? About our mom?'

'Hard to say with Ben. If he does, we didn't see it. So, listen. You were in New York, right? I heard you were in New York. I heard you work in one of the World Trade Center towers, but I'm guessing that's one of those small-town, get-it-wrong things.'

'No, that was true. Past tense, though. I *worked* in the towers. Nobody works in them now except forensic specialists and fire crews. And even then it depends on your definition of the word 'in'.'

'Right. I knew that. So . . . where were you? When it happened?'

'Home. I was a little late getting out of the house.'

'Whoa. So you would've been . . . '

'Yeah. I would have been. But, as it turns out, I'm not.'

'So, did you hear it, or turn on the TV, or . . . ?'

'I live right across the river from lower Manhattan. I had a perfect view.'

'You watched it?'

I didn't answer. It wasn't a decision so much. More an absence of emotional fuel. Instead I watched as Larry pressed the lighter to the end of his cigarette, then puffed until it was drawing well. He cracked the window to draw out some of the smoke.

'How'd you feel?' he asked.

And I thought, Oh, crap. Now I'm on a therapist's couch? And then I thought, You really need an answer to that? Like you're thinking I might say great? I watched it and felt great? But I knew it was just my exhaustion, and really not so much Larry's failing. So I said nothing at all.

Larry took a long pull off the Marlboro, tucked high in the crook of his first two fingers.

'Christ,' he said. 'That must've been something.'

'Look. Sorry. I'm just really tired. I haven't slept in days. I mean, maybe an hour once or twice, but nothing really. I've been on the road this whole time. We'll get together. Catch up. I just need a couple nights' sleep.'

'Have to be soon, though. I'm shipping out.'

'To . . . ?'

'Don't know yet. We'll see. I'm National Guard. I been National Guard six years, man. Nearly as long as you been gone. We been ready for six years. Three of us from Norville: me and Paul Kager and Vince Buck. You remember them, right? The National Guard Three. We'll be the first to ship out. First, I think they'll put us on defending some key US targets. But if we go to war the Guard'll be the first ones over there. You know. Afghanistan. I hope so. I'd like to give 'em a fresh look at what they started.'

'Sounds pointless,' I said.

I didn't mean the part about defending. I

meant the part about what he wanted to give them. I actually hadn't mean to say it at all. Any of it. I'd thought I'd only thought it. But then I heard it in my ears.

'What?' Larry asked. 'What'd you say, man?'

It was clear, in the way he said it, that he'd heard me just fine.

'Oh, crap, Larry. Look, I'm sorry. I'm just like the freaking walking wounded right now. I don't know what I'm saying at this point.'

A long silence. Then I felt his hand clap down on my shoulder.

'Yeah, well. Look. We got you home.'

I looked up to see him pull into the driveway of the house I'd lived in for eighteen years. From the day I came home from the maternity hospital to the day I went off to college, believing in my heart that I'd left Nowhere-ville for good and for ever.

I still refused to call it home.

*   *   *

I went first to the Jesperses, next door, thinking they had Ben.

I stood in front of their door with my oversize pack at my feet, and knocked, expecting Phil to answer. Instead I got his wife, Patty. She looked pretty ruined, not to mention more than six years older. Her long hair was uncombed, and she brushed it off her face with her hands. I was pretty sure I saw some gray I'd never seen before.

'Oh, my God,' she said. 'Oh, thank God. You finally made it.'

'Yeah. Sorry it took so long.'

'Well, honey, it's not your fault.' She moved in and trapped me in a bear hug I'd have been happier without. 'I mean, no planes. I heard all the rental cars in the country were rented out, even.'

'Yeah. I heard that, too. From every rental car company I called.'

'Well, we're just so relieved to see you. And, first of all, before I say another word, we are so, so sorry about your mom. Poor baby, you must just be devastated. I didn't want to miss saying that. But . . . and please don't take this the wrong way, honey . . . we love Ben. No way we'd let him be on his own, even for a couple or three days. But, honestly, honey, we had no idea. We really don't have the patience for it. Not at all. We raised two of our own, and that's enough for the whole 'Are we there yet?' thing.'

'Yeah. How *is* Mark, anyway?' One of the other guys I'd gone to high school with, not to mention a same-age next-door neighbor for eighteen years.

'Oh, fine, but now he's talking about enlisting, and I'd like to wring his neck.'

'Lot of that going around,' I said.

'Well, I guess folks figure something needs to be done.'

That's when it hit me that I had no energy for digressions. Even though this one was my own fault. I'd have to be more careful.

'But . . . back to Ben. You told him about . . . '

'Oh, sure, honey. We told him everything, as nice as we could, we even took him in to your

25

mom's doctor so he could explain to Ben all about what an aneurysm is. And then on the way home he asks, for about the hundredth time, when she's coming back. We're just about running out of . . . well, we just can't take much more.'

'Send him out, then.'

'Oh, he's not here.'

'He's not? Mr Jespers said — '

'We tried, honey, God knows we tried. But you know how your brother is. Everything's got to be familiar. Got to be his own little routine. So we've been putting him to bed in his own bed, and then the last few nights Phil slept on the couch over there, case he needed something in the night, or got scared. But tonight we figured, from when you called and all, that you'd be in soon enough. Ben goes to bed at eight. Every night. Eight. Not a minute sooner. Not a minute later. Wait, let me get you the key.'

She disappeared from the doorway, and I stood, shivering slightly. I looked up into the yellowish, bug-repellent porch light and squinted. I was so tired that just for an instant I lost track of my surroundings. Things whited out, the way they do in that split second just before you lose consciousness.

Part of me was wishing she wouldn't come back. Because I didn't have the energy for her. But that was stupid, of course. I needed the key.

A second later she reappeared, and pressed it into my hand.

'You'll have to take him to work in the morning. He goes in early.'

'Ben has a job?'

'Oh, yeah. Sure, honey. You didn't know? Ben's been bagging groceries for near on to two and a half years. It's working out real good. Everybody likes him. Somebody has to drive him there and pick him up, though. He can't ride the bus. Your mom tried to teach him to ride the bus, but he got lost every time. Every damn time. One time it took her half the day to find him again, even though the whole damn town was on alert to be looking out for him.'

Mom's older son got a job bagging groceries right around the time 'her baby' got a job with one of the best ad firms in New York. Much as I was accustomed to Ben's condition, this seemed weird.

I needed to get out of this conversation. I needed sleep.

'I don't have a car, though.'

'Take your mom's car.'

'Oh. Right. Do you know where she keeps her keys?'

'No. I don't. Sorry. But maybe Ben does.'

Sure. Cling to that, let's.

'Well, goodnight,' I said. 'Thanks for looking after him.'

'It was an emergency, honey, but thank God you got home. That's all I can say. Phil and I are just too old for the whole Ben thing. Maybe you'll do better, cause you're young. Good luck.'

'Thanks,' I said.

'You're gonna need some luck.'

I didn't answer that one. I just cut across the lawn to my childhood home, thinking, Don't you

27

really figure that last comment would have been better left unsaid?

★ ★ ★

All the lights were off in the house, but when I opened the front door with my key and stepped into the living room, I could see everything clearly. Too clearly. The room was suffused with a sort of ghostly glow. In my altered state of exhaustion, it seemed nearly supernatural. But it didn't take long to figure out there was a night light in every room.

I wandered over to the mantel first, because the photos drew me.

My mom and dad at their wedding. My mom and dad with Ben and me, ages maybe four and ten. I looked at the sharp focus in Ben's eyes, the slight glint of defiance and mischief. I'd known Ben that way for the first eight years of my life. Then I'd lived with the changed Ben for ten. I wondered if I was really sure who I expected to meet again in the morning, though my rational mind certainly knew what was what in that situation.

Then there was the photo of me winning statewide track in high school, and Ben at age twelve, holding a twenty-inch trout in a tippy canoe (the tippiness didn't show in the photo, but I remembered) on Council Grove Lake.

I looked again at the photo of my parents, and was hit with a strange and disturbing thought.

I'm an orphan.

Then I shook it away again. Orphans were

28

little waifs, dependant minors. I was a grown man whose parents were both dead. Lots of adults fell into that category. Granted, most were older than me.

Oddly, that chain of thought did not bring me dangerously close to tears. The next one did.

I looked at the mantel itself, and got a sudden flash of our family's Christmas village.

Every year my mom would take down all the photos and knick-knacks and construct the village with decorations that spent the rest of the year hiding, boxed, in the attic, just waiting for their season to shine.

She used stacks of books for hills, then covered them with chicken wire and cotton batting. The little houses had holes in the back for the bulb of a Christmas light to be inserted, so the houses on the hills glowed with light, as though occupied. A little horse-drawn sled spent the whole season headed down a cotton hill toward a mirror lake it would never reach. On the lake, a tiny porcelain skunk ice-skated, and a family of inch-high deer drank from the silver water.

And that was the spot where I nearly lost it. But I held tight. I was too unguarded to let anything like real emotion happen now. It would flip me and pin me, and I would lose. Maybe permanently. I had to rest and be strong enough for that fight.

I wandered into the glowing kitchen in search of something to eat. But I only got smacked again. On the door of the refrigerator, held on with food magnets (an ear of corn, a strawberry, a carrot, an ice-cream cone, a banana), were all five of the postcards I'd sent my mom from New York.

First I was merely struck by their dullness and lack of imagination. The Empire State building. Rockefeller Center. The Statue of Liberty. The Brooklyn Bridge. Had I really put so little time and attention into my choices? Or had I thought my choices would seem appropriate from this end of the world? Now I stood on this end of the world with them, and they just seemed sad.

The fifth card was a photo of the World Trade Center. The Twin Towers. It zapped my body with a jolt of electricity. I could feel it buzzing for many seconds, eerie and slow to fade. I pulled the postcard off the fridge, dropping its ice-cream cone magnet on to the kitchen linoleum. I bent down and picked it up, feeling vaguely dizzy, and stuck the postcard back on the fridge with the photo side in. So I wouldn't have to look at it.

Of course, that left the message side out.

It was dated 30 April 1999. 'Dear Mom,' it said. 'Here it is, the job of a lifetime. I'm on top of the world. Wish me luck. Love, Rusty.'

Rusty? Why did I sign it Rusty? I'd left that name behind on my way to college.

Amazingly, none of that was the genuine zap I referred to.

It was the role reversal. The surrealistic role reversal. I'd sent those postcards from a place I viewed as the true world, the only important world, as if dropping them into a void. Almost as if the address on the card had never existed, or at the very least, was not entirely real.

Maybe that's why I had signed it 'Rusty'. What did it matter, in fiction?

Now I stood on the wrong end of the cards' journey. And this place was all too real. And the place I'd believed in so strongly, invested in so fully, had crumbled like a house of cards.

I shook my head a little, and tried to clear away any stray thoughts and feelings. I told myself I'd feel better after something to eat.

To my surprise, the fridge was brimming with food. Casserole dish after casserole dish, some covered with foil, some with plastic wrap, some with their own matching Pyrex covers. And Tupperware. Tupperware abounded.

Then I realized I shouldn't have been surprised. Family friends and neighbors had been bringing food for Ben. Of course they had. People do that when somebody dies. Even if the survivor is fully capable. Even if the grieving survivor isn't Ben.

I rummaged through a few casserole dishes and settled on a noodle dish with some kind of ground meat in a creamy-looking sauce. It looked like a genuine stroganoff, and very unlike anything that could be purchased at a gas station mini-mart.

I heated a mound of it in the microwave. But I only ate two or three bites.

It tasted like something made from a mix, out of a box. The sauce tasted like chemicals. Like butter and milk stirred together with a packet of artificial flavoring. But that wasn't the worst of

31

it. It tasted familiar. It tasted like my childhood. My personal past.

I dumped it into the garbage and left the plate soaking in the sink.

I stuck my head into my old bedroom. It had been converted into a TV room, with two stuffed chairs, and Mom's sewing machine on a table in the corner. But my trophy case was still there, my track trophies still on display.

The door to Ben's bedroom was closed, but a spill of glowing light under the door told me his night light was brighter than all the rest. Maybe brighter than all the rest put together. I didn't open the door. I let sleeping brothers lie.

I wandered into my mom's room, knowing I didn't want to sleep there, and also knowing it was the only bed available to me.

I hauled in my backpacker's five-day pack and pulled out my running shoes, my clean underwear, my dirty laundry from the trip.

I used my mom's bathroom, and while I did, I looked at the oversize clawfoot tub and decided a bath would be just the thing. So I ran one. It was deep and it was hot.

I eased my tired body into it and lay back, eyes closed. I sighed.

Next thing I knew, I was bolting upright in the tub, sputtering, spitting bathwater out of my nose and mouth. So that was too dangerous. I was too sleepy for a bath.

I dried off and put on a pair of clean boxers. A tee-shirt would have been nice to sleep in, but I didn't have one clean. I took a deep breath and climbed into my mom's bed. Where I knew I was not allowed. With only one exception: if I'd had a nightmare.

Silently, in my head, I told my mother I believed this just might qualify.

13 September 2001

Two days after the towers fell, I caught a ride in the dark at a little after five thirty in the morning. I knew I was on Interstate Route 70, and that I was west of Indianapolis, but I didn't know if I was still in Indiana, or if I had passed into Illinois some time in the night.

Lots of things are a mystery in the dark. Maybe that's why as many people are afraid of the light as the other way around.

'I don't usually stop for hitchhikers,' the driver said, before I was even granted permission to get in. He was sixtyish, with hair that could have been blond, or gray, or both, shaved in an old-fashioned buzz cut. He wore a jersey in a most alarming shade of orange. 'But I know people are still having trouble getting around. Getting home. Is that your situation?'

'Yes, sir, it is. I'm trying to make it from New York back to Kansas for a funeral, and I booked a plane, but . . . well, you know.'

'Go on and get in, then,' he said.

We drove in silence for a time. How long a time, I'd be hard-pressed to say. Could have been ten minutes, or it could have been half an hour. Or maybe I even dozed briefly and never knew.

'Whereabouts in Kansas?' he asked suddenly, startling me.

'Nowhere-ville,' I said, forgetting, for just a brief second, to censor myself. Forgetting that some things were meant solely for the silence of the inside of my head. 'Sorry. I meant Norville. Norville, Kansas.'

'I wondered . . . '

'When we were kids, we always called it Nowhere-ville. You know. Norville. Nowhere-ville. The temptation was irresistible.'

He didn't comment on that, though I expected he was a man who could have resisted the temptation. Instead he just said, 'I never heard of Norville, Kansas.'

'Thanks for helping me prove my point.'

Another long silence. Long enough to lull me back into the hypnosis of the road.

'Piece of tough luck,' the man said, startling me again. 'To have to add a funeral on top of all this. Someone close?'

'My mom.'

'Oh dear. Sorry I even asked.'

'It's OK. Yeah. Bad timing. Especially since nearly everybody I knew was in one of those towers.'

He seemed to consider that for a time. As though it were a thing that might or might not be true.

'Which one?' he asked, and it seemed like an odd question.

'North Tower. One World Trade Center.'

'Anybody you know make it out alive?'

'Just one that I know of. He was late getting

35

in, like me. My office was above the . . . you know . . . the floors that took a direct hit. I heard on the radio news they're figuring nobody survived above the hit line.'

Interesting. Interesting how I talked about it as though I were describing the plot of a movie I'd seen two days previously.

We didn't talk for a few minutes. I looked out the window to see that the stars had faded, and the barest hint of morning was glowing in the side mirror, to the east. Directly behind us.

My cell phone rang, and it felt as though someone had dropped a heavy object into my stomach from a long way up. Maybe a cinder block. Maybe an anvil.

I thought, Please don't be Kerry. I looked. It was Kerry.

'Mind if I get that?' I asked my driver.

'No, why would I mind?'

'I don't know. Just seemed rude.'

'Go ahead.'

I flipped the phone open. 'Kerry,' I said.

My mouth felt dry. Like flannel. I could feel a pounding in my ears.

'They found him,' she said.

But I was already armored for it. So her words just hit the armor and slid off.

'Jeff?'

'Who the hell else, Russell? Who the hell else would I call you and say, 'They found him' about?'

True, it had been a dumb question. But this was a new side of her. There was no reason for her to speak in anger to me. Other than having

36

just lost her husband. I decided to consider the circumstances and let it go by.

'They actually found his body? I thought that was impossible under — '

'He jumped.'

I felt a pinching sensation at the very back of my tongue, on both sides, like a hit of lemon juice, and my stomach tipped dangerously. I opened my mouth to speak, but nothing came out. I closed my eyes and tried not to see the image. The view I'd seen through my telescope two days earlier. Of course, that hadn't been Jeff. At least, reason held that it hadn't been. But it really didn't matter. Because it had been somebody.

'When are you coming back?' Kerry asked, a needy, gaping black hole in her voice that I'd never heard before. Then again, these were remarkable times.

'I haven't even gotten there yet.'

'But . . . what do you think? How long do you think you'll have to stay?'

'I have no idea.'

'It takes, like . . . what? Five days or so to plan a funeral?'

'Kerry. I haven't even figured out who's going to take care of Ben.'

That was a lie. Actually. I had. I'd figured out that I was the only candidate.

'I need you here,' she said, breaking down.

My heart went out to her . . . then turned and ran like a spooked coyote.

I glanced at the driver in my peripheral vision. That was why I hadn't wanted it to be Kerry.

That was why I hadn't wanted to take the call.

Well. One of the reasons.

'Can we talk about this later?'

'What's going on there, Russell?' Between sobs.

'Nothing. Really. I just got a ride. This nice gentleman is driving me through Indiana — '

'Illinois,' the nice gentleman said. In case there was any doubt as to whether he was listening. How could he not hear, though? It was the front seat of a goddamn car.

'Illinois. And I would just feel better if we could talk later, in private.'

'This feels bad, Russell. What're you saying? You're coming back, right?'

'I'd rather talk about this later.'

'I'm going to see you again, right? Because I've got nothing here. I lost everything, Russell. You're coming back. Right?'

I swallowed a little of the flannel in my mouth with great effort. The silence lasted too long, and we both knew it.

'He was my best friend, Kerry.'

'What are you saying?'

'Not over his dead body. You know.'

'I think I'm going to be sick,' she said.

And, though it's strange to report, I sat still in the car, my cell phone to my ear, realizing I didn't know this woman at all. Realizing that the phenomenon of attraction — all attraction, not just mine — is a form of illusion. Under the illusion lies a real person. But which one? What person? That's the part you don't get to know. Until it's too late.

'I'll call you when I'm in-between rides. Do you have anybody you can call? Anybody who can be with you?'

A couple of loud sniffles. 'I could call my mother. See if she's home.'

'You called me before you called your mother?'

'I thought . . . '

'Never mind. I'll call you as soon as I can.'

I flipped the phone closed. Awkward silence.

What exactly do you say to a stranger who just overheard all that? What does he say to you?

Apparently nothing.

'You got quiet,' I said after a while.

'It's none of my business,' he said.

I watched the sky lightening.

'I guess I should've let that go to voicemail.'

'I could be wrong,' he said, 'and if I'm wrong I apologize. And even if I'm right, I know it's none of my business. But it's sounding like you were having an affair with your best friend's wife. And I don't know what to say to a man like that. Even if it *is* none of my business. It sort of found its way into my car, though. Otherwise . . . '

'I never touched her. We never touched each other. In any way. Ever. It was just something that happened . . . you know . . . on a feeling level. It was just feelings.'

'Where I come from,' he said, his knuckles pale on the steering wheel, 'you don't even have *feelings* for your best friend's wife.'

A flare of my own anger surprised me.

'Oh, thanks,' I said. 'Thanks for letting me know. You seem to know everything, so . . . care

39

to let me know how I go about not having feelings?'

A long silence. I watched him chew on the inside of his cheek. Then I looked in the side mirror and watched the sky reddening. I figured he was just looking for a place to pull over and let me out.

I looked back to see his right hand extended in my direction, as if he were waiting for me to shake. Which, it slowly dawned on me, he was.

'Accept my apology?' he asked.

'Oh,' I said. A bit dumbfounded.

I still had not shaken the hand.

'You're right,' he said. 'You're absolutely right. I'm sorry. Hearts pretty well do what they do. Can't tell 'em much of anything. I guess it's mostly what you actually *do* that you gotta answer for. So . . . forgive my outburst?'

'There's nothing to forgive,' I said, staring at the hand. I shook it. It felt calloused and dry. 'Everybody's just a little on edge. More emotional than usual.'

'Got that right.'

We rode in silence for a long time. I watched him pull an individually wrapped toothpick from the pocket of his orange jersey and peel back the paper. I expected him to pick his teeth with it. Instead he just held one end in his mouth. The world's smallest cigarette, without all that dangerous smoke and fire.

Insects were hitting the windshield. We were driving through an agricultural landscape, and big bug after big bug tapped the glass, each leaving a whitish splotch to mark the moment of its death.

'Besides,' he said, as if we'd never paused the conversation. 'You told her just exactly the right thing. Not over his dead body.'

I stared at the bugs some more.

'It wasn't as noble as it sounded,' I said.

I remembered a joke my friend Mark had told me in grade school. Well, my acquaintance Mark. I grew up next door to him. But we never really fit quite right.

What's the last thing that goes through a bug's head when it hits your windshield? Its ass.

I didn't think it was funny.

Maybe it's an overload of empathy on my part, or maybe I just have a too-well-developed sense of fairness. The problem with that joke is that it's only funny if you're not a bug. Call it weird, but I can't help putting myself in bug shoes. Hey, that was my uncle Joe's ass. That's my friend Hector on that windshield. And it's not so damn funny.

'It's like this,' I said. 'I just have this . . . aversion . . . to her. Since . . . you know. After what happened. It feels like one of those places you go to stop smoking, and every time you reach for a cigarette, they zap you with electricity. No. That's not a good analogy. Because that's a lot of little things. This is one big thing. It feels like when you eat a whole bunch of a certain kind of food and then get sick. And maybe the food didn't even make you sick. Maybe you ate three plates of fettuccini Alfredo, and then got the stomach flu. And all

41

night you're up, throwing up fettuccini Alfredo. You'll never eat it again. Guaranteed. It's knee-jerk. So don't give me more credit than I deserve.'

We stared out the windshield a while longer. It was light now. It was officially morning.

My driver was chewing up one end of his toothpick. I wasn't sure how he could even see the road through all those bug splats.

As if reading my mind, he said, 'I'll have to stop at the next filling station. Clean the windshield proper. Won't help to put on the washers. That only makes it worse. Smears it. Damned inconvenient.'

'Not as inconvenient as it was for the bugs.'

He laughed, one little snort.

'Good point.'

'I lied to her.' I was in full-on confession mode. And we both knew it. 'She told me to go get my telescope. I have this telescope. A guy at work gave it to me. It's not so much for astronomy. You can't see much of the stars in the city anyway. For him I think it was a peeping Tom thing. I used to use it to look at the towers. Mostly the North Tower. My tower, I used to call it. It was such a dream for me . . . to actually work there. I used to find the one-hundred-and-fourth floor with the tele-scope, and then find my actual office window. It was just a thing I liked to do. At the beginning. I hadn't done it for a while. So Kerry knew I had this telescope. So she told me to go get it. We were talking on the phone. She was watching on TV, and I was watching

42

out my window. I live in Jersey City, right across the river from lower Manhattan. We watched the second plane hit. While we were talking. And we were, like . . . this is not happening. So she said, 'Get your telescope.' And I did. And I told her I couldn't see anything. Just smoke.'

Silence. I think he was waiting. In case I'd restart on my own.

'But you saw something more.'

'I watched somebody jump.'

Out of the corner of my eye, I saw him quietly cross himself.

'And I kept thinking, how hot does it have to be? In your office. How hot does it have to get? You're more than a hundred floors up. And the certain death, well, that goes without saying. Obviously. You know you're going to die, one way or the other. But just to be able to push off. Or even let go. Just to override that hard-wired survival instinct. How hot does it have to be in your office? And that was my office. I mean, not the very person I saw. But it was the same in my office. And I knew Jeff was up there, along with just about everybody else we knew. So I told her all I could see was smoke.'

More bug hits. I wondered if thousands of bugs were meeting their death in eastern Illinois this morning, and if the bug community would mourn. If their friends and relatives suffered trauma. Were diagnosed with post-traumatic stress disorder. Yeah. It was that bad inside my head.

'You're never going to see her again,' my driver said. 'Are you?'

'Nope. And I'm not sure that's a good thing. She needs comfort. And I don't have any for her. And we were friends. I mean, above and beyond anything else we might've been, we were friends. And she needs a friend right now. So it's not noble. I'm falling down on the job. I'm failing.'

'You're being too hard on yourself,' he said.

But not all that vehemently, I noticed.

'No. I don't think so. I think I'm being just hard enough.'

He let me off another forty miles up the road, because he had to bear farther north than I needed to go. I never found out where he was from. And I still don't know his name. And he doesn't know mine.

I really think it's better that way.

12 **September 2001**

It was the day after the towers fell, and the interstate through central Pennsylvania was lined with sign after handmade sign. About one every mile. In some stretches, more. They all said the same thing: 'God Bless America'.

They were beginning to get on my nerves.

Now, in retrospect, I see I should've kept my mouth shut about it. At the time, I saw nothing. Except the signs.

My driver was fortyish, maybe older, in a BMW sports car. Maybe the car was an instrument of his midlife crisis. I wasn't sure. I was busy enough with my own crises.

'That bugs the crap out of me,' I said.

'What does?'

He had a brusque voice. And gravelly. Like a smoker. Though neither he nor his car smelled like smoke.

'Those signs.'

Long pause. Long and . . . not good.

'You have a problem with 'God Bless America'?'

'I do.'

'What's the problem?'

'It's not self-evident?'

'Not at all. I can't imagine. So explain.

Enlighten me. Please.'

'Well,' I said, not even sure where to begin. 'It's *God*. If there's a God, he has to be for everybody. How can you ask God to take sides?'

'Nothing wrong with asking him to be on the side of right.'

His voice was tightening at each turn. And I heard it. And I recognized what it meant. But it was too late to stop.

'Fine. Let's ask him to be on the side of right. Let's say, 'God bless all the peaceful people of the world.' How about that? That way we're blessing the victims and not the perpetrators. But this idea that America is always on the side of right is laughable. They don't hate us because we're free. They hate us because we armed the Afghani rebels against the Russians and then walked away and let them get slaughtered. And a hundred other bad foreign-policy decisions. I just can't get behind asking God to take care of us in some kind of exclusive sweetheart deal no matter how we behave.'

'That's a pretty unpatriotic bunch of sentiments,' he said.

'And that's another thing that I don't get. Patriotism. And that doesn't mean I hate America. Or even that I don't like it. I like it fine. But I live in New York City. So why not God Bless New York City? Or state? Plus we also live on planet Earth, but there are no boosters for planet Earth. Why is it just the *national* boundaries we're so passionate about?' I literally couldn't stop. Even though I could tell I was pissing him off. And he was my ride. 'I'll tell you why. Because planet Earth doesn't have an army. And neither does New York. It's just a safety move. Buddying up to a power structure to feel less vulnerable.'

'You're full of shit,' he said.

'I'm sure you'd feel much safer if I was.'

I felt the bumpiness of gravel under the wheels, and suddenly realized we were off on the emergency shoulder of the interstate.

'Out,' he said.

I sighed.

I opened the passenger door and stepped out, and he gunned it back out on to the highway before I could even close the door. He swerved sharply back on to the pavement, and corrected, and the veering motion slammed the door for him.

And then he drove off with my pack.

'Hey!' I screamed at him. 'My backpack!'

I jumped up and down. Waved my arms, hoping he'd catch that in his rear-view mirror. He didn't.

I sighed, and began walking west with my thumb out, my back to traffic. Not the most effective way to get a ride. 'No more editorializing,' I said out loud. 'Keep your damn feelings to yourself, Russell. Idiot.'

About a quarter of a mile later, I found my backpack tossed into some weeds by the shoulder of the road.

★ ★ ★

Later in my morning of walking and not getting another ride, my cell phone rang.

It was Kerry.

'You'll never guess who just called me,' she said, her voice bouncing between strangely upbeat and dangerously hyper. 'Not Jeff. Unfortunately. But guess.'

'I have no idea. Tell me.'

'Stan Harbaugh.'

'He's alive?'

'He's alive!'

'He got out?'

'No, he never got in. He was late to work. You'll never believe this. He was just stepping into the elevator. I mean literally. He'd just picked his foot up to step into the elevator, but he hadn't put it back down again, and the plane hit. And he just ran out again. Along with everybody else. He asked me to give you his cell phone number. Do you have something to write with?'

'Just tell me. I won't forget.'

'Oh, that's right. I forgot you don't forget.' She read off the number. 'So, listen. See? Weird things happen. Miracles happen. Nothing is definite, you know?'

'Right,' I said. 'You never know.'

Her point being that Jeff might still be alive. Despite the fact that he'd called her briefly from the office a few minutes after the first plane hit. Despite the fact that he hadn't called since.

'I better call Stan,' I said.

I was hoping my anxiousness to get off the

48

phone would be interpreted as eagerness to call Stan Harbaugh.

I was not eager to call Stan Harbaugh.

I stood right there by the side of the road and punched in the number. One ring. And then a car stopped. So I disconnected the call.

The woman who stopped for me was probably eighty. Or maybe I'm flattering her. Ninety might've been a better guess. She was small, and her spine was bent, and I worried that she could barely see over her own dashboard.

But I'd been waiting all morning for a ride, and she'd made it this far, so I got in.

'Thanks for stopping,' I said.

'I don't usually.' I noticed a tremor. Her head jerked back and forth. All on its own, it seemed like. 'But nobody can get around, so I'm trying to help. I can't believe all this. Can you? Can you believe this really happened?'

She pulled back on to the highway, and accelerated to about twenty miles under the speed limit.

Maybe it was a toss-off question, but I didn't treat it that way. I took it seriously. It was a hard moment in time to take anything less than seriously.

'It feels like a dream,' I said. 'I still feel like I dreamed it.'

'I never thought I'd see a thing like this happen in my lifetime. Nothing like this ever happened before.'

'Well, that's not entirely true.'

The minute it came out of my mouth, I realized I was editorializing again. Just what I'd

49

promised myself I wouldn't do.

'How so? When did this ever happen?'

'Never mind. Sorry. Forget I said it.'

'No, really. Go ahead and say. I want to hear what you meant.'

'Well. Terrorism isn't new. War and violence is nothing new. Look at the Middle East. Look at what happened in Rwanda in ninety-four. Look at — '

'Oh,' she said. 'I meant here.'

Of course she did. Of course she meant here. It's always different when it's here. To my credit, I didn't say so out loud.

I remembered something my mom told me once about Winston Churchill. Or at least, that's the way she remembered it. Someone was arguing with him about the loss of nearly a million in the Second World War. And Churchill corrected the man and said the death toll had been more like sixty million. The man's answer? 'Oh, if you count foreigners.'

I couldn't help wondering why this was making everybody else more patriotic, and me less so.

'I guess I should have counted those,' she said.

'I should've kept my mouth shut. I'm sorry.'

'No. Don't be sorry. You're right. I should've counted those. I have to stop up here and get some gas. I need some more gas.'

'Good,' I said. 'I could use a quick rest stop.'

While running for the gas station men's room, I pulled up Stan's number and hit 'call'.

He picked up on the first ring.

'Stan?'

'Russell. My God. I'm so glad you called. Kerry told me you might call. I was hoping you'd call. Did you try to call before?'

'Yeah. Sorry. Something came up.'

I didn't know what to say next. And I needed to pee. So I just did, with the phone tucked between my shoulder and ear.

'I think it's just us, Russell. I think the rest of them are gone.'

'Well, we don't know. Don't be too quick to say. I didn't know *you* were alive until just now.'

'But somebody did,' he said. 'I've been calling around like crazy, and the rest of them . . . nobody's heard from them. At all.'

A long silence, during which I made my way to the sink to wash my hands.

I looked at myself in the mirror. My hair was a mess, and I had five o'clock shadow. I hadn't shaved since the previous morning. My eyes were puffy and red, as though I'd been doing nothing but cry for a whole day. But I hadn't cried. Or . . . just for a moment I doubted myself. Maybe I'd cried and I hadn't even known it. But that was crazy. I'd have known. Right?

'Kerry told me about your mom,' Stan said into my left ear. 'I'm really sorry about your mom.'

'Thanks,' I said, thinking I wanted badly to wash my face, but not sure how to do it without damaging the phone.

That's when I realized I was dangerously disconnected from the emotion of the conversation.

51

And another thing that hit me as I stood looking into my own eyes in the filthy bathroom mirror: I really didn't know Stan Harbaugh. I mean, I'd met him. I'd worked with him. But nothing that went beyond a thirty-second conversation in the elevator. He was a good twenty years older, a senior partner to my junior ad man. Not much in common. But now we were tied together. For ever. Like war brothers. When I was eighty, I'd still be getting Christmas cards from Stan. It was a bond that nothing would ever break.

It felt weird to be irreversibly bonded to a relative stranger.

'You wanta know the goddamn truth?' Stan asked.

'Sure,' I said.

But I didn't.

'I forgot about the damn meeting. I forgot Sturgis asked us to come in at eight thirty. I didn't think I was running late, I thought I was early. Even after I ran outside and all. It wasn't until later that afternoon that it hit me. I was supposed to be in at eight thirty. If Sturgis hadn't called that early meeting, they'd all still be alive.'

'He did, though.' What else was I supposed to say? What else could I say? 'Take down my cell number.'

'I've got it now on my phone.'

'Oh. Fine.'

'Where are you?'

'I'm not sure. Pennsylvania, I think.'

'How are you getting around?'

52

'On my thumb. It's all I've got.'

And, in that most benign of conversational moments, Stan Harbaugh broke down and began to sob.

'Why not us, Russell? Why them and not us?'

'I haven't the faintest idea,' I said, wanting out.

'Do you think we have something important left to do in the world? Do you believe like that?'

'Maybe. I'm not sure. I'll have to think about it. Look, I have to go. Sorry. My ride is gassing up, and I have to get back there before she goes. She's old. She might forget about me. She might forget she has all my stuff.'

'Yeah, OK,' he said, but he sounded devastated to lose me. 'Call me later, OK?'

'Yeah, we'll talk,' I said.

And I clicked off the phone.

I knew it would be downright painful to force myself to call him again. But I would. Or he would. Or we both would. In each other's lives, we were an inevitability. The only two left standing.

When I got back to the car, the old woman had just barely completed the process of authorizing the gas with her credit card. She didn't look equal to the task of pumping.

'Here, I'll do that,' I said, realizing I should have offered sooner. 'Let me do that for you.'

'Well, that's very nice. You're a nice young man.'

Just for a moment, I wondered. I wondered if that was true.

Later that evening, just before the sun went down, I got a ride from a middle-aged woman in a Volkswagen van. An old one. A real throwback to an earlier time.

I should have known, just to look at the van, that I wouldn't be ejected for lack of patriotism.

'It's terrible,' she said, without even bothering to introduce herself, forcing me to tell my story, or making small talk. She had to speak up to be heard over the straining engine. 'But what's even more terrible is what we're about to do back. We're going to go in and bomb them off the map. Aren't we?'

'I would guess so. Yes,' I said. Loudly.

'I know we never will . . . I know this is idealistic. But I wish we'd just do nothing.'

'Nothing?'

'It would be an example for the world.'

'Amazing,' I said.

'What is?'

'I'm not sure. I guess that I met someone to the left of me.'

'You don't think we should do nothing?'

I sighed. I was already stunningly tired.

'I'm trying to imagine if I were in charge. Like, if my neighbor threw a fire bomb into my house. And I had to decide what to do. I don't think I'd do nothing. Would you? I mean, if he was still out there. Probably planning to do it again.'

She thought that over for a time.

'I wouldn't bomb his house and kill his entire family.'

'No, neither would I. But I'd call the police.'

'Yeah, but who do you call for this?'

'I don't know. But I still think there's the concept of justice. In-between doing nothing and bombing them off the map is justice. We could find who's responsible and haul them into The Hague and put them on international trial.'

'We won't, though,' she said.

'No. Of course not.'

'I'm sorry I said what I said. It was stupid. And naïve.'

'No. It was refreshing. More than you know.'

Then, just when I thought I might've skated by it, she asked where I'd been at 8:46 and 9:03 the previous morning. And I had to take a deep breath and tell my story all over again.

11 September 2001

I opened my eyes and looked at the alarm clock. It was 8.13 a.m. And I was supposed to be in to work at eight thirty for Sturgis's meeting. Apparently I had pushed the ten-minute snooze button at least five times without realizing it.

The next few minutes of my morning were an exercise in speed. Speed showering. Speed shaving. Speed dressing.

Then it hit me. What a waste of energy. It was all for nothing. I was going to miss that meeting no matter what I did. I could be on the platform right now, waiting for the PATH train, and it would still be a no-go. I could be on the train, heading out of the station, and it still wouldn't work. So I took a minute for four or five gulps of too-hot coffee, which had already brewed on a timer.

I wanted to call Sturgis and tell him I'd be late and I was sorry. But by then it was almost 8:35 a.m., and I thought it would be worse to interrupt his meeting.

Crap. Crap. Crap. This was the worst. The absolute worst. The worst possible thing that could have happened to me. The job meant more to me than anything, than my own life, than the world. Why did I keep screwing up like this? Why?

I sat a second or two with my head in my hands, then headed out the door.

The phone rang.

'Great,' I said out loud. 'How absolutely perfect.'

I almost didn't get it. But then I thought, Sturgis. It's Sturgis, wondering where I am. Then I thought, No. Couldn't be. He'd call on my cell, thinking I'd be most of the way there. Then I thought, Just let it go. To hell with it. Then I thought, I already missed the meeting. I'm already late.

I decided to pick it up. If it turned out to be important, I'd ask whoever it was to call on my cell while I headed for the train.

'Hello?' I said. Probably telegraphing a lot of irritation.

'Rusty?' A man's voice. 'Is this Rusty?'

I felt a pinch in my chest. Not long later it would grow into a crushing sensation. Like a vise clamped on to my heart. I had no idea, at the time, how long it would choose to stay. And how little power I would have to send it packing. I only knew that somehow, for some reason, I was receiving a call from a world I'd left behind. This fictional place called Kansas. Because nobody called me Rusty. Not in the real world.

'This is . . . Russell. This is Russell Ammiano.'

'Rusty. Good. This is Phil Jespers. From Norville. Remember me?'

'Oh. Mr Jespers. Right. Sure. Mark's dad. From . . . next door.'

'Right.'

'I'm kind of in a — '

57

'Hold that thought a minute, son. This is hard. This is bad. I wish . . . oh, hell . . . well, it doesn't matter what I wish, does it? Are you sitting down? You might want to sit down for this.'

That's when the pinch turned into a vise.

Something happened to Ben, I thought. Sad. How sad. But I'd survive. But my poor mom . . .

I sat.

'It's about your mom,' he said.

'My mom?'

'Oh, God, Rusty. I wasn't gonna be the one. The doctor was gonna call you. But I said, 'No, let me.' I said, 'Rusty knows me. It'll be better from someone he knows.' Now I wish I'd kept my damn mouth shut.'

A long pause.

'My mom?' I said again.

'I'm really sorry, Rusty. She passed away.'

Some time went by. I think. I'm not sure how much.

'That doesn't . . . seem . . . I mean . . . What happened?'

'Well, we're not exactly sure yet, but the doctor thinks either a stroke or a brain aneurysm. He's gonna do an — He'll look into it. We'll know more soon.'

Some more time went by.

'Where's Ben?' I asked.

'He's with us. Just right at the moment, we've got him. But that can't last. God knows, Rusty, I hate to hit you with everything at once like this. Just hate it like the devil. But this has got to be said. You need to get back here and take him off

58

our hands. The sooner the better.'

I looked out the window. At my office across the river. I thought, I can't do that. I'm already late for work.

I looked at my watch. 8.39 a.m.

'I can't drop my life and take care of Ben,' I said.

'Well, then drop your life for a minute and figure out who can. Because I sure as hell can't. And somebody sure as hell has to. Look. You have to come home anyway, to make arrangements for your mom. While you're here, you'll just have to make some choices about Ben. Maybe you'll decide he needs to be in some kind of a home. Nobody can make that decision for you. Or maybe you can figure out somebody else he can be with. But one way or another, you've got to get yourself out here. Sooner, not later.'

I watched, as if from some other location than my own body, as all the fight drained out of me. All the resistance. He was right. This was unavoidable. I'd just have to call Sturgis and tell him my mom died. I wasn't even late for work any more. I hadn't overslept. My mom died. So I couldn't come in at all. He would understand that.

Anybody would understand that.

Wait. My mom died?

'Right,' I said. 'I'll get online right now, and book a flight. I'll keep you posted. Let me give you my cell number.'

'I've got it. It was on the side of your mom's fridge. Along with this one.'

'Right. So . . . I'll get back to you.'

'Rusty? I'm sorry. Patty's sorry. Mark's sorry.'

Wow, I thought. I must be one sorry son of a bitch.

I hung up the phone and found a plane ticket online. It took no time at all. Outrageously expensive, but what did I expect? Same-day tickets are like that. And I had no idea how I'd get . . . there . . . from the airport in Wichita. Would the Jesperses pick me up? Long drive. How much would it cost to rent a car? A lot, I figured.

But I still hadn't called Sturgis.

I glanced at my watch again. 8.44 a.m.

I had him on speed dial. I figured I'd get his voice-mail, because he was in a meeting. But he must've checked his caller ID. Because he picked up.

'Ammiano,' he said. 'Where the hell are you?'

'Home.'

'Home? What are you doing home?'

'My mom died.'

The words sounded weird coming out of my mouth. And I thought he wouldn't believe them. Because *I* didn't.

'Oh, my God. That's terrible. What happened?'

'They're . . . not exactly sure yet. Maybe aneurysm or stroke. So listen. I booked a flight. I have to go.'

'Of course you do. Go. Take care of things. Don't worry about us. We'll manage. God. I'm sorry, Russell.'

'I'll call you when I know more about when I'm coming back.'

'No worries. Just go.'

I clicked the phone off.

I sat for a minute or two with my head in my hands, the heels of my palms pressed too hard against my eyes. So when I lifted my head and opened my eyes, my vision was weird. Spotty. So it took me a minute to realize that it wasn't any kind of optical illusion. There really was smoke and fire coming out of the North Tower.

I've told the story many times since. More times than I can count. But I've never told this part. I've never answered the question of what I felt in that exact moment. I'll answer it now.

Relief.

This sweeping wave of relief. I actually laughed a little short bark, out loud. And then I said out loud, to the empty room, 'Of course.'

I should have known it was just a dream.

I mean, my mom suddenly dies and I have to drop this whole life I've worked so hard to earn, and go back to Kansas and take care of Ben? I should've known right then. I shouldn't have had to look up and see my tower burning to know it was only a dream.

Now everything made so much sense.

Except it didn't feel like a dream. But a lot of times dreams only feel like dreams later. After you wake up.

My cell phone rang. It was still in my right hand. It startled me.

I clicked it on.

It was Kerry.

'Oh, my God. You're there. You're answering. Nobody else is answering. Wait. Where are you? Are you at work?'

'No, I'm home.'

'Turn on the TV. Oh, no. Wait. You can see it out your window.'

But it was too late. I was halfway to the TV. So I went ahead and turned it on.

And, as I'd gotten up, as I'd put one foot in front of the other, I'd known. I was awake. I just knew. I could just tell.

'Jeff called me,' she said, 'and we talked for a minute, but then he got cut off.'

I was trying to listen to her and the TV at the same time.

'A plane?' I said, only vaguely aware that I was answering the TV, not Kerry.

'I tried to call back,' she said, 'but all the circuits are busy. I called everybody's work number, but I couldn't get through. And then I remembered to call Jeff on his cell. But it was weird, Russell.' She started to cry, but kept talking. 'He just said it was hot. And that he loved me. That's all he would say. And then I called you. Because I know your cell number. Can you see what's going on?'

'Wait,' I said. Under no circumstances could I keep up with all this. 'How could you have had time for all those calls in . . . like . . . a minute?'

A brief silence.

'It hasn't been a minute, Russell.'

I looked at my watch. 9.03 a.m. Somehow, impossibly. 9.03 a.m.

'Get your telescope, Russell. Tell me what you see.'

But I just stood. For a second, I just stood. I didn't want to go get my telescope. If I did, I would see.

'Oh, my God,' Kerry shrieked. 'Do you see that?'

I looked up to see the second plane heading for the South Tower.

'Do *you* see that?' I asked.

I didn't know how she could see that. She lived in mid-town Manhattan.

'I'm watching it on TV. Oh, my God!'

We both watched the second plane slice into the South Tower. Just slice in. Like a door opened up and let it enter. On an angle. With a burst of fire around the corner, as if it might burst its way back out again. But I can't remember if I could see all that from out my window. Or if I'm remembering what I saw on TV.

'Russell,' she screamed. 'What's happening? Why is this happening?'

'This is not happening,' I said. It was a theory, anyway. 'Is it possible that this could be a dream?'

'No, it's happening. Get your telescope.'

'Hang on,' I said, and threw my cell phone on to the couch.

I got my telescope.

Here's what I saw.

Smoke. Tons and tons of smoke. Gray and black. Both. And it didn't only come from the diagonal gash, but from the windows of upper floors. And the roof line. It seemed to come from the roof line.

And paper. I saw lots of paper. It looked like a ticker-tape parade, except I could tell that each tiny bit of confetti was a whole sheet of paper.

And then I saw him. But who? I don't know. Somebody. I knew he wasn't one of ours, because he was in a window at least two floors down from my office. Maybe three. He was standing in a broken-out window. Standing on the ledge.

And then he just sort of . . . fell forward. It was a broad move. It was purposeful. He didn't lose his balance. He pushed off.

Believe me. I had a telescope. I know. I saw.

I followed him with the telescope part of the way down.

I watched his tie fly upward in the air current, standing straight up beside his neck. I watched the open flaps of his suit jacket flutter out toward his outstretched arms. He had his arms outstretched. As if he could fly.

And the fabric of the jacket reached out. Almost to his wrists. Not quite. And it made it look like he had wings.

And just for a minute I thought, He'll fly. He wouldn't have fallen forward if he didn't think he could fly. He'll fly.

He didn't.

I lost him behind a building a little more than half the way down.

I could hear Kerry yelling something from the couch.

I picked up the phone and held it to my ear. She was yelling, 'What do you see? Russell? What do you see?'

'Nothing,' I said. 'Just smoke. I can't see anything. All I can see is smoke.'

Part Two

That's a Hard Question

15 September 2001

It was about seven in the evening. Still my first full day . . . back.

I was plowing through my mom's papers. A little stack of files I'd found in a drawer in her bedroom. I can't even really say what I thought I was looking for. But I knew it when I found it.

It was a thin file marked: 'Final' decisions. Just like that. With quotes around the word final. As if it might not turn out to be so final as she'd thought.

Inside, I found papers informing me she'd chosen cremation. And had already paid for it.

'Whoa!' I said out loud.

It was something like saying, 'Bingo!' which was too old-fashioned. Or, 'Oh, snap!' which was too hip-hop modern. But this was good. I mean, as good as something can be when it relates to your mother's recent death.

It filled me with an unfamiliar feeling. At least, recently unfamiliar. Like I'd been cut a break. For a change. Something had actually gone right. Even righter than expected.

'What'd you say, Buddy?' Ben called in to me.

He was in the TV room by himself. Watching cartoons. With the volume up loud. Even out here in the living room I could tell that Daffy

Duck thought it was 'wabbit' season, and Bugs Bunny thought it was duck season, and each thought Elmer Fudd should shoot the other and not them. Following every sound of a cartoon shotgun blast, a dribble of low-pitched laughter from Ben.

'Nothing, Buddy. I just found something.'

'Something bad?'

'No. Good. Very good.'

It was good for so many reasons. I was still counting all the reasons as I spoke.

Good, because it meant I didn't have to somehow find thousands of non-existent dollars for a traditional funeral. Even better because I didn't have to stress that I was making the wrong choice, handling things in a way she wouldn't have wanted. And another reason. I had my doubts about Ben and the traditional funeral. You know, with the open casket, and the dear departed dressed and made up to look remarkably lifelike. How would Ben react to a sight like that? He was still waiting for her to come back. Obviously. I'd been having a nightmare fantasy that he'd pick her up from the coffin and carry her home, and no one would be able to stop him.

And a final blessing: a memorial, with a nice photo, and an urn of ashes, was not nearly so time-sensitive. Which made it more Ben-sensitive. We could wait a month if we needed to. Two, even. Give him more time to adjust.

I looked up to see him standing in the TV room doorway, his head nearly pressing the top of the door frame.

'What'd you find?'

'Some plans Mom made.'

'Why good?'

'Because they let me know what she wanted me to do.'

'Oh. What?'

Now, how was I going to answer that one? Sometimes the truth just doesn't fit the moment.

'Kind of a long story.'

'Why don't you just ask her when she comes back?'

'Because ... Buddy ... she's not coming back.'

Ben turned and disappeared back into the TV room.

I decided I'd be a better brother if I didn't just let it go by.

I joined Ben in the TV room, where I picked up the remote and muted the sound on his cartoon.

'Hey!' he said. 'I'm watching this!'

'But I want to talk to you.'

'Leave it on, though.'

'I can't think and talk to you with all that noise.'

'Leave it on quiet.'

'But then you'll listen to Bugs Bunny and not me.'

'No. I'll listen.'

'Promise?'

'Yeah. Promise.'

I de-muted the sound and turned it down to barely audible. I watched Ben lean in a little closer to try to hear. But then the cartoon ended, and a commercial came on, and I muted the sound again, and he turned his head toward me. But still with his gaze off at an angle toward the rug.

'I don't think you know what it means when somebody dies,' I said.

'What?'

'It means you don't see them again.'

No answer from Ben.

'Like Sandy. Remember Sandy?' I asked.

'No.'

'Our dog. Our collie dog. Remember?'

'No.'

'Oh. Too bad. I thought you might remember Sandy.'

'I don't, though.'

'Let me see if I can find a picture. Maybe that'll help.'

I leapt to my feet and hurried into the living room, hoping the old photo album was right where it had always used to be. In the compartment under the end table next to the living room couch.

I opened the little compartment door with the brass handle, reached in, and there it was. I felt it immediately. It was huge, an ancient antique wooden scrapbook with leather hinges. It had lived in our family much longer than I had.

I heard the volume come up to blasting again on the TV. Sylvester and Tweety Bird.

I rummaged through photo after photo of my mom and dad, doing my best not to get distracted by emotion. I could always do that later. Right at that moment I had an important brotherly role to perform.

And then, there she was. Sandy. A perfect Lassie lookalike. A beautiful dog. It stretched my heart painfully to look at her photo. She'd been there when I was born. Sometimes I think she was the first thing I saw when I opened my eyes. Sometimes I think I mistook myself for a puppy at first. I'd loved her abjectly, completely. I'd been devastated by her death. I'd been maybe six when she died. And I hadn't understood. I'd wanted to see her again, and I couldn't understand why no one would help.

In the photo, I was there with her. I was not even two. Leaning on her, holding her fur in a way that must have hurt her, while she smiled. Patient. Proud. I'd learned to walk by holding her that way.

I took the album back into the TV room.

I turned the TV volume down to almost nothing again.

'Hey!' Ben said. 'I'm watching this!'

'This was Sandy.'

I set the album on his lap.

His eyes came away from the TV for the first time I could remember.

He touched the photo.

'Oh!' he said. Hushed. Reverent. 'She's a good dog! She's a nice dog!'

Bingo. Oh, snap. I'd done it.

'See? You remember.'

'No.'

'Then how do you know she's a good dog?'

'Well. Just look. Just look at her.'

Nice try, I thought. Next time I wouldn't be so

quick to congratulate myself.

'Hey. Ben. Wait a minute. If you don't remember her, how did you know she was a she?'

I hadn't used any gender-specific pronouns.

Ben didn't answer for a long time.

Then he said, 'That's a hard question.'

He closed the wooden scrapbook and dropped it on the rug, and his eyes returned to the TV.

I sighed.

'Let's try this a different way. Maybe instead of expecting to see Mom the old way, the way you're used to, maybe you could be open to something new.'

I was pretty sure he wasn't listening.

Until he said, 'What?'

'Like, maybe you won't *see* her again. But maybe you can *feel* her here.'

'Why wouldn't I see her?' He sounded agitated. Suddenly alarmed.

'I just meant, maybe you'll feel her looking over your shoulder. You know. Still with you.'

'But why wouldn't I *see* her?'

Ben struggled to his feet and began to pace in that special way that only Ben paced. I'd forgotten all about it.

The refresher course didn't take long.

My brother Ben didn't pace in a straight line. And he didn't go around in a circle either, though the effect was similar. Ben paced endless squares. Out with the left foot, out with the right, sharp ninety-degree left turn, repeat. Around and around in a clumsy box of his own creation. All he had to do was miss a turn to escape the box. But he never did. Until he was damn good and ready.

'Why wouldn't I see her?' he wailed.

'Ben, I — '

'You tell me why I wouldn't see her, Buddy. Why wouldn't I see her?'

And that was my second fast refresher. After the pacing box, the broken record. Once Ben got off on a tear like that, repeating the same impassioned question more than two or three times, his clutch seemed to stick. No more shifting gears for some time.

I was in for a long night.

Brilliant, Russell, I thought. You sure did a stellar job on that.

Unclear for the moment on how these situations used to be handled — I was remembering each phase of this as I went along — I jumped up and tried to stop him. I stood in front of him, so he'd have to stop his obsessive box-pacing to keep from bowling me down.

Then I was on the rug looking up at the ceiling, and wondering how badly I'd twisted the muscle I felt twanging in my back.

He hadn't struck me. He hadn't even pushed me out of the way. He just hadn't stopped.

'Buddy,' I said, absorbing his panic. 'Stop.'

'But why wouldn't I see her?'

I ducked out of the TV room, and into the living room, where I breathed long and deeply. I could still hear him, repeating the same question. Over and over. And over. And over.

What did we used to do, my mom and me?

Well. I knew the answer to that. *We* didn't. *She* did.

Then I was hit with a strange thought. Here I was telling Ben to be open to feeling Mom with him. Was I willing to try the cure I was prescribing?

'OK, Mom,' I said. 'What did you used to do?'

Chalk it up to the fact that I'd turned my mind a hundred per cent to the question. Because I don't forget things. So if I hadn't known before, it's because I hadn't yet tried to remember.

'Cookies,' I said out loud.

When Ben would get stuck, our mom would bake cookies. And Ben's tantrum would last just about as long as it took her to bake them, and let them cool a bit. And then she'd bring them in to Ben and say, 'Look, honey. Cookies.' And by then he'd be tired and run-down, and enough of a distraction could break the cycle. And cookies were enough of a distraction.

There was only one problem. I didn't know how to bake cookies.

'Well, Mom?' I asked.

And then I had another remembering. When we were little, she'd made them from scratch. But then later, when she had enough to do looking after Ben, she'd given that up. Gone instead to the type you buy at the market, as unbaked tubes of dough. Because the difference was lost on Ben anyway.

I ran to the kitchen. Even in the kitchen I could hear him.

'You tell me, Buddy! You tell me why I wouldn't see her!'

I rummaged through the freezer and found no cookie dough. Just my luck these days. But then I thought, maybe you don't freeze them. Maybe you keep them in the refrigerator. I opened the fridge door, purposely not looking at the postcards.

And there it was. Granted, I had to lift two casserole dishes to see it. But I found it. Two-thirds of a tube of chocolate-chip cookie dough in a plastic ziplock sandwich bag.

My luck seemed to be changing.

I set about following the directions on the tube. But it was hard, because the first couple of words of each sentence had been cut off for previous batches.

But I got the oven temperature. Three hundred and fifty degrees. And I figured out that you cut the dough into one-inch rounds and cut the rounds into quarters. And then baked them for . . . that part was cut off. I could only see a two. So, two minutes? Twelve? Twenty-two?

I reminded myself not to panic, or hurry. After all, Ben wasn't going to hurry his tantrum. The whole idea was in the timing. In the way we would meet up at the end.

'Cool on a wire rack.'

I plowed through what seemed like every cupboard, and found no wire rack. They'd just have to cool on something else.

I cut eight, and then sat at the kitchen table with my head in my hands while they baked. I purposely didn't go back into the TV room with

Ben. I couldn't. I couldn't unhook from his tantrum. Watching him, listening to him, made me feel like I was falling apart, just as surely as he was.

After a while I put my hands over my ears. Hard.

About fifteen minutes after that, I was using a spatula to lift eight cookies on to a yellow plastic plate, noting that Ben's voice had gotten hoarse and quiet. In fact, I couldn't hear what he was saying.

But I still knew.

I stood at the open door of the TV room, cookies in hand. I think he smelled them. I saw him miss a step.

'Look, Buddy. I made you cookies.'

He stopped.

Oh my God. He stopped.

It's hard to describe the relief.

He'd been crying. His eyes were red, his face streaked with tears. And his nose was running. I mean *running*. Not a little. Buckets.

I got him a box of tissues from my mom's bedroom, and, when I got back, he was sitting in one of the stuffed chairs, eating a cookie.

I handed him five or six tissues, but he just held them in one hand and kept eating. So I took them back, and wiped his nose.

It was a low moment in our relationship.

I threw away the tissues and then just sat watching him.

'Can I have a cookie, too?' I asked.

'Yeah.'

And then, after a long pause, he held the plate

76

out in my direction. But all I could think about was the running faucet of his nose.

'Never mind,' I said. 'They're all for you.'

'Mom's are better.'

And that's what I get for being a nice guy. That is, if I am.

'They're both made from exactly the same dough.'

'But hers are baked right. This is burned. Right here.'

He showed me the bottom of the cookie. He was right. It was blackened all around one edge.

'Sorry. I did my best. But I'm not much of a baker.'

Oddly, as I said it, I thought about that girl who was. Even though I'd only met her the one time.

'It's OK. I'll just give the burny part to . . . '

I waited for him to finish the sentence. But he never did. But he tipped his hand on where he'd been headed with that thought. He reached the burned edge of cookie out and down toward the floor. To about dog level.

So, he remembered. Even though maybe he didn't remember that he remembered. Or maybe I'd just gotten him thinking about dogs by showing him the picture.

But . . . no. You can think about dogs all you want, but if you've never had one, as best you can recall, you don't automatically give them your only-slightly-less-than-edible leftovers. That's not instinct. That's habit.

'Who?' I asked.

'Who what?' As if he'd forgotten the entire proposition.

He set the burned edge of cookie on the very outermost edge of his plate.

'Who were you going to give that to?'

Ben thought that over for a time.

'That's a hard question,' he said.

He looked up to the TV screen. The cartoon show was over. I glanced at my watch. Seven minutes after eight. So much for Patty Jespers's declaration of 'Not a minute sooner. Not a minute later.'

I watched his eyes go wide.

'Time is it?' he asked nervously.

'Seven minutes after eight.'

He dropped the plate on to the floor. Cookies rolled in every possible direction.

'Past my bedtime.'

'It's just a few minutes.'

'But I go to bed at eight.'

'It's just — '

'I have to brush my teeth. I have to go to work tomorrow. I can't be tired. Mr McCaskill wouldn't like it if I was tired.'

He hurried off — as best Ben knew how to hurry — while I searched for cookies under the furniture.

I was down to one missing cookie when he called in to me.

'You have to come tuck me in.'

'Of course,' I said. Out loud. But not to him. Not loud enough for him to hear. 'Of course I have to go tuck him in.'

I also had to give him a kiss on the temple,

78

right at his hairline. Just the way Mom used to
do. He pointed carefully, so I'd get just the right
spot.

'Night, Buddy,' I said.

'Hey. Buddy. Want to know . . . something?'

'Sure. What?'

'Why wouldn't I see her?'

I tried not to sigh. But the sigh more or less
sighed itself.

'Night, Buddy. See you in the morning.'

I turned out the light. But the world's
brightest night light must have been on at all
times. All day as well as all night. Because it
didn't get much darker in Ben's room.

16 September 2001

I cruised by Nazir's Baked Goods at six forty the following morning. Stopped out front.

If anything, the street, the town, seemed even more deserted than it had the morning before. Then again, it was Sunday. So it had some excuse.

It struck me that the bakery might be closed on Sunday. A lot of non-essential businesses were, in this Christian town. And maybe that glow of light in the kitchen was like Ben's night light. A constant.

But then I saw a flash of her head, on her way to the oven, through the window.

I shifted my mom's old Buick into park, and shut off the engine.

That's when I noticed the issue with the bakery window. Right on the word NAZIR'S, someone had hit the glass with two raw eggs, which dripped their yolks obscenely down the window and on to the brick below.

I wondered if she even knew yet.

I reached for the front door. Her head came up, and she motioned me around the side. I walked around to the tiny bakery parking lot and saw an employee's entrance into the kitchen. It was open.

She smiled when she saw me come in. That felt good. Seemed like it had been a while since anyone had.

'So,' she said. 'You came back, Ben's brother.'

I was so tired and disheartened that I was almost willing to accept that as my new name. I offered no answer of any kind.

'We don't open till eight on Sundays. So I don't even have the donuts cut yet. But come in and talk to me. It won't take too long. And I have coffee made. No offense, but you look very bad. Worse than you did yesterday. I was hoping you would feel a little better by now.'

'I had a bad night with Ben. Have you got a bucket? Something I could put soapy water in? And maybe a scrub brush or a big sponge?'

She looked at me strangely.

'Your mother didn't keep such things at your house?'

'It's not for me. It's for you. For your front window. Somebody hit it with eggs.'

Her smile disappeared. I heard her mutter a couple of words under her breath, but I didn't make out what they were. I'm not entirely sure they were English.

'Right on my father's name?'

So that's who Nazir is, I thought. That's the other half of her 'we'.

I guess I wasn't answering fast enough. So she went on.

'So maybe the donuts won't just be a few minutes. I have to tend to this other matter first.'

'No, that's fine,' I said. 'You do the donuts. I'll get the window. I just need a bucket and

81

something to scrub with.'

She looked into my face for a long moment. 'You're sure?'

'Absolutely.'

She disappeared into a back storeroom and came out with an aluminum bucket. I watched her partially fill it with hot water at the big industrial double sink. She added a shot of dishwashing liquid.

The bucket steamed as she handed it to me. I thought she'd forgotten the scrub brush, but I looked in and saw the end of it sticking up out of the sudsy water.

'I don't know why you're doing this,' she said. 'But it's nice. Thank you.'

'I don't know why you gave me coffee and donuts for free yesterday. But sometimes people are nice to each other. Not everybody's an ass. I guess I'm apologizing to you for the egg thrower. On behalf of my entire nationality.'

She laughed a little. It was nice to see a bit of lightness return.

'It's not your fault,' she said. 'You didn't do anything wrong.'

'Right. If I ever catch the son of a bitch, that's what I'll tell him about *you*.'

Now her face seemed to have returned to its original relaxed smile. And I thought, What a small price to pay for such a good thing.

'There's a hose on the other side of the building. In the alley between here and the bank. It's very long. We use it to hose off the sidewalk out front.'

'Fine. I'll be back in a bit.'

I stepped out into the cool morning, glad to have a simple, predictable mission. It was that hour of morning my dad used to call civil twilight — the first few minutes you can see your hand in front of your face. Plus the streetlight on the corner helped. Still, it felt for all the world like a movie set. I still was not convinced I was in a real place.

I carried the bucket to the front window, and, thinking very little about who put them there and why, scrubbed away the raw eggs. They were freshly thrown, and still wet, so it didn't take much. I listened to the sound of the scrub brush bristles against the rough brick under the window, and found it comforting for reasons I couldn't pin down. I felt the pinch of the muscle I'd pulled in my back the night before. But it was OK. It wasn't too bad. I fetched the hose from the alley and blasted away the soap, using the force of the water to wash it, and the eggshells, off the curb and into the storm drain. I replaced the hose, turning it off and then releasing the water still trapped inside. Because . . . I don't know why. It's just the way I was taught to do things. I poured the soapy water from the bucket down the storm drain and went back inside.

She looked up and smiled at me. She was just, in that exact moment, slapping an enormous mound of dough — that would soon be my morning donut — on to the table. I stood at the door a moment, watching her roll it out with a heavy wooden rolling pin, in motions almost too fast for my eyes to follow.

'You can just leave the bucket under the sink

for now. And you can wash your hands in that sink, or you can use our bathroom. Thank you.'

'Oh, that was nothing.'

But it was something. It was just something I didn't mind.

When I got back from washing my hands, she pointed with a flip of her head to a high stool, which I sat on.

I watched her cut the donuts.

In her right hand she held a metal cookie cutter — well, donut cutter — and she moved along the sheet of dough with blinding speed, leaving classic donut shapes marked into the dough, complete with holes. With her left hand she followed along, pulling them up, leaving the centers on the table, placing the perfect circles on a wire rack.

'You want to talk about it?' she asked.

'What?' I asked, thinking I sounded like my brother. I could only imagine she was referring to the eggs on the window, and that didn't require much processing. At least, not on my end.

'You said you had a bad night with Ben.'

'Oh. Right. Well. Not a bad *night*, so much. More a bad evening. Then he went to sleep at eight and forgot the whole thing, and I was so rattled I was up till three thirty, and then at twenty after six he gets me up to drive him to work. So that's why I look tired. I mean, even more so.'

'Grab a coffee.'

'What a good idea.'

And I did.

'So,' she said, when I came back and sat. 'You want to talk about it?'

I laughed. It felt good. I wondered when I last had.

'Thought I just did.'

'Well, that's fine. If that's all you want to say about it, that's fine. That's up to you.'

I blew on the coffee and took a few sips. I'd never drink any other coffee again. If I ever had to, it would never be good enough.

'He doesn't get it about my mom. Our mom. It's like he literally doesn't understand the concept of death. Not that I blame him. I mean, he only has just so much to work with, and he can only understand what he can understand. But he still thinks she's coming back, which is heartbreaking. So I was trying to find a nice way to help him with it. I just said that maybe even though he can't see her any more, he might still be able to feel her. Feel her with him. And that turned out to be a mistake. He completely flipped out. For ... well, I don't want to exaggerate and say for hours. Twenty-five minutes, maybe. But ... let me tell you. It felt like hours.'

She lowered a rack of donuts into the fryer, and a rush of sizzle startled me.

She looked over her shoulder.

'If he flipped out, then he understands.'

'On some level. Yeah.'

'What about you? Can you feel your mother still with you?'

'I did last night.'

'Good.'

Silence. For a long time. Long enough that the donuts came out of the fryer, and I watched her glaze them with a big ladle, right on their rack, the excess glaze running back into the well of the metal glazing table.

She brought me one on a paper plate.

'Careful,' she said. 'Hot.' Then, just when I least expected it, 'Are you going to put him in a home?'

'Oh, no,' I said, without even thinking. 'I couldn't do that to my mom. I've hurt my mom enough for one life-time.'

She cocked her head to one side, but didn't ask any questions.

I didn't want to elaborate, but it was too late. I'd stuck my foot in it. Now I had to go on. Otherwise what she was imagining would be even worse.

'It's just . . . I should've stayed and helped her take care of him. I know I should have. I've always known. But I didn't stay. The minute I turned eighteen, I ran. And I've felt like shit about it all these years. And obviously it's come back to haunt me. Like karma, but all in the same lifetime. But . . . to put Ben in a home . . . '

'I'm glad,' she said. 'I think he would be unhappy.'

'He'd be miserable. And my mom. My mom would roll over in her grave.'

And, as that last word came out of my mouth, I broke. I cried.

So, there it was.

For five or six days, nothing. Oh, a little sweating and shaking and screaming here and there, but no tears. But when I said what I said, there it was. My mom was in her grave. Figuratively speaking. The denial cracked like river ice in the first good thaw. The kind of cracks that won't stop once they get going. They travel. They craze. The whole structure just . . . well, we all know what it does. It comes tumbling down. Things are like that. You can build them all you want. But they tumble down.

It would not be exaggerating my case to call this 'The moment I realized my mother was dead.' And I thought, You should be more understanding with Ben. He gets it on an emotional level, but can't wrap his brain around it. You did almost exactly the same thing, but in reverse.

She came close to me, but did not touch me in any way.

'Poor Rusty,' she said.

It surprised me so much that I almost stopped crying.

'Who told you my name is Rusty?'

'It isn't? I was in the market yesterday, and I saw Ben. And I said, 'Ben, I met your brother.' But I hadn't thought to ask your name. So I said, 'Ben, what's your brother's name?' And he said 'Rusty''.

'Childhood nickname. I go by Russell now. Ben is having trouble making the switch.'

'Well, I won't have trouble making the switch. Poor Russell.'

And she reached out and handed me two paper towels. I wondered if my nose was running. It didn't feel like it.

'It's the best I have,' she said.

I took them from her. And looked into her face. And fell for her.

Yes. Just like that.

I won't say fell in love, because I don't quite believe that. I think you have to know someone better to earn that phrase. But I fell. That's all I can say. I fell into . . . something. And hit hard.

Like being hit by a car. And almost as painful. But mostly I mean, just that sudden. There's no beginning, middle and end to that experience. The split second it happens, it's happened. In its entirety. The only time that really elapses is the time it takes you to catch up. To absorb what just happened to you. And nobody ever thinks it's going to unhappen. Do they?

'Now you're looking at me strangely,' she said.

'Was I? Sorry.'

I looked away.

But a minute later, when she went back to her donuts, I looked at her some more. I wanted to do nothing else from that moment forward.

There were just two problems.

One, whether she would ever return my feelings. And two, if she ever did, how to keep Ben from sitting between us on the couch every night.

I took a big bite of my glazed donut.

Three problems. And if it worked out, I would be very fat.

Yes, it's interesting, isn't it? Suddenly it was lighter inside my brain. Funnier. Things were looking up.

When I got into the driveway, Mark Jespers was standing out in front of his parents' house, watering the lawn with a hose.

I waved, and he waved, and then he ran to turn off the hose, and my heart sank. I've never been Mark's biggest fan. And I'd been seriously looking forward to taking a nap. And daydreaming.

Lady bakers, maybe.

He met up with me right in front of my mom's front porch.

'You look terrible,' he said.

'I just need some sleep.'

He'd changed, Mark. Literally. Physically. He'd bulked up. Gotten into bodybuilding, apparently. He wore shorts and a sleeveless tee, a muscle tee, obviously proud of what he had to show. I wondered if he used steroids. It looked like he might.

'Hey,' he said, careening off in another conversational direction entirely. 'We're going out tonight to celebrate Larry and Vince and Paul. It's their last day.'

I had an irreverent thought. I thought, Yeah, seeing as they're already trained by the National Guard and they'll be part of the first wave into Afghanistan, it's probably at least one of their last few. I shook it away again. I didn't want to think that way, especially about Larry. I liked Larry. At least, better than I liked Mark. And I knew him better than I knew Vince or Paul.

'Yeah, Larry told me they were shipping out.'

'We're gonna go out tonight, all the guys. Get drunk. See them off. Come with us. You should come.'

I just stood there a minute, looking at him. Not into his eyes. That's always hard for me. I was looking at the girth of his neck. I was hoping he'd get it on his own. Belatedly. Without my having to say it. Didn't pan out.

'You know I don't drink,' I said.

'Ooooooooh,' he said. It was the 'oh' that almost never ended. 'Riiiiiight. I forgot that whole thing. Shit. Well, come with us anyway, though. Just come with us. Have a pop.'

Pop. Right. Mid-westerners don't say soda. They say pop.

'I don't think I'd do too well around all that. But thanks.'

I turned to go inside.

'Yeah,' he said. 'I shouldn't be surprised. I remember.'

I turned back, sighing. I didn't ask any questions. I just waited. Obviously it would spew forth on its own.

'You always were way up here,' he said, reaching one hand up high, above his head. 'And we always were way down here,' he said, reaching the other hand down low, below his waist.

'I think you're remembering wrong.'

'I'm looking at it. Right now.'

'I just don't want to be around all that drinking. You'd feel the same if it'd happened to you. I'm going to go inside and try to get some sleep. And maybe later I'll go by and see Larry. Does he still live with his folks?'

'Oh, hell no. He's married and got kids.'

'Where does he live?'

'He's in the phone book,' Mark said, simply, turning his back to me.

Then he stomped back across the lawn. Just as I let myself in the front door, I heard the hose start up again.

*　★　*

I took a long, hot bath and got back into my mom's bed.

Then, just as I was closing my eyes, I saw my cell phone. It was sitting on the bedside table.

I hadn't carried it with me. I hadn't turned it on. I hadn't checked messages.

No, I thought. No. I'm going to sleep.

But I couldn't stop thinking about it.

So I sighed, and turned on the phone, and checked voicemail.

Two new messages. Could have been worse.

The first was from Kerry.

'I'm not trying to change your mind,' she said. 'I get it. I get it, I get it, I get it. But we can still talk, right? I mean . . . can we? I'm having a bad night, not that they're not all bad lately, and I know you're having a bad night wherever you are, you must be, and I just thought we could talk. So, if we can, call me.' I could hear a break in there, right around the word 'can'. A little crack, letting emotion through. 'And if not, well . . . I get it.' Click.

The second was from Stan Harbaugh.

'I'm lost,' he said. 'Russell, I'm lost. And I

can't think who to talk to. The people who would know are dead, and the people who aren't dead don't know. So I called you . . . And you're not there. OK. You're not there. Call me. If you can. Or I'll call back. Or maybe it's OK. I don't know. I'm sorry I called. No. I'm not. Call me. OK?'

I pressed disconnect. Turned off the power again on the phone.

I would call them. But not now. Later. When I could.

Funny how they both seemed to figure I had some of what they needed. Funny how people think that. Like they're lost but you must be found. Everybody looks at you and judges you more stable. Because they can't see inside.

If and when I was vaguely found — or even just a little better rested — I would force myself to call.

In the meantime, I was determined to sleep. And I did.

★ ★ ★

Larry lived in one of those old housing projects from the fifties, now turned into cheap duplex apartments. Over on Hardwood Court, on the south side of town. The other side. Right. All the way over on the other side of town. Took me almost four minutes to drive there.

I hadn't called first. I'm not sure why I hadn't called first. I'm the kind of guy who usually calls.

I could hear children shrieking as I knocked on the door. More than one. That ear-splitting, discordant child shriek that could be fierce indignation or could be all in good fun. The lines are so blurry at that age.

Larry looked surprised to see me.

'Rusty,' he said.

His face looked . . . now how was I going to finish that sentence? Older, but not literally. Burdened. I wondered if it was just now catching up with him, or if I was just now seeing him in the full light of day.

'Yeah. Hey, I won't take up much of your time. I know you're trying to get ready to go. It's just . . . Mark wanted me to go out with you guys tonight, and I can't. I mean, I'm not going to. But I didn't want you to think it was because I didn't care that you're shipping out. So I thought I'd just come around real quick and say bye.'

'Come in, Rusty. Come in.'

I stepped into his modest — to put it mildly — living room.

Two boys, about four and three, came barreling into the room, the little one chasing the big one. When they saw me, they stopped dead. A ridiculously pregnant woman stepped out of the kitchen, and they hid behind her legs.

'Trish, this is my old friend Rusty. You remember when I told you about Rusty, right?'

'Oh, yeah,' she said, her voice full of hushed awe. As though he'd told her I was an axe murderer, or something.

'And this is Petey and Jack. Sit down, Rusty. Sit down.'

I did as I was told. The boys ran outside, into the back courtyard, screaming.

Trish came and stood over me. I tried not to look at the horizontal mountain of her belly.

'Larry told me so much about you,' she said, still in awe of . . . something.

'Sounds like it was all bad.'

'Oh, no, I didn't mean it like that. He didn't say anything bad about you. He just told me you worked in the World Trade Center. So the day it . . . When it . . . He said you must be dead. I mean, until the other night, when he picked you up on the road.'

'Yes and no. I did work there. I'm not dead.'

'Well, obviously. Oh, God. I'm sorry. Is everything I've said so far just the worst, most tactless thing I could have said?'

'Not at all. I appreciate the concern.'

'Can I get you guys some coffee? Or a beer?'

'Nothing for me, thanks,' I said. 'I won't be here that long. I know Larry's trying to get ready to go.'

'I'll just let the old friends talk, then.'

And she waddled away.

I looked at Larry, trying to gather what I'd been wanting to say. It had all seemed so clear before I got there. But now I was there. And nothing was clear.

No words came.

'You should come tonight,' he said. 'It'll be fun.'

'I can't. I don't drink. Remember? And I don't do real well when other people are drinking . . . '

'Oh, shit. Oh, yeah. Hey, I'm sorry, Rusty. I forgot. I forgot about that whole disaster with your dad. And Ben. Oh, God. Too much

94

heartache for one family. That's what my mom used to say. And that was before your mom went and died. Well, screw tonight. Who cares? You came to say goodbye. That's what counts.'

'I think I got into it a little with Mark. Without meaning to. He thought I was being high and mighty when I said I didn't want to go.'

'Yeah, well. Mark is a butt.'

'Huh,' I said. 'Interesting. I always thought that was just me.'

'Definitely not just you.'

'So, listen. Larry. This has been on my mind. So I wanted to tell you again I was sorry for what I said. You know. The other night. When you picked me up out on the highway.'

'No worries, Rusty. No worries. You were tired. You had a lot of crap going on.'

Petey and Jack came back. Ran in through what sounded like a kitchen door, shrieking. I didn't even bother to try to answer. It wouldn't have been heard.

Larry leaned closer to my chair.

'Come on outside,' he shouted. 'It'll be quieter. And I can smoke.'

I followed him out on to the front porch, where we sat in two rusty folding lawn chairs. The sky was the color of steel. It was a color I remembered. He lit a Marlboro and drew deeply.

'I did want to ask you, though,' he said, 'but not like I'm trying to bust your chops or anything, it's just, usually when people are really tired like that, they say what they really mean. They may be sorry they said it, and they maybe wouldn't have said it at a better time, but they

95

still mean it. So I was wondering. Did you mean it?'

'Oh, hell, Larry, I don't know. I guess I just feel like we're going around in a circle. Everything that happens is in retaliation for something else, and so how is it ever going to end? I just get frustrated. You know? But I didn't mean to —'

'Hey. I asked.'

'Yeah. You did. So . . . when I'm talking to Mark today . . . he lets loose with this accusation that I've always tried to act like I was above you guys. But it's not like that. I mean, not as far as I know. I'm being as honest as I can. It's not an 'up here, down there' sort of thing. But we're different. And I think we all know it. So, listen. I'm going to head out.'

'You just got here.'

'You got a lot to do, though. And that's really all I wanted to say. Oh, no. One more thing. Come home safe. You better. That's a lot of kids.'

Larry laughed. 'Yeah, no shit, huh?'

'And tell Vince and Paul I said come home safe, too.'

'Will do, pal.'

I got up and ambled off his porch. A couple of steps later, I heard him call me.

'Rusty.'

I turned, and found myself looking right into the sun. I shielded my eyes as best I could with one hand.

'You gonna put Ben in a home?'

'No.'

'Oh. What're you gonna do, then?'

'Not a clue,' I said. 'Not the first clue.'
Then I drove away.

★ ★ ★

I picked Ben up at a quarter after three. Not a moment sooner. Not a moment later.

'Hey, Buddy,' he said. 'You want to know . . . something?'

'Sure,' I said shifting into drive.

'Don't go! Don't go yet. I have to put my seat belt on.'

'Right. Sorry.'

'OK, now you can go.'

I turned out of the parking lot and down the street. I felt a tug of apprehension. Staring down the barrel of another night with Ben.

'What were you going to tell me, Buddy?'

'Oh. Right. You know that gas station?'

That was a partial thought if I ever heard one.

'Which one?'

'The one we always stop at when Mom takes us to the farm store. The one that has two hot dogs for a dollar fifty. Mom calls it the no-name one. But it has a name. I just can't remember it.'

'Right. She called it no-name because it's not one of the big brand names.'

'Whatever. Can I tell you this?'

'Sure.'

'Somebody got shot at. There.'

'Seriously? Around here?'

'Well, it's outside town. But pretty close to around here. Everybody at the store today was talking about it. All day.'

'Anybody know why?'

'Yeah. It was his head.'

'Whose head?'

'The guy that got shot at. He had that thing wrapped around his head. What's that thing?'

'I don't know, Buddy.'

A brief silence, and then a muffled noise exploded from him. I looked over to see him banging his head against his knees. Hard. Barely missing the dashboard. His seat was back absurdly far, to give him room for his legs, but the top of his head still barely missed the dashboard. If he'd been sitting straighter, he'd have knocked himself out.

'Hey, hey! Buddy!' I pulled over to the curb and shifted into park. 'Stop! Stop! What are you doing?'

Amazingly, he stopped. He just sat forward a moment, curled over his own knees, his spine curved in defeat.

'I worked on this all day,' he said. 'So I could tell you.'

'It's fine, Buddy. You're telling me. You're doing fine. We just need to work out this one thing about the guy's head.'

'There's these people,' he said, gesturing wildly with his hand. 'Who wrap a thing around their head.'

'Like a turban?'

'Yeah!' he shouted, bolting upright. 'That's what it was! That's why somebody shot at him.'

I sat still a minute, breathing.

'That's a bad reason,' I said.

98

'That's what most of the people in the store said.'

Most of them? Not all of them? Then again, if everybody agreed it was a bad reason to shoot at a guy, nobody would've been shot at.

'Was he hit?'

'No. It missed. But it hit the car. And he was gassing up his car. So his car got burned up.'

'Holy crap.'

'I worked all day on that. So I could tell you.'

'You did fine, Buddy. You did great.'

'What did you do today?'

Oh, let's see. Scrubbed eggs off a window that wasn't even mine. Had a small fight with an old acquaintance. Said goodbye to an old friend going off to war. Ducked two important phone calls. Took a nap. Fell for a girl.

'Nothing much, Buddy. Nothing much.'

*   *   *

It was an uneventful night with Ben.

We both went to sleep at eight. Not a moment sooner. Not a moment later.

I needed to sleep, so I built a wall. I closed my eyes and pictured it. It was built tough. Made of bricks and cement.

It was taller than Ben.

On the other side of the wall, I put wars. Arguments. Hurled eggs. Falling buildings. Temper tantrums. Butts named Mark. Desperate phone messages. Dead mothers. Dead friends. Multiple sons of Norville headed off to war. Bullets fired at men in turbans. Burning cars at

99

no-name gas stations.

Brain-damaged brothers.

The only thing I allowed on my side was a girl. She had jet-black hair, and flour on her hands. And I still didn't know her name.

17 September 2001

I woke up early the next morning. Not earlier than Ben, but early. Before he could amble into my room and tell me I had to drive him to work.

I found him sitting at the breakfast table, eating kids' cereal in the shapes of cartoon characters I didn't recognize.

He ate slowly, too. Then again, I guess Ben did everything slowly.

'I could take you in a little early,' I said.

'Why early?' he asked, his mouth revoltingly full.

'Why not? I'm up.'

'Fine. Be up. But why early?'

'Your boss doesn't like it when you're late.'

'On time isn't late.'

'True. But neither is early.'

He put down his spoon and looked into my face, his own face open and childlike.

'Is earlier better?'

So, what was I going to do? Lie to him? Take advantage of the guy because I wanted to see a girl, and I couldn't hang on ten minutes?

'Maybe not. I don't know. We should probably just go at the regular time.'

★ ★ ★

101

We were cruising by Nazir's Baked Goods, on the way to the market, when I saw it.

Someone had spray-painted both front windows, in letters several feet high. The first window said, 'GO'. The other said, 'HOME!' With an over-sized exclamation point that dribbled on to the brick under the window.

'Oh, shit,' I said.

'That's a bad word. You said a bad word.'

I hit the brake. Stopped dead. Right in the middle of the street. Nobody else was on the road with us, though. So it hardly mattered. Except to Ben.

'Don't stop here!' he shouted. 'Why are you stopping?'

'I'm looking at that. I'm looking at what someone did to the bakery.'

'Oh,' he said. 'Oh, no.' Like it was his job to clean it up. 'That's bad.'

I was looking for her in the kitchen. But I couldn't see any movement.

A honking horn startled me out of my coma, and I jumped the clichéd mile. There was a car waiting behind me. It was Monday. And somebody else was awake. I waved to him in my rear-view mirror and drove again, nursing a sick feeling at the very bottom of my gut.

'Do they sell hardware-type stuff at your market?'

'What kind?'

'Like a can of paint stripper?'

'What does the can look like?'

'I don't know.'

'I'm not sure, then.'

'Can we ask? When we get there?'

'I guess.'

I pulled into the parking lot, shut off the engine, and walked to the market door with Ben. It was hard to slow my stride enough to match his.

He didn't have to knock. A perky blonde woman walked by the door, caught sight of us, and smiled. She unlocked the door with her key, and levered it open a couple of feet.

Ben ducked by her into the store and disappeared.

'You must be Ben's brother,' she said. 'Ben talks about you constantly.'

'He does?'

Great. Complicate my thinking even more, why don't you?

'Every day. All day. We're glad you're safe, by the way. We were all worried for you. Plus if something had happened to you, too, I don't know what Ben would have done.'

Nice, yet distracting. What was I going to ask about, again? It was important. Oh. Right.

'Thanks. I was wondering if you guys sell paint stripper.'

'Funny you should ask. I just checked when I got in this morning. We have one can. But I'm wondering if I should save it for the El Sayeds. Did you see what someone did to their windows?'

A last name. Progress.

'That's actually why I wanted it. I was going to go by and help them with that. With their windows.'

'Oh. Good.' She seemed a little surprised. Or maybe more than a little. 'Good for you. I'll be right back.'

I waited, blinking, in the near-dark, staring into the glow of the closed market. Then she reappeared with a rectangular metal can.

'How much do I owe you?'

'Nothing.'

'Really? Nothing?'

Was there something wrong with my money in this town?

'I think it's terrible, putting that on their window. They're citizens. They're naturalized. They *are* home. I thought it was disgusting, so if you're going to help get it off there . . . no charge.'

'Thanks,' I said.

'Anything for Ben's brother.'

So maybe that really was my new name.

★ ★ ★

When I pulled up in front of the bakery, there was a man out front. The light still wasn't good, and I couldn't see him well, but I figured I was about to meet Nazir El Sayed.

I thought, She called her father when she saw it, so he could help.

Too bad. I could have helped just fine. It could have been the two of us.

He was scraping at the paint on the window with a carving knife. He'd barely managed to make a dent in the letter G.

When he heard me shut off the engine, he

spun defensively. He stood straight and ready, and watched me approach.

He was only a couple of inches taller than me, but he somehow managed to appear formidable. His body was stocky and thick, his face heavy. His skin was dark, even darker than his daughter's. He wore a rather imposing black mustache.

'What is it?' he barked in that now-familiar accent. 'What do you want?'

'Just coffee and a donut. I brought paint stripper. I thought that would make me welcome.'

I watched him breathe some of the volume out of his shoulders, some of the stiffness out of his neck.

'I apologize sincerely,' he said. 'I am a little on edge.'

'Understandable. I think everybody is. You must be Nazir.'

He peered at my face more closely in the dim light.

'Should I know you?'

'No. I'm just going by what it says on the window. I know your daughter. A little. I've been coming in early for coffee and donuts. She's been very kind.'

'Oh,' he said, as if all of life were suddenly laid out at his feet, sorted and clarified. 'You are Ben's brother. Anat told me about you. I am very sorry for the loss of your mother. A tragic turn of events.'

'Thank you. Where's Anat this morning?'

'Home. Sleeping. She is off on Monday and

Tuesday. Nobody should have to do the morning donuts seven days a week. The early schedule is too hard on the constitution.'

Of course, my heart fell. Wednesday was forty-eight hours away, which felt a little like having been told I'd see her in my next lifetime. But I had a task at hand. No point mourning when I could just as well get at it.

'I'll need gloves, and some kind of cleaning rag for this,' I said, attempting to perform that complicated squeeze-press-and-turn motion that's supposed to keep the paint stripper cap from coming off accidentally, or in the hands of a child.

By the time I got the cap off, and saw that there was a thin safety film of metal underneath, it was too late to ask him to bring me something I could use to puncture it. He came around the dark corner and handed me rubber gloves and a linen dish towel.

'It'll ruin the towel, you know.'

'Go ahead and ruin it. I just want to get this off here.'

My eyes landed on the carving knife he'd been using to scrape paint. It sat on the edge of the brick under one window. The 'GO' window. I picked it up and placed the point of it down on the inner metal cap, and hit the handle of the knife hard with the base of my palm. It punctured easily. So I did it again, at an angle, to form an X. I figured we'd need a lot of paint stripper.

I pulled on the gloves, soaked the rag and then rubbed hard on the top of the G. At first

106

nothing. Then, in a few swipes, it started to smear. In a few more swipes, the G had no top.

'Oh. I just thought. Will this hurt the good paint?'

'Good paint?' he asked.

'Your sign.'

'The good paint is on the inside of the window.'

'Ah. Good.'

I looked over to see that Nazir had more gloves and another towel. I watched him soak it in paint stripper and go to work on the H.

'Anat told me you washed off some eggs yesterday. We don't know why you would do that. We hope you are just a nice young man.'

I hope so, too, I thought. But I didn't say it out loud.

'Purely selfish. I wanted her to keep working on those donuts.'

He said nothing in return. In time, I turned and looked at him. He was studying me closely, seriously, his hand still scrubbing at the letter H.

'But that is more like a joke,' he said.

'True. You're right. Honestly? I'm not sure why. I didn't take a lot of time to think it out. It just seemed like the right thing to do. I guess I thought I could do it more unemotionally than she could. It wasn't an insult directed toward me, so I guess I felt like, if she never even had to see it, then the insult would never be fully delivered. Which was good.'

I looked over again. He was still staring at me.

'You are a nice young man,' he said.

'I hope so.'

107

I finished the G and moved on to the O. It was going fast. Hearteningly so.

'This is what will be hard.' He indicated the bottom of the exclamation point. 'Paint on glass is better. Paint on brick is bad.'

I watched him scrub at the bricks with his towel, but it only smeared the paint around.

'Maybe we should just soak a towel with paint stripper and let it sit on there for a while. Really soak in.'

'I guess that's worth a try,' he said. 'I have the donuts nearly ready. I started them because I did not see. I did not see this. I could not see it from the inside until it got just a little bit light.'

'You came in through the kitchen,' I said. Not really as a question.

'No. I slept last night in the room over the store. We live in the country, a long drive away. I sleep upstairs when I have to open. I don't like to take the drive so early, because I am sleepy and it doesn't feel safe. In any case, when we are done here, you will come inside, please, and have coffee, and eat anything you want as my guest. You will be my guest.'

★   ★   ★

Nazir and I stood side by side at the industrial double sink. Washing our hands. And washing. And washing. And washing. At least four times so far we'd washed, rinsed and dried, smelled our hands, then started over again. Even through the gloves, the paint stripper smell was slow to fade.

'You see?' he said, startling me. We had fallen into silence for some time. 'That is the problem with a thing like this. You think you know how to fix it. How to make everything all right again. But that method to fix it leaves a bad smell behind, and it stays to remind you. When anything is very bad, usually the method to fix it is also bad, and keeps you from putting it completely behind you.'

'Hmm. I'll have to think about that.'

'You seem like a smart young man. I think you know what I mean.'

'I do,' I said. 'I know what you mean.'

★ ★ ★

I sat up front, drinking the only true coffee on earth and eating a jelly-filled donut. Nazir made the donuts in a slightly different order. Now and then I raised my head and watched him work in the kitchen.

'Did you hear about the Sikh?' he asked. After a lot of time silent.

'The what?'

It was a spelling issue. I was thinking s-e-e-k, and so the sentence made no sense.

'The Sikh man at the gas station.'

'Oh, God. Yeah. Ben told me. Made me sick.'

'Imagine how sick it made me. This is why, when you came up to me in the dark, I was not kind to you.'

'I wasn't worried about that.'

'For myself I don't even care so much. But when I think about my daughter.' His voice

109

hardened as he spoke. Rose in volume. 'Even the thought of some anger directed at my daughter.' Reached a crescendo. 'Makes me want to explode.' The last sentence felt explosive.

I felt my face break out in a cold sweat, my stomach turn weak.

'Please don't explode,' I said. 'Too many things have been exploding in my life lately. I couldn't take much more.'

'I am sorry. I can't help being protective of her.'

We fell into silence for a while longer. I looked at the remaining half of my donut and waited for my stomach to settle again.

'I need to tell you something about my daughter,' he said.

And, of course, that foreclosed upon any chance for a settled stomach. I pushed the plate a few inches farther away.

'Anat is a good Egyptian girl. And that is unlike an American girl. An Egyptian girl is raised with traditions of morality. An American girl, you meet her, you text her, to her cell phone, you talk two or three times. Then you 'hook up', and she is OK to 'hook up' with you, because she is raised to think that way. That is not how I raised my daughter.'

I actually put one hand on my stomach. It was that tipped.

'I have no dishonorable intentions toward your daughter,' I said.

I guess it sounds like I was stretching the truth. But it didn't feel that way. I didn't want to text her three times and then hook up. It was nothing like that. And he didn't say it was

110

immoral to think I might love her. Or at least that I could.

'Good,' he said. Sounding completely convinced. Apparently not doubting my word for a moment. 'Good. That is as it should be. You will forgive me for speaking this way to you, but you are a man, and you have been around early when no one else is around.'

'Only because I have to take Ben to work before seven.'

'Understood. Please, you will forgive me. But, as I say, I am protective. You will have something else to eat?'

'No. Thank you. I'm all done.'

'I sincerely hope I have not made you lose your appetite. Anat said you have a big appetite.'

'Oh. Well. When she met me, I had some catching up to do.'

'The first of the bread is about to come out. You will take some bread home with you.'

'You have to let me pay you, though.'

'No. I will not hear of it. I owe you. Besides, it will only go to waste. We make half what we used to make, and we throw more than half of that away. It's a crime. I don't know what we will do.'

'I think people will get over this after a while.'

'I hope so. I hope they get over it soon. Sooner than we will be out of business.'

★   ★   ★

Just as I was leaving, my arms laden with not one but three loaves of bread, Nazir asked one last question.

111

'Who does such a thing, and why? Can you tell me this?'

'People get scared,' I said. 'And it brings out the worst in them. Probably somebody was drunk. Most people know better, till they get drunk. And then they do stupid things. Probably a bunch of guys went out and got drunk. And put each other up to it.'

But then I thought, It was Sunday night. Who goes out and gets drunk on Sunday night?

And then I remembered.

But that was a circumstantial indictment of my old gang. At best.

Wasn't it?

★ ★ ★

I went for a run. Finally. I was finally rested enough to give it a try.

There was only one problem. I was not running in New York. Not in Manhattan. Not in Jersey City. Not in any city.

Another piece of the ice floe of denial breaking loose, I guess. I'd been refusing to take a good look around me and accept where I'd landed. But the ice shifted as I ran, and I missed New York so much that, at one point, I actually had to stop and lean on my own knees. Try to breathe it out. Anyone driving by probably thought I was just out of breath.

Good way to disguise grief. I'd have to remember it.

Then I was forced to admit to myself another problem. Meeting Anat had thrown a wrench into the gears of my half-baked plans. I think, until that moment, I'd believed I would sell the house and take Ben back to New York with me. Even though transplanting Ben was a plan with many potential flaws. But I purposely hadn't examined them fully in the light of day.

Now I had something in Nowhere-ville, someone I might not be willing to leave behind. So I ran through the streets of that town, fully understanding that I was staying. My reaction was to run harder, and faster, counting on endorphins to save me.

Then I saw Vince Buck. He and his parents and his sister — who I went on dates with twice in high school — were getting into the car in their driveway. Vince was in uniform. And I knew this was their actual moment. I could tell by the gravity on the faces of the family. They were taking him to the airport, or the train station. Or wherever you take your son at a time like that.

Vince had been famous for his shaggy long black hair in high school. Now he was shaved close to the scalp, especially on the sides.

I stopped. I broke my run.

'Hey,' I said. 'Vince.'

By then Vince was the only Buck not in the car. So I couldn't really say hi to Hannah. I wondered if she'd done that on purpose, or hadn't even seen me.

'Rusty,' he said.

'Sorry I missed you guys last night.'

'No big deal. Mark was being weird about it,

but you know how Mark is. Nobody agreed with him or anything.'

Then we just stood there, no sounds except my breathlessness. Already out of things to say.

But I noticed something. I'd said I didn't know Vince or Paul the way I knew Larry. But now I knew I was wrong. They were all guys I'd gone to school with. Larry only seemed head and shoulders above the rest because I'd just seen him. Now I was seeing Vince, too. And knowing I didn't want Vince to come home in a body bag, either.

'So come home safe,' I said. 'OK?'

'You bet,' he said. Not seeming the slightest bit nervous. 'You know I'm doing this for you.'

It seemed like a bizarre thing to say.

'For me?'

'Well. You and everybody else who was in those buildings.'

'Oh. Right. Got it.'

I couldn't help thinking about Afghani civilians who would inevitably die. Civilians always do. Along with young men in uniforms. And I thought, Don't do it for me. But I got smart and didn't say so. I didn't say a word about pointlessness. I was learning.

I just shook his hand and then ran again.

It was a weird morning.

★   ★   ★

It was after dinner, and I had just finished washing the dishes.

I looked around and realized that I didn't

114

know where Ben was.

I stuck my head in the TV room. His bedroom. No Ben.

'Ben?' I called, already at the edge of panic.

No answer.

I checked the bathroom. No Ben.

I found him in the living room. Thank God. And I breathed for what felt like the first time in a long time.

'Buddy. Why didn't you answer me?'

'What?'

'I was calling you.'

'Oh.'

I walked over to where he was standing. In front of the mantelpiece. Standing staring at the mantel, the way I'd done my first night back. I'd been thinking about the Christmas village. What was Ben thinking about?

As I moved closer, I saw that one of the pictures of Mom and Dad was missing. But I found it. Just a split second later. In Ben's hands.

I reached up and put my hand on his shoulder, but he pulled away from me. Which hurt my feelings. I wasn't prepared for it to hurt my feelings.

'You miss her,' I said. 'Huh?'

He didn't answer for a long time. I'd begun to think he never would. He didn't take his eyes off the picture.

'She's not coming back,' he said. 'Is she?'

I took a big, deep breath.

'She would if she could, Buddy. But she can't. No.'

Another long moment.

Then I said, 'Hey. Isn't it time for those cartoons you like so much?'

'I dunno.'

'It's six thirty. Isn't that when the first one comes on?'

'I guess.'

'Want to watch it with me?'

'I guess.'

He ambled into the TV room with me, still clutching the picture. I sat him down in one of the big stuffed chairs.

'What channel, Buddy?'

'I dunno.'

I knew that, if left to his own devices, he'd find the cartoons. But I didn't want to argue with him. So I just started looking for the TV listings.

'Where's the TV section?'

'The what?'

'The TV listings. From the paper.'

No answer, so I just kept looking. I looked on the coffee table. Under the chairs. On top of the TV.

Then I heard a sound. A muffled banging sound. Like an impact of some kind.

I spun around to see that Ben had dropped the framed photo on to the rug, and was sitting, leaned forward in his chair, his hands balled up into fists, hitting himself in the head with the heels of both hands. And I mean *hard*.

'Buddy! Hey! Don't do that! Stop that!'

But he didn't stop.

'Hey! Don't hit yourself!'

But I might as well have been talking to the picture, or the rug.

I tried to grab his arms. In fact, I did grab his arms. But he just kept hitting, pulling me closer to him on each strike. Pulling me right along.

Then I suppose he got tired of the restraint, because he pushed hard, with both arms at once, and I landed on my tailbone on the rug.

And that was the start of *my* temper tantrum.

I'm ashamed to admit this next bit, but I was tired, and beaten down, and emotional. And so I started yelling at my mom.

'Why did you leave me with this?' I screamed. 'I can't deal with this! I can't do this! I don't know how you did this all those years, but I can't! You should've left me some kind of instructions or something!'

I paused, and listened to the sound of wrist bones on skull.

'I don't know how to help him! I'm not helping him! This is not fair to me! This is not fair to any of us!'

Then I started to cry.

I cried quietly for a few seconds before I realized the room was silent, save for an occasional sniffle from me.

A moment later, I felt his hand on my back.

'Why are you crying, Buddy?' he asked, plunking himself on the rug beside me and draping one long arm over my shoulder.

'I miss her, too, you know. Don't you think I miss her, too?'

Silence, while he thought that over. I expected him to say it was a hard question.

'But you never saw her.'

I started to say, Not never. Just not for six

117

years. But then I realized that, to Ben, six years was for ever.

'But I always figured I could.'

'I don't like it when you cry.'

'Yeah? Well, I don't like it when you hit yourself in the head. I can't deal with that. At all. How can you hurt yourself like that? I can't watch that. That must've hurt like hell. Doesn't your head hurt now?'

'Sort of.'

'You must've given yourself one hell of a headache.'

'I guess.'

'Want some aspirin?'

'No. I don't like pills.'

'Now I feel like I should take you to a doctor. Make sure you don't have a concussion.'

The arm disappeared from around my shoulder.

'I don't like going to the doctor.'

'It makes no difference what you like, Ben. Sometimes we have to do things we don't like.'

God knows.

'But I don't like doing things I don't like.'

I laughed. In spite of myself. 'Nobody does, Buddy.'

'Please? I feel fine.'

'Tell you what. This time I'll figure you don't have a concussion. This one time. But if you ever hit yourself in the head again, we're going to the doctor.'

'OK. I won't, then.'

'Promise?'

'Promise.'

He pulled himself to his feet. I stayed, rooted to the rug. A moment later I heard the cartoons come on. Full blast. The roadrunner and the coyote.

I sighed, and got myself up off the floor. Picked up the picture of Mom and Dad from the rug.

'I'm going to put this back now. Is that OK with you?'

But I asked just as the coyote ran over the edge of a cliff, felt around gingerly in the air with one foot, then waved goodbye and fell.

A hearty, deep laugh from Ben. I knew better than to try to regain his attention.

I carried the picture back to the living room and put it back in its place on the mantel. As I did, I looked at my mom, and thought I knew what she would tell me, if she were here.

She'd say, See? You're figuring it out.

'Not fair,' I said, out loud. 'Not fair that I should have to. Especially all by myself.'

Tell me all about it, she said.

At least, in my head that's what she said.

18 September 2001

I woke up early the next morning. Quarter after six. No point going back to sleep. Ben would be in to wake me in just a few minutes, anyway.

I lay awake in the night light glow, trying to decide if I wanted to go into the bakery that morning. God's honest truth? I was a little bit afraid of Nazir's intensity. Not afraid in any real way. Not in a way that would have held me back a week earlier in the history of the world. But in my depleted state . . . I closed my eyes and felt around in the empty hole inside myself. It felt short on resources, short on resistance. For reasons I couldn't quite put my finger on, it asked that we please not see Nazir. At least, not this very morning.

I opened my eyes to see Ben standing over my bed.

'I'll be up in a minute, Buddy,' I said.

'I don't want to go to work today. I don't feel good.'

'Your head?' I asked, more than a little alarmed.

I sat up fast.

He has a concussion, of course he does, I thought, and I should've taken him to the emergency room, whether he liked it or not, and now it's come back to bite us, and I am a terrible, terrible brother.

'No. Not my head.'

'What, then?'

'Oh. Uh. My . . . stomach.'

'What about it?'

'It . . . hurts.'

'Do you feel like you're going to throw up?'

'No. It just hurts. Just a little bit. Not enough to go to the doctor.'

'If it's just a little bit, maybe you should go to work anyway.'

'No. It's too much for work. But not enough for the doctor.'

'You sure it's not your head? I'm still worried you have a concussion.'

But I wasn't. Not by then. I was just exploring the boundaries of his increasingly flimsy complaints.

'I think my head does. Hurt. A little. But not like I had a concussion. Some other way.'

'Some other way. That's interesting. So what do you think we should do?'

'You should tell Mr McCaskill I'm not coming.'

'*I* should? Why not you? It's your job.'

'I don't know his phone number.'

'How can you work there and not have the phone number?'

'Because Mom had it for me.'

I sighed.

'Got it. OK. You go on back to bed. I'll see if I can figure this out.'

I got up and got dressed, then looked for

121

phone numbers on the side of the refrigerator. I only succeeded in finding mine. Nobody else's. I dug up a comically thin phone book — for the whole county — in the drawer under the kitchen telephone. I looked up Gerson's Market.

I called, but got only a recording with the store hours.

I found Ben in his bedroom, curled up on his side under the covers.

'You OK here by yourself for a little bit?'

'Yeah.'

'You sure?'

'Yeah.'

'Good. Because I don't have a direct number for him. So I'll have to drive over there and tell him.'

'Good. Tell him I'm really sick.'

'Really sick?' I asked, noting he'd gotten sicker in the last couple of minutes.

'No. Not really sick. Not enough for the doctor. Just too much for work.'

★ ★ ★

I slowed on my way by the bakery, and tensed. I felt a bracing, an armoring, in that weak spot inside of me. The spot that asked not to see Nazir that day. The spot that couldn't handle much more.

But it appeared all had gone well in the night, El Sayed-wise.

I parked in the market parking lot and made my way through the civil twilight to the door, only to be spotted by that same perky woman.

Of course, she unlocked the door and pushed it partway open.

'Ben's brother,' she said.

'That does seem to be my name, doesn't it?'

'I'm sorry. Rusty.'

'I go by Russell now, actually.'

'Sorry again.'

'Don't be. It's fine. Is Mr McCaskill around?'

'Sure. I'll get him. Everything OK with Ben?'

'Probably. But he thinks he's sick.'

'Really? That doesn't sound like Ben. He hasn't missed one single day in two and a half years.'

Then she disappeared, leaving the door to drift closed and me to think that over.

McCaskill appeared what seemed like seconds later. I knew his face. I knew I'd grown up in the same town with him. But I didn't know him, not even well enough to connect his face with his name. Until that moment.

'Everything OK?' he asked.

'Probably,' I said. 'But Ben thinks he's sick. He thinks he either has a stomach ache or a headache. Or both. Just enough to keep him home, but not enough to warrant a doctor visit, which he doesn't like.'

'That doesn't sound like Ben.'

'So I'm hearing. It may help to know that he just finally got it last night about our mom being gone for good.'

'Oh. Poor Ben. I mean . . . poor you, too. My condolences about your mom. So . . . '

'So. I just needed to come and tell you.'

'Am I missing something?' he asked. 'Do you

123

need my help with this in some way?'

'No. I'm just telling you he isn't coming in to work today.'

Amazingly, he continued to stare at me in obvious confusion. I almost said something short to him. I almost said, What part of this are you having trouble with? It seems straightforward to me.

'Ben doesn't work today,' he said. 'It's his day off.'

I dropped my head back and looked up at the barely light sky.

'Are you kidding me?'

'He's off Tuesdays and Wednesdays.'

'And he doesn't even know that?'

'God's honest truth? I don't know what he knows. I just know he's working out good here. I just know he shows up every Thursday through Monday, without fail, and never showed up on a day off yet. I don't know if he knows it, but then he got upset and forgot, or if your mom used to keep his schedule for him.'

I brought my head down, and into the shelter of my hands.

'You have no idea,' I said, quietly, 'how much I wish I knew where she kept the owner's manual on him.'

'I can imagine.'

'Sorry to take your time for nothing.'

'Oh, hell, don't worry about that.' Then, just as I was walking away, 'Rusty.'

I stopped, and turned.

'Russell. I go by Russell now.'

'Russell. Sorry. I don't really know you. But in

another way I do. I mean, I sort of watched you grow up, but from a distance, you know? Anyway . . . if you don't mind my asking . . . you going to put him in a home?'

'No.'

'Really?'

'Really. No.'

'Good for you.' Just when I thought that would be all, he added, 'Probably shouldn't tell you this . . . '

But you will, I thought. And I was right. He did.

'We were sort of . . . taking bets. Almost. Not that money changed hands or anything. But a lot of us figured you wouldn't come back at all. Just make a phone call and get him put somewhere. But then we knew you'd have to come back for your mom's funeral, so that was a stupid thought. So most of us figured you'd come home for maybe five days and get him put somewhere. Can't recall that anybody thought you'd come back and really take care of him. That can't be easy.'

'It's not.'

'I can imagine. Anyway. My point is . . . I didn't know you well enough to judge you, I guess none of us did. And we obviously got it wrong. So, sorry about that.'

I examined the inside of myself for a moment to see if it was worth being offended. It felt like too much trouble.

'Oh, hell,' I said. 'I'd probably have bet against me, too.'

He smiled. And that was my chance to break

free. But I didn't. I walked closer to where he stood, still framed in the sliding door of the market.

'Let me ask you a question,' I said. 'Ever patronize the bakery?'

'I don't, no.'

'Any special reason?'

'Gluten allergy.'

'Ah. Good reason. Still, you could do me a favor. You see a lot of people every day in your work. So if you could encourage anybody to go back in, that would be great. The El Sayeds are hurting. Think how you'd be hurting if practically nobody came in your store for a week. And no end in sight . . . '

'I know, huh? And just because they're Arab.'

'They're Egyptian.'

'Oh. Middle Eastern. Middle Eastern, I guess I meant.'

'I better get back to Ben. I don't even know if I'm supposed to be leaving him alone. I don't know if my mom left him by himself. I don't know . . . '

'Good luck finding that manual.'

And he laughed. Even though we both knew it wasn't funny.

I think we also both knew I'd end up writing my own from scratch.

★ ★ ★

Driving by the bakery, I couldn't help looking into the glow of the kitchen. I saw a figure cross by the window. It was not Nazir. It was Anat.

126

My foot hit the brake as if of its own accord, and the tires skidded slightly.

By the time I'd managed to pull up to the curb, my heart was pounding so hard I thought it might burst free. And not in a good way. I couldn't breathe, which didn't help. And I thought, Why doesn't love feel good? Why does it make you feel like you're about to die? Why doesn't it make you feel like you're about to live?

My thighs felt trembly, and barely got me to the door.

It was open, so I stuck my head in.

'Have I got my days mixed up?' I asked, wondering if I sounded as breathless as I felt.

She looked up, and her face lit up to see me. And that made it all worse, though in a wonderful way. But the heart rate, the breathing, the standing up straight or lack of same. Worse.

'I don't know, Ben's brother. I give up. What day do you think it is?'

I stepped inside, feeling like I was walking in a dream again. Or still. Had I ever wakened up in-between? I wasn't sure.

'I think it's Tuesday. And I think your father told me you're off on Tuesday.'

'Normally, yes. Normally I would be off. But he wasn't feeling well last night and this morning. What would you like? He says your money is no good here, so whatever you like. He specifically said that, just as I was leaving. Whatever you eat here, there's no change. He told me what you did to help him. So what will you have?'

I dream-stepped up to the dream counter.

'What's still warm?'

'I just finished the chocolate glazed.'

'Sold.'

I leaned on the counter and watched her choose one for me. I tried to look casual, as if leaning was the thing to do. Not as if I might topple otherwise.

'So, is he OK, your father?'

'Oh, I think so. I think he just takes everything too hard. Too seriously. Like he can't let things roll off his back. You know what I mean? And so the stress takes a toll on him. I don't mean to make light of the situation, because he really is worried about money. But he's just so . . . I can't quite get the word, but he's more of it than he needs to be.'

'Intense?'

'Yes. There you go. He's too intense.'

She brought me the donut, careful not to look into my eyes. Or, anyway, that was my observation. And though I was definitely the sort to doubt myself, some inner knowing-place observed this with unshakable confidence. It felt strange to know anything for sure again.

And something else came clear to me in that moment: why I'd been a little afraid to see Nazir. It wasn't his protectiveness toward his daughter, or even his extreme candor on that subject. It was even simpler. He was unable to deal with his stress. And I'd been taking on that stress when I was with him.

I took a deep breath and sat down with my donut, grateful for the clarity.

'Lot of that going around,' I said. 'Ben thinks

he's sick today, too. Last night he seemed to have a sort of breakthrough. Figuring out that our mom isn't coming back. So today he has a stomach ache. But I suspect stress.' I lifted the still-hot donut to my mouth. And then it hit me. 'Oh, crap. I can't sit here and have a donut. I left him alone. I'm not even sure if it's OK to leave him alone.'

'No problem,' she said. 'Don't worry. I'll wrap it up to go. Get some coffee, and I'll bring you a lid for the cup, and give me the donut back, and I'll wrap it all up to go.'

'Thanks,' I said, wondering if I was successfully disguising my disappointment. Here I was about to sit down, unexpectedly, and enjoy a stolen morning with Anat. And now I could feel the expectation of that pleasure pulling out of me, leaving an empty, deflated space in my chest.

I felt like saying, This is so not fair. But that would made me sound more childlike than Ben.

I gave her back the donut.

'I'm wrapping a jelly-filled for Ben. You tell him it's from Anat. Will you? Tell him I hope he feels better soon.'

'I will,' I said, making myself a coffee to go and feeling sulky.

'Oh, my goodness,' she said. 'Will you look at that? We have a customer. And it isn't even you!'

I looked up to see McCaskill come through the front door.

'You open?' he asked.

Then he noticed me, and nodded at me, and I nodded back. It was a good moment.

'Open enough,' she said.

'Sorry I never come in,' he said, 'but I'm allergic.'

'Gluten?'

'Yeah. Gluten.'

'I used to make gluten-free bread, but I stopped, because not enough people were buying it.'

'I'd buy it.'

'Good. I'll make some any day, if you say you'll be by to get it.'

'OK. Maybe I will. Thanks. For now, how bout you pick me out a dozen donuts. Just a nice assortment — you pick. Thought I'd put some in the employee break room this morning. Everybody's been feeling down lately, you know. Been a tough time. It'll be a treat for them.'

'What a nice idea,' I said.

And I made my way to the counter to pick up my to-go bag.

'Here, for you and Ben,' she said, as she handed it over. 'Don't forget to tell him Anat says get well soon.'

As I took it from her, my hand touched hers. And, in that split second, we looked into each other's eyes. And I knew. I knew she felt the same.

But I couldn't hang around and express what I knew. I had to put the whole incredible moment on hold until that 'next lifetime' of tomorrow morning.

So much was out of my control. Had so much of my life always been out of my control? I couldn't recall. I could no longer connect with what my life had used to be. That was so long ago. It was . . . I did the math in my head. The tenth of September was 'before', and that had been . . . eight days ago.

It was all so impossible that I couldn't think about it any more. I had to file it away under Things That Might Make Sense Later. At that moment, it sure as hell made no sense.

★   ★   ★

I still wasn't breathing normally when I got back. Oh, I'm sure it looked and sounded normal. But it was conscious. Not reflexive. The slightest distraction, and I'd just stop breathing. Or, anyway, that's how it felt.

Ben was in bed, right where I'd left him. Thank God.

'How's your stomach?'

'Bad.'

'Oh. Too bad. Anat sent you a jelly donut.'

Ben sat straight up in bed.

'I could eat a jelly donut.'

'You sure it won't hurt your stomach?'

'I don't think it was my stomach. I think it was more my head.'

'But not like a concussion.'

'No. Not like that.'

'Well, you better come to the table for this,' I said, unwrapping the donuts.

'Why can't I eat it in bed?'

'Because it has jelly that squishes out when you bite it, and it's all covered in powdered sugar.'

'I'm getting up,' he said.

131

He dragged his long, only partially responsive legs to the table, still in his flannel pajamas. I put our donuts on plates and set them on the table. Ben bit his donut hard, and directly, squirting jelly out on to his plate. And the table.

'Sorry,' he said.

'Never mind. I'll wipe it up later. So. Listen. Tell me something, Buddy. Do you know which days are your days off from work?'

'You mean when I don't go in?'

'Right.'

'Yeah.'

'Which ones?'

'The ones when I have to make my own cereal because Mom's getting ready to drive me to work are the days I go in. The ones when she makes me pancakes and goes back to bed are the days I don't.'

I sighed, and took a bite of my chocolate donut. It was still slightly warm, and made me think of Anat. Then again, what didn't?

'Got it. So I need to keep your schedule. That's another page for my manual.'

'What is that? What you just said?'

'A manual? It's like a book you use to figure out how something is done.'

'I could use that,' he said.

'We all could. Oh, and I forgot. When she gave you that donut, Anat said to tell you to get well soon.'

He looked up at me. Right into my eyes. For the first time since I'd been back. It startled me. I thought he never looked into anybody's eyes.

'You like her!' he said. Loudly. Strongly. A sort of proud accusation.

'Why do you say that?'

'Because you do!'

'But why did you say it?'

'Because it's true!'

'Let's try this another way, Buddy. How do you know?'

'It's right there,' he said.

And he pointed, with two fingers of his right hand. Two powdered sugar-covered fingers, pointing right at my two eyes.

★ ★ ★

If I'd had any doubt at all that Ben's health problems stemmed from missing our mom, his temper tantrum at dinner would have cleared things up.

I'd thawed and heated up a lasagna I found in the freezer, and I was just cutting it when I looked up to see him standing in the kitchen doorway.

'I want that macaroni and cheese you make from a box,' he said.

'Well, we're having this,' I said.

'But I want that.'

'I'll make it tomorrow, then.'

'Mom always makes me macaroni and cheese when I ask for it.'

So, there you have it. That's simple enough.

'Maybe because you told her in time, and she hadn't already gone to the trouble to make something else.'

'No. Always. If I ask.'

I doubted that. Having known my mom. But I didn't say so.

'Well, I'm not Mom.'

I more or less knew that would set him off. But it needed to be said.

He said nothing, but his face twisted, and he launched into his box-pacing, his hands clenched into fists and pounding at his hips, angry tears leaking.

I tried an experiment.

I sat down on the kitchen floor and acted out my frustration in a very big way. Highly visible. And audible. I put my head in my hands. I made a strangled sound in my throat. It had worked once. Maybe it was a key.

No response from Ben.

So I cried.

Not literally. I hate to have to say I faked it. But it was something like that. I made a show of crying.

A second or two later Ben plunked on to the kitchen linoleum beside me and draped an arm over my shoulder.

'What's wrong, Buddy?'

'I went to a lot of trouble to make you a nice dinner, and it hurts my feelings that you don't want it.'

'I want it,' he said.

'You said you wanted macaroni and cheese.'

'No. I don't. I want what you made. Really.'

'Good. I'm glad. That makes me feel better.'

He helped me to my feet and we ate in peace and silence.

Note for my manual: Ben prioritizes my sorrow over his own.

★ ★ ★

I didn't sleep well that night. I lost most of the night thinking about it.

What does it mean when someone loses the use of most of his brain, and it makes him more kind?

I couldn't wait till morning, so I could talk it over with Anat, and get her opinion. But I knew what she would say. She'd say it must have returned Ben to his original nature.

But she didn't know Ben like I did. She hadn't known him before. This was nothing like Ben's original nature.

Part Three

Sinking

23 August 1981

When I was four, my brother Ben told me there was a monster lurking in the drain of our bathroom sink, drinking the water we provided him and living only on toothpaste and hand soap. So far.

'Listen,' he said, tilting his head over the sink. He turned on the tap for the count of three, then shut it off again. 'Hear that? You can hear him swallowing.'

And he was right. I could.

I backed all the way up into the hall, and slammed right into my mom's legs.

'Brush. Your. Teeth,' she said. As if I'd better not make her say it again. Then she walked on.

I took one step closer to the bathroom sink. Just one.

Ben shot me one of those maniacal smiles.

'How can he just eat toothpaste?' I asked, hating that my voice was shaking, and that I knew Ben could hear it. 'And soap?'

'He can't,' Ben said. 'And that's just the problem. Sooner or later he's going to have to reach out and try to grab something better. So be extra careful when you first lean over. And right when you turn the water off. Because sooner or later he'll get hungry. Now brush your teeth, Wussy Boy.'

And he laughed and went off to his room.

Usually I fought back hard at the Wussy Boy insult. But that night I was too scared to open my mouth again.

I sidled up to the sink and stood up on my tiptoes. I didn't pull the step bench around, the one I was supposed to use at the sink. I figured it would be better if my feet were firmly planted on the bathroom tiles. In case I had to run like hell.

I grabbed my toothbrush, bruising the underneath of my arm on the edge of the porcelain. And pulling my hand back fast. Nothing. But I didn't dare reach for the toothpaste. This time he'd be tipped off. He'd know to expect me.

I stood in the middle of the bathroom, brushing my teeth with a dry brush.

Then it hit me that I could use the water from the tub.

I ran some tub water on the brush, then stood leaning over the tub, brushing my teeth and hoping neither one of my parents would come in and tell me to cut the crap and do it right.

Just as I was rinsing my mouth and my toothbrush, Ben stuck his head in the bathroom again.

'Well, I hope you don't think that's going to save you,' he said.

'It's not?'

'It's all one pipe. Under the house.'

'How can it be all one?'

Ben sighed, like he just couldn't tolerate my

stupidity. But I was used to that.

'It all goes into the sewer as one pipe. Right?'

'I dunno. I guess.'

'So then it splits off and goes to all the different sinks and tubs. So he came up from the sewer. Right? All monsters come up from the sewer. So he can be in any pipe he wants.'

'Even in Mom and Dad's bathroom?'

'Yup. And don't forget the kitchen sink. I think the reason he mostly hangs out in here is because you do.'

I said nothing, knowing I couldn't hide my terror if I did.

'Because you're the smallest. You know. The easiest to pull back down the pipe.'

I dropped my toothbrush on the floor and ran to bed, where I waited for my mom to come tuck me in.

Ben walked by my bedroom doorway and stopped suddenly.

'What was that?' he asked, sounding startled.

'What?'

My heart pounded so hard I could hear it and feel it in my ears.

'Thought I saw something go by the window. Well. Maybe it was nothing. Night, Wussy Boy.'

I pulled the covers over my head and called for my mom. A split second later, Ben appeared in the doorway again.

'Do *not* tell Mom there was something outside the window,' he said.

'Why not?'

'Because she has a weak heart. Didn't you know that? You could scare her to death. You don't want to scare her to death, do you?'

'No.'

'Then keep your mouth shut.'

And he disappeared again.

About a minute later my mom stuck her head in my door.

'Why is your toothbrush on the floor?'

'I dunno. I guess it fell. Could you come here a minute?'

She came to my bed. Sat on the edge of it. Smoothed my hair back off my forehead. 'What are you all in a tizzy about? You're shaking. Are you sick?' She held a warm palm to my forehead. I wished it, and she, would never go away.

'No.'

'What's up, then?'

'Nothing. Can you send Dad in?'

She sighed deeply. 'Now, what can your father do that I can't?'

'I dunno. Could you just get Dad?'

'OK. Fine.'

And she left me alone with the monsters again.

My dad appeared in the doorway about a minute later.

'What? I'm right in the middle of my show.'

'This is big.'

He sighed, and came and sat on the edge of my bed.

'Will you go look outside? See if anything's out there?'

'Like what?'

'Like a robber. Or a monster.'

'No such thing as monsters.'

'Robber, then.'

'Why would you think there's a robber out there?'

'Ben saw something go by the window.'

'Ben,' he said. Like he was saying, 'The source of all evils in the world.' 'If Ben saw somebody out there, why didn't he come tell me? Or your mom?'

'He said we can't tell Mom. That she has a bad heart and it might scare her to death. How come you never told me that?'

He straightened his legs and rose to his feet, towering high over my bed.

'I'll be right back. I have to go have a little talk with your brother.'

But it wasn't really going to be a talk. I thought it was. At first. But then I heard him open the front closet. Instead of going straight to Ben's room. If he'd gone straight, that would be a talk. Stop at the hall closet, that's a strapping. That's where he goes to pick up the strap.

Then I got even more scared, more than I'd been so far that entire night. Because monsters and robbers were in a sort of maybe category. But Ben, if I got him strapped . . . which I guess I did . . . that was more dangerous than anything.

I heard him yelping. I counted the number of times Ben yelped. Fourteen. Fourteen lashes. Fourteen welts on his butt, or on the backs of his legs. So maybe no more public pool for a few weeks, or maybe he could just wear bigger, longer trunks.

I heard my dad saying things to him, but I

couldn't make out the words.

Then silence.

I wondered if anybody would even remember to come tuck me in.

My dad came in, the strap still hanging from his hand.

'Your mother does not have a weak heart,' he said.

'Oh. Good. Why would Ben say so, then?'

'Kiddo, I have no idea why Ben does half the things he does. In the future, just figure if Ben says it, it isn't true.'

'So you think maybe nothing went by the window?'

'I can just about guarantee nothing went by the window.'

'What about the monster in the bathroom sink?'

'Did he tell you that?' His voice rose sharply, and he turned back toward my door, like he was going to go strap Ben again.

'No,' I said. 'Please don't. You already did.'

'Right.' He came and sat on my bed with me. 'If there was a monster in the sink, you'd see it.'

'No. It's in the pipe.'

'Oh. In the pipe. But I told you there's no such thing as monsters.'

'But you can hear him drinking.'

'Rusty. Kiddo. That's just the sound water makes when it goes down the drain.'

'Oh. But . . . '

My dad sighed. 'Go ahead. But what?'

'What if Ben's a big liar *and* there's a robber outside? Both?'

He sighed again. More deeply this time. 'Want me to go look?'

'Yeah. Thanks.'

He wasn't gone thirty seconds when Ben appeared in my doorway and shut off the light, throwing me into darkness.

'You are so dead, Wussy Boy,' he said.

But he knew my father would be back. So he'd have to kill me later. Like the monster in the pipe, he'd just have to lie in wait for the perfect moment.

★　★　★

I'm sure he killed me later, but I don't specifically remember the incident. He killed me an awful lot of times.

5 July 1983

Ben let out a whoop and jerked the end of his fishing rod high, just like my father was always trying to teach him not to do. But he paid no price for impetuous fishing — this time. A trout landed in the bottom of our canoe, right at my feet. In fact, it landed *on* my feet, then flipped its way off again.

I watched in horror as it began the process of dying.

Of course, Ben laughed at me.

'Don't look so horrified, Wussy Boy,' he said.

But it's horrifying. I'm sorry, it just is. I've never been a vegetarian, and I don't have a moral issue with killing an animal for food, but nothing could be worse than fishing. Because you just sit there and watch the fish die. Watch it flop around, desperate for air, until it's too weak to flop any more. At least hunters try for a clean kill. They try to end the animal's suffering on the first shot. They don't hold the deer's head underwater and watch while it drowns.

I've been told that many fishermen hit the fish once in the head, hard, to minimize its suffering. Needless to say, my brother Ben was not one of them.

'Hold it up, Ben,' my father called over from

his canoe, paddling closer.

Ben held the fish up and smiled widely, and my father raised and aimed a disposable camera. I smiled, too. But later, when the picture was developed, I found out I wasn't in it.

I popped the end of my fishing rod up and down, like I was trying to interest a trout in my worm. But I had no worm. As always, I'd snuck my hook into the water baitless, careful to work while Ben wasn't looking.

Later, when I reeled it in, he would laugh at me and say something like, 'Ha, ha, your bait got stolen and you didn't even know it, and you've been fishing without bait this whole time, Wussy.'

'Reel in,' my father yelled at us. 'We're going to paddle over to that bank.'

My father was about twenty feet away, in his own canoe. He pointed to a brushy/reedy area on the shore of the lake.

My father drank a lot of beer while we fished. A lot. Much more than he would drink later in camp. Though it never occurred to me at the time, I now think his love of fishing was closely wrapped around his love of beer, and our mother's hatred of watching him drink it.

I noticed something just now. I said 'my father' and 'our mother.' So maybe Ben's insecurities, which I'll get to soon enough, were not so far off track. But now I'm getting off track.

When my father said he was paddling ashore, he meant he needed to pee. Again. Granted, it's not impossible for a man to pee over the side of a canoe. But every time my father peed he also needed to offload an armful of beer bottles, usually behind some vegetation. And we needed to paddle along with him, so we weren't too far out on the lake by ourselves. After all, we were only six and twelve. Too young to be out in a canoe alone. Or with a drunken father. But of course I'm stacking on that last observation after the fact.

I reeled in, and Ben and I watched as my bare hook broke the waterline.

He said something new this time. He said, 'You think I'm stupid? You think I don't know you always cast it in there with no worm?'

I said nothing. Just felt my face grow hot and — probably — red. I looked down at Ben's trout, which now lay perfectly still. I wondered if it was dead, or just accepting the inevitability of its fate.

Ben shook his head and began to paddle.

We watched my father land his canoe on the muddy bank and step out, his rubber boots sinking into the mud up to his mid-calves. He cursed loudly, embarrassing me. I looked around to see if anyone could hear, but saw no one on the shore, no one within sight on the lake.

'Scared of the worms, Wussy Boy?' Ben asked.

'No.' A little grossed out, maybe. 'I just don't want to kill them.'

'The fish? Or the worms?'

'Both, I guess.'

I could hear the sucking sound my father's boots made as he pulled them up out of the mud, step after step. He struggled for balance, his arms loaded with empty brown-glass bottles.

I looked up at Ben, and his face was dark. 'So

I'm a killer? Is that it? You're saying I'm a killer?'

Of course it's easy to look back and know what I should have said. But everything just happened so fast. I looked at the blank, open eye of the trout, lying in the bottom of the canoe. And I nodded. It just seemed so obvious.

I realized my mistake quickly enough, but too late. My father had disappeared behind the vegetation, where he couldn't save me. I felt myself lifted by the back of my shirt and propelled up and through the air. I broke the water and swirled down into the greenish lake for a frightening space of time, increasingly desperate for oxygen. If I had known Ben was about to throw me in, I'd have taken a deep breath and made it last. But I'd had no such preparation.

I thought of the trout. I thought, I know now. Just how you felt.

I began to push for the surface, and it wasn't until my face broke out into the air, and I gasped for breath, that I looked at my hands and saw they were empty.

I no longer had my dad's ultra-light rod and reel.

Ben wasn't laughing. Or taunting me. But he had a satisfied look on his face that I found deeply disturbing.

I treaded water for a minute or two before I heard my father.

'What the hell just happened?' he yelled.

I looked over to see him struggle back into the canoe without taking time to rinse the mud off his boots. If I hadn't been in the water, he would have dangled and swished his boots in the lake, one at a time, while half the canoe was still grounded, to keep all that mud out of the rented boat.

'He fell in!' Ben yelled back.

My father said nothing. Just paddled over to me. He couldn't pull me into his canoe without tipping it over, so instead he handed me the end of a rope, which I held on to as he paddled me over to the shore.

'Can you stand up now?' he asked.

I put my feet down, and they sank deeply into the silty mud. When I pulled my right foot up again, it came up bare. The mud kept one of my good sandals. I fell over into the water, hands buried in the silt, popped up blubbering, and pulled out my other foot, careful to bend my foot to grip the sandal. As if it really mattered to hold on to your one remaining sandal once it had lost its mate. My father had the canoe landed by then, and he picked me up by the shirt, much the way Ben had, rinsed me off by dunking me in the lake a few times almost to my neck, and then loaded me in.

He used the paddle to push off from the shore, and it came up with a deep half-moon of mud on the blade. My father looked at me as he paddled on one side only, turning the boat toward camp.

'Where's my ultra-light?' he asked. Quietly.

I pointed straight down, and he nodded. As if he'd known that much already.

'Sorry,' I said, miserably.

'Not your fault,' he whispered. But he didn't elaborate. Not at the time.

We paddled the rest of the way in silence.

150

My mother was waiting for us back in camp, looking artificially cheerful. And Sandy was there, wagging her whole body. She barked once, sharply, as if to insist that Ben and my father paddle faster.

'You weren't out very long,' our mother said. 'Already catch your limit?'

Ben climbed out of the boat and held up his trout proudly, to show her. He had it on a stringer now. I wondered when he'd put it on the stringer.

My father jumped out of our canoe, stepped up behind Ben. I was behind them, so I couldn't see his face, but my mother's face served as a mirror. I saw the trouble reflected in hers, and I know Ben saw it, too. He'd just barely begun to turn when my father smacked him across the back of the head, sending him sprawling into the dirt. The trout landed three or four feet away, and flopped once, weakly. Sandy sniffed it. Oh, dear God, I thought. It's still alive. How can it still be alive?

'Heeeey!' Ben's voice was whiny, wounded. He struggled to his feet. 'What was that for?'

'You think I'm stupid?' my father roared. Yes, *my* father. So long as we're being specific about it. 'I don't know what pisses me off more: when you torture your little brother, or when you treat me like I'm stupid. If Rusty had fallen out of the canoe, he'd've tipped it over. He didn't fall. Did he, Ben? *Did he?*'

Silence. I still hadn't gotten out of my father's canoe. Nobody moved or spoke for a long time. My mother's eyes fell on me, as if just now

151

noticing I was dripping wet. Sandy slouched into our open tent and lay down, looking guilty.

'Get your things,' my father said, more quietly. 'I'm taking you home.'

'But, Bert,' our mother said. 'We just got here.'

'Not you,' he said. 'You stay here. Rusty stay here. Ben's going back.'

'Bert, he can't stay alone,' she said, a model of artificial patience. I think, looking back, that she always knew when my father was drunk, and tried to correct his mistakes without mentioning that obvious fact. 'He's only twelve.'

'I'll ask the Jesperses to look after him, then. But me and Rusty and you, we're going to have a decent vacation. For a change. We're not going to let Ben mess it up for us. Not this time.'

Ben said nothing. Just ducked into our tent and began to stuff a few things into his duffel bag. My father stood by the tent flap like a prison guard, watching and waiting, arms laced across his chest.

I climbed out of the canoe and stood in front of my mother, and she looked down at me, and noticed I was wearing only one sandal. I could see it register on her face, see the loss of something recorded in her eyes. Sandals cost money. So that was one more expense to add to all the other expenses we boys were constantly wringing out of the family budget.

I hobbled over and picked up the trout by its stringer. Determined that its death would not be in vain. I brought it to my mother. But she was busy watching the drama play out. We watched together as Ben and my father loaded up the

152

truck with Ben's things. They drove off without further comment.

I stood, holding the stringer, feeling the sun burn the back of my neck and the tops of my ears. I'd already gotten too much sun without realizing it. It seemed to take her for ever, and I didn't know why, but eventually she broke her statue-like status and took the fish from me.

'Go get into some dry clothes,' she said.

I didn't. I sat in the tent for a while, stroking Sandy's ears and watching my mother make a fire. She still hadn't said another word since they'd left.

Suddenly she looked in at me. 'You don't want trout, do you?'

I shook my head.

'I knew that. I knew that once you'd watched it die, you wouldn't eat it. You're my sensitive guy.'

I winced inwardly, figuring that was her polite way of saying 'Wussy Boy'.

'Hot dogs?'

I nodded.

I climbed out of the tent after a while. When I could smell them. When the smell made me realize how hungry I was. I sat by the fire and watched them sizzle on the iron grate, watched Sandy lick the air, as if the aroma could be stolen.

'You know he's just jealous of you,' my mother said.

I had no idea what she was talking about.

'Ben?'

'Yes. Ben.'

'How *could* he be?'

My mother sighed deeply. Rolled the three hot dogs over with a long barbecue fork, exposing blackened ridges on their undersides. 'He doesn't see his father any more, and he probably never will again, and your father isn't Ben's father, and Ben knows it . . . and . . . I don't think he ever stops testing that. At least, it doesn't seem like he does. I think Ben feels like your father . . . loves you better. You know. Because you're his.'

'Does he?'

I looked up at her face for the first time in quite a long while. She had a little bit of gray at the part line of her hair, and I don't think I'd ever noticed it before. She wasn't very old.

She sighed again. 'Oh, Rusty. You ask the hardest . . . I don't know . . . I think he *tries* to love you both the same. But Ben makes it so hard. And it just keeps going around in a circle like that.'

I think I didn't know, at the time, what she meant. I didn't know *what* kept going around in a circle. I do now. I know for a fact that I didn't believe her. I didn't think she was lying to me, I just thought she was wrong. Ben wasn't jealous of me. That was impossible. He just hated me. For a number of very concrete reasons.

I should note that my father was too drunk to be out on the road, and we both knew it. And that cast a pall over lunch. Well. It was hard to tell what was what inside that pall, but I think drunk-driving was a big part of it. Not that he didn't go out on the road in that — or an even

154

more advanced — condition pretty regularly. But you still worry every time.

But he made it back. He dropped Ben at the Jesperses' house and made it back to the lake safely. His drunkenness didn't come back to bite us.

Not that time.

★   ★   ★

Later that night, when I couldn't sleep, I got out of the tent and walked down to the lake shore in the moonlight, Sandy padding along behind me. My feet were bare, and the cool ground felt good. I stripped out of my shirt and pants, and stood at the edge of the lake, in the dark, in just my underpants. When I stepped into the water, the silty mud felt funny but nice squeezing between my toes. The bank was firmer at camp, and I didn't sink in any deeper than the tops of my feet. The moon was full, casting a stream of silver on the water, and I fell forward and swam into it. Sandy barked once, not wanting me to go beyond her reach. I swam back and stumbled to her and gently held her graying muzzle shut for a moment.

I told her, 'Shhhhh.'

She sank into a down position on the muddy bank, her long muzzle touching one front paw. She still didn't like the idea. But she wouldn't question me again. She placed the judgement of her humans ahead of her own, as a matter of courtesy and pride, even if she was always right and we were always wrong. Good dogs are like that.

I swam out into the silver light and paddled in place for a few minutes, treading water. Savoring the feel of the coolness against my skin. Savoring the knowledge that I existed, for that brief moment, in a safe window. There was no one to hold my head under the water just to be mean.

Then I thought of lake monsters creeping up in the dark behind or underneath me, and I scrambled out of the water as fast as I could. Ben had left a mark on me, just the mark he had intended. Whether he was present or not, I would always feel the seeds of fear he had planted in me. I was still only six, and didn't know how not to be willing soil.

★ ★ ★

But, anyway, we had a decent vacation. For a change.

2 October 1984

I was sitting on my bed reading a comic book I'd probably already read fifteen times. I couldn't afford new ones every time I wanted them.

Ben opened my door and stuck his head in.

'Come 'ere in my room for a minute.'

I reflexively pushed against the bedspread with my feet, pressing my back tighter up against the headboard. This felt like the beginning of a game I was destined to lose.

He noticed.

'I'm not gonna do anything to you. I promise.'

I tried to swallow, but only half-succeeded. 'Promise?'

'I just want to talk to you.'

'What about?'

'I want your help with something.'

My help. With something. That didn't seem to add up right.

'What?'

'The one thing you're really good at. You know the one thing you're really good at, right?'

I chewed that over for a minute. I could think of a couple of things, but I was pretty sure Ben would disagree with them.

'Um . . . No.'

'Memorizing.'

157

'Oh. Memorizing. Right.'

I *was* good at something. Something even Ben couldn't deny. I jumped off my bed and followed him into his room.

Ben's room was all but unnavigable. All of his clothes, school books and sporting equipment lived permanently on the floor, along with many other items that not only resisted categorization but identification. But I picked my way through to his little round table and sat, and he sat across from me. Oddly, there was nothing on its surface. Everything that might have sat on the table lived on the floor. It defied logic.

'I'm going to be a famous actor,' he said.

'You are?'

'I am.'

He spoke as though there was no possibility, not even a remote one, that he could be wrong, that the world would not support him in this endeavor. It was as though he'd already made his dream come true just by declaring it.

'OK,' I said.

'But I need you to help me learn my lines.'

'For what?'

'I got a part in the school play. We all have to start somewhere!' he shouted, as if I had disparaged his announcement between sentences. 'There's this one part where I have to take a sword and fight a duel with this guy, and the whole time we're dueling I have a speech. It's kind of long. Well . . . like six sentences, but they're long sentences, and they don't make a lot of sense. So I want you to help me learn my lines.'

I looked up into his face, and it was open, unguarded. Nothing hostile or dangerous. It was a look I wasn't sure I'd seen before.

'I don't know if I can help you,' I said. Stupidly. 'It's not like I can memorize it for you.'

I watched the gates slam shut again in his eyes.

'Well, just go over it with me,' he said.

He had to read it to me. I was barely eight, and it was a bit beyond my reading level. But it wasn't beyond my memorization level. Nothing was. When I hear things, or read things, they remain printed on my brain and I can access them again anytime I want. I don't know why. It's just always been that way.

Here's what Ben had to memorize. Note that I'm now twenty-four years old, and I can still recite it word for word. At least one of us learned it that day.

'' 'I come to defend her honor, the honor granted to her by right of her station in the realm. And when I have won my battle she shall reclaim the keys to her kingdom, and all will be put to right again. Did you fancy no one would see, would notice your treachery, your crimes against your own fellows, or did you only think no one would be brave enough to fight you for it? I will lay down my life for my country and for its rightful ruler. Though, more likely, I will lay down yours.' And when I say that last bit,' Ben added, 'I stab the guy with the sword.'

'That's five sentences,' I said.

'What?'

'It's five sentences.'

'Fine, it's five sentences. Who cares?'

'You said it was six.'

Ben sighed. 'I guess it just feels like more.'

He got up from the table, rummaged around in his closet, and pulled out two hiking poles. He tossed me one. I wasn't expecting it, so it just hit my shoulder and fell on to the rubbish heap of the floor.

I stared at it. I had no idea where we were going with this.

'Who wrote this play?' I asked, thinking it wasn't very good.

'Shakespeare. He was just having a bad day.'

'Seriously?'

'No, not seriously, stupid. Ken Friedman. He's a sophomore. You want to pick up the pole?' Ben was already fiercely impatient with me.

'Why? Are we going hiking?'

'No, we're not going hiking, stupid. Why are you so stupid? We're going to work on my big scene. That's your sword.'

'Oh. My sword.'

I got up from the table and picked up my sword. I wasn't sure how one would go about sword fighting in the middle of a landfill. I wasn't even sure how to move closer to Ben.

He kicked a backpack halfway across the room and made a swath in the mess with one foot. Then he approached me, hiking pole raised, and I winced. It was all I could do to keep from running back to my room. He looked quite sincere about running me through. But I steeled myself and raised my 'sword'.

I could almost see the wheels spinning in

Ben's head as he tried to remember his first line.

'I have come to . . . to honor . . . '

'I come to defend her honor, the honor granted to her by right of her station in the realm.'

'I have come to defend the honor granted by the realm. *Her* honor granted by the realm. By right of the realm.'

'I come to defend her honor, the honor granted to her by right of her station in the realm.'

We went on like this for a few minutes. Every sentence came out wrong at least three or four times, then came out close enough to right that I didn't correct him. But when we came around to the first sentence again, I found Ben was no closer to mastery. I've heard people use the expression 'mind like a steel trap', but in Ben's case the trap seemed designed to keep anything from getting *in*.

'*You* do it all the way through,' Ben said. 'So I can hear how it sounds. But leave the last line for me. I think I know the last line.'

I raised my hiking pole.

'I come to defend her honor, the honor granted to her by right of her station in the realm. And when I have won my battle she shall reclaim the keys to her kingdom, and all will be put to right again. Did you fancy no one would see, would notice your treachery, your crimes against your own fellows, or did you only think no one would be brave enough to fight you for it? I will lay down my life for my country and for its rightful ruler.'

'Though it's more likely I will lay down yours,' Ben shouted, and jabbed me in the solar plexus with the tip of the pole.

I fell over backwards, and a notebook rammed painfully into my back. I remember thinking that it hurt to be around Ben even when we seemed to be getting along fine.

'Ow,' I said, rubbing the spot on my chest, though my back hurt more.

'Sorry.' He held a hand down to help me up. 'Can't afford to piss you off. I still need a lot of work. Don't I?'

'I'll say.' I got up by myself, without taking his help.

I sat down at the bare table and he sat across from me, a look in his eyes like he might be about to eat me up. Like somehow ingesting me would help him gain access to something. Something I had that he needed.

'How do you memorize things like that?'

'I don't know. They just go in and stick.'

'I wish I knew how you did it. That's one thing about you . . . Well, two. Actually. Something else you do, and I wish I knew how.'

'What?'

He waited a long time, appearing lost in his own thoughts. I would have bet money he'd never spit it out. But he surprised me.

'How do you always make Mom and Bert like you?'

I was short on tact when I was eight, I guess. Because I just told the truth. You'd think I'd have known better by then.

'You just . . . don't be bad.'

162

And that was Ben's detonator.

Looking back, it seems clear that I was triggering my brother by suggesting he was wrong and bad and irredeemable. But at the time it just felt more like stating the obvious. And Ben's reactions were about as understandable to me as advanced calculus.

He pushed away from the table so hard that the table lurched in my direction, and my recoil upended my chair, and I fell back and hit my head on something on the floor. I was never sure what.

'Screw you!' Ben yelled. 'Get the hell out of my room! I'll learn these lines on my own! I'll be fine without you, you little shit!'

I got the hell out of his room. Locked myself in my own room to nurse my wounds. Physical and otherwise.

27 October 1984

When the night of the school play came around, Ben was anything but fine.

I sat in the third row of the auditorium, between my mother and my father. They had to lean over me to talk to each other. To say all the things I didn't want to have to overhear. It was painful.

My mother was prepping my father on how not to hurt Ben's feelings regarding his first dramatic performance.

'Now, you say something encouraging to him, you hear? Even if he's bad.'

'Well, I don't think that's much of a way to raise a boy. Calling bad good.'

'I didn't mean you had to say it's good if it isn't. Just be encouraging.'

'Like how?'

'Oh, I don't know . . . ' she said impatiently. 'Why do I always have to think of these things for you? You have a brain. How about you say something like, 'Well, Ben, if you keep going with this acting thing you might really get somewhere.''

Long silence.

Then my father said, 'Just keep your fingers crossed that he's good.'

When Ben finally marched out on to the stage holding a painted wooden sword, I could feel the jolt of electrical tension that ran between the two of them.

Ben raised his wooden sword to another boy who stood about eight inches shorter, and glanced nervously out into the audience.

'I come to claim . . . ' he said, and then trailed off, and I knew we were in big trouble.

Honestly, I was surprised. I knew he was bad at memorization, but I also knew this was hugely important to him. So I figured he'd found a way to solve the problem somehow. Hard work, maybe. Or maybe that's just what I would have done.

The whole audience picked up on the tension, and shifted slightly in its collective seat. Out of the corner of my eye I saw my father sink his face into one big hand.

'I come to claim . . . the right . . . '

More painful silence.

I whispered, 'I come to defend her honor, the honor granted to her by right of her station in the realm.'

When nothing happened, I rose to my feet, ready to call out the line loudly enough for Ben to hear it. I felt my mother's hand on the crown of my head. She pressed down, and I was returned to my seat. She put a finger to my lips.

'He's on his own now,' she whispered into my ear. 'No matter how bad it gets. We're not trying to be cruel. It just has to be that way.'

Then we heard the line, but not from Ben. It

came from offstage, and in the voice of a grown-up.

Ben repeated the line, then opened his mouth to say the second line, and ended up right back where he started from. For many, many painful seconds.

'Shit!' he said, really belting it out, and threw his wooden sword down on to the boards of the stage, where it clattered loudly.

I winced. My parents winced. The whole audience winced.

Ben stormed off the stage.

In the excruciating silence that followed, my father leaned across me and asked my mother, 'What was it you wanted me to say to Ben, again?'

A long silence. Then she said, 'Maybe just don't say anything at all.'

'No problem there,' he said.

A grown-up, probably a teacher, took the stage, picked up Ben's sword, and fought the duel while reading the lines from a script clutched in his other hand.

I thought we might leave, and go find Ben, but we didn't. Not until the play was over. To this very day I don't know whether my parents thought it would be unconscionably rude to leave mid-play, or if they simply chose to hide the fact that Ben's performance was in any way connected to them.

★ ★ ★

Afterwards, we found Ben sitting out on the front steps of the school, in the dark, talking to

166

two girls. They both sat disturbingly close to him — disturbing to me, anyway — one on each side, laughing in a way that sounded forced and artificial. One had her hand on his forearm.

All mirth ended when they looked up and saw us standing there.

My father said, 'Ready to go home, son?' Speaking of forced and artificial, my father had been calling Ben 'son' for the better part of a year, ever since legally adopting Ben, but he still couldn't manage to sound like he meant it.

The prettier of the two girls stared into my face, and I looked down at some squashed gum on the concrete and blushed.

'Oh, Ben. Your little brother is so cute,' she said.

'*Him?*' Ben asked. Like there were several.

'Yeah. He's adorable.'

'Hmm,' Ben said. 'I don't see it. But OK.'

'*Now*, Ben,' my father said.

Ben sprang to his feet.

'You were great, Ben,' the other girl said.

Ben was, of course, stunned. We all were.

'I was?'

'Oh, yeah. So much passion!'

Ben smiled and followed us out to the parking lot, a good ten paces behind me. And I was a good ten paces behind my parents.

I heard my mother say, 'See? That's how you find a compliment.'

And my father snorted and said, 'Yeah, right. I think there's some romantic interest required for that one.'

Then behind me I heard one of the girls say,

167

'Maybe we'll see you later, Ben.'

And Ben said, 'Yeah. Maybe you will.'

I wondered what that meant. It definitely sounded like it meant something.

* * *

Later that night, much later, there was giggling in Ben's room, and some other noises I struggled to identify. It woke me, and I lay awake for a long time, clarifying beyond a doubt that I was hearing more than one girl in Ben's room.

I didn't even try to go back to sleep until I saw their shadows creep by the shrubbery outside my window on their way out.

I never said a word to anyone about it. Maybe so he wouldn't kill me. Maybe because I was grudgingly impressed.

31 December 1984

This is a brief memory of my brother Ben 'before', but a disturbingly vivid one.

Ben had a New Year's Eve party in our 'recreation room' downstairs, which I guess is a nice name to call a basement with some old couches, a ping-pong table and a dartboard.

Hard to imagine that room packed with at least thirty reveling fourteen-year-olds, but I don't need to imagine. I saw it with my own eyes.

My parents stayed upstairs and didn't really chaperone. I guess they thought being right on the other side of the living room floor would be close enough. The one thing they absolutely insisted on: at fifteen minutes into the New Year, party over. All fourteen-year-olds, except theirs, would clear out on time, as agreed.

I sat in the living room with my parents, and we watched that New Year's Eve entertainment show that ends with the ball dropping. There were moments when I had to physically hold my eyelids up with my fingers.

My dad had an old starter pistol, and, right after the ball dropped, he went off to get it. Brought it back into the living room with us.

'I'm going to go down there and fire this off,'

he said, 'and that'll get their attention, and then they'll know the party's over.' Then he looked right at me and said, 'Unless *you* want to.'

'Yeah, let Rusty,' my mom said. 'It'll be cuter coming from him. Not so embarrassing to Ben as having his father come down there and chase them all out.'

I felt the cold metal of the pistol in my hands when I took it from him, and the weight of it. I had to remind myself it wasn't a real weapon.

'What am I supposed to do again?'

'Just go down there, point this up at the ceiling, pull the trigger, and say, 'Party's over.' I guarantee you'll have their attention by then.'

Nearly paralyzed by the responsibility, I made my way down the basement stairs.

It was crowded. And loud. There was supposed to be no alcohol, of course, but it was plain by the stumbling around that someone had sneaked some in. I got my foot stepped on twice before I made it out to the middle of the room.

I saw Ben lying on the old green couch. On top of a girl. Just lying still, his face buried in the crook of her neck. He wasn't kissing her, or giving her a hickie. He wasn't doing anything. Just burying his face in her.

I raised the pistol and put one finger in my ear. Which was silly, because of course it could only be the other ear. The wrong ear. And I pulled the trigger. The sound was deafening. Almost literally. I could hear nothing but a ringing noise in my right ear for quite some time.

I looked up to see all Ben's friends holding

perfectly still. Staring at me. Then one fell down, laughing.

'Party's over,' I said.

There were a couple of disgusted groans — even though all had agreed to the rules in advance — and Ben's friend Kurt said, 'Ben, do we really have to go?'

It took Ben what seemed like minutes to raise his head from its hiding place on that girl.

'Yeah,' he said. 'Go. Or Bert'll be down here in, like, thirty seconds.'

They filed out with surprising speed.

I stood in the middle of the rec room, staring at Ben. And Ben lay on the couch — on the girl — staring back. His eyes were cool and completely placid. It frightened me. Looking back with the wisdom of years, I know he was probably on something. Something stronger than the flask or two of booze someone had undoubtedly snuck into the punch. At the time I just had the weird sensation that he had turned into someone else . . . but not really. Like Ben squared.

We stared at each other like that for a truly bizarre length of time.

Then Ben raised one hand and made a gun of his fingers. He sighted me down, and aimed at me for a few chilling moments. Then, in cold blood, he pulled the imaginary trigger. His hand even recoiled from the kick of the shot.

The look in his eyes never once changed as he murdered me.

Then he put his head back into its hiding place, and I ran back upstairs.

My parents were in bed already. They didn't tuck me in. They didn't check on Ben. I don't think they took any special notice of when — or even whether — Ben came back upstairs.

I have no idea how long he stayed down there with that girl or what they did. I don't even know who she was.

I just knew I couldn't shake the look in Ben's eyes as he pulled the trigger on me.

I'd always made comments about how Ben would kill me, or was lying in wait to kill me, but it was always a figurative murder. And I'm not saying this was a literal one, or even pointed to the possibility of a literal one. It was more that, suddenly, nothing was out of the question. I just wasn't absolutely, positively, one hundred per cent sure any more that such a thing was impossible.

30 June 1985

My father baited my hook for me. Unfortunately.

'Here,' he said. 'I know you don't really like the worms.'

Ben smirked at me.

I liked the worms OK. It was running them through with the worm version of a bayonet that didn't much appeal to me.

We were back at the lake, after taking one year off following the great canoe disaster. This year we'd rented a motor boat big enough for all three of us. My father never said so, but I'm sure he felt safer within arm's reach of both me and Ben. I couldn't help noticing that he'd bought a case of beer — not a six-pack or a twelve-pack but a full thirty-six-bottle case — at the dock store, and had the guys load it into the bottom of the boat for him. My mother would never have to know.

I opened the fishing reel and lowered my worm slowly into the water. I had one small split-shot sinker on the rig, just enough to take the worm down to the bottom of the lake, where I sincerely hoped I could snag the hook on some weeds and break the line.

I watched my father twist the cap off another beer.

I reeled back in. I felt a resistance, which I was sure was the snag I'd been hoping for. A second later I felt a sharp tug, and my heart fell. I held the rod perfectly still. What I should have done, by fisherman standards, was pull back quickly to set the hook. Instead I just froze, hoping the fish would finish the worm without hooking itself, and move on. The strategy backfired on me. He swallowed the hook, though I didn't know it at the time. At the time I just kept hoping there'd be an opportunity to lose him again.

'You got one!' my father shouted. As if this should be one of the shining moments in my life.

I slowly reeled in. What choice did I have?

'It's a beaut!' my father called out when it came to the surface.

I didn't bring it into the boat. Sometimes they'll wiggle off the hook if you allow a moment of pause, and a slack in the line tension. That is, if they haven't already swallowed the hook. Which I didn't yet know this one had.

'It's not so great,' Ben said. 'Maybe twelve inches, is all.'

My father shot him a grim look, and he turned his gaze down to the bottom of the boat.

'Sorry,' he mumbled.

Meanwhile my fish was still struggling just under the surface of the water, reinforcing the gravity of what I'd done to him.

'Reel him in, Rusty. Get him in the boat.'

I looked up at my father, but it involved looking right into the sun, and I could only screw up my face and press my eyes closed. It was three thirty in the afternoon, with the sun at a slant. We'd been out a long day already.

'I want to let him go.'

A long silence, during which I'd have liked to have seen my father's face. But the sun was in my eyes.

'You sure?'

'I'm sure.'

He leaned over the side of the boat and grabbed my line.

'Don't take him out of the water!' I yelled. 'He won't be able to breathe.'

My father sighed, and grasped the fish by the lower section of its jaw. 'He swallowed the hook,' my father said, and my heart sank even further. 'Ben, hand me that knife.'

I watched in horror, thinking my father was going to stab the fish dead, or maybe even perform surgery to retrieve the hook. Instead he made a loop of the line close to the fish's mouth, held it tightly so it wouldn't pull on the swallowed hook, and sawed through the line. He let go, and the fish disappeared.

Before I could even ask, my father said, 'It'll rust out. That hook'll just disintegrate in a week or two.'

'I don't want to fish any more,' I said.

And Ben, who had his back to my father, smirked at me again.

'Can I go back?' I asked.

'No,' my father said. The kind of 'no' that leaves little room for dissent.

'Why not?'

'Because it's a family outing. You don't want to fish, fine. Don't fish. But be with the family.'

It was literally after sundown when I started begging him to turn back for camp.

'It's only civil twilight,' he said.

'The sign said all boats off the lake by sundown.'

'This is the best time to fish,' he said. 'Catfish bite right around now, when it's so dark you can barely see your hand in front of your face. I want to hook one of those big channel cats. I don't want to go in empty-handed.'

Bizarrely, I was the only one who'd had any luck all day. If you can call my previous experience luck.

I looked down at the case of beer and saw only three bottles left with their caps on. I wondered if it was more about the channel cat or more about not wasting good beer.

I forced myself to be silent for another few minutes, then whined, 'What if we can't see to get back to camp?'

'That's why I brought that great big flashlight. Get it out, Rusty. It's in that little backpack under your seat.'

I pulled out the pack and rummaged around. I found the last sandwich and sniffed it, disappointed that it was only peanut butter. Then I found the flashlight. It was heavy and vaguely comforting. I sat in the front of the boat, chewing miserably on the sandwich and shining the flashlight off into the dusk. It was a strong light, but it didn't help you see very far. Just what was right in front of you.

But I didn't dare say more.

What felt like hours later, but was probably fifteen or twenty minutes, my father's head came up, and he looked around as though his surroundings were entirely unfamiliar to him.

It was close to full-on dark.

'We better get back. Reel in,' he said, apparently having forgotten that I hadn't been fishing, and Ben had reeled in over an hour ago and seemed to be napping curled up on his bench. 'Shine that light, Rusty,' he said, pulling the outboard motor into noisy, smelly life.

I shined the light in what I was sure was the direction of camp.

My father took off in the exact opposite direction.

'You're shining the light the wrong way,' he shouted to be heard over the motor.

'No, you're driving the boat the wrong way!' I yelled.

Ben raised his head to complain. He said, 'What are you guys yelling about?'

I leaned in close to him and said, 'Dad's going the wrong way.'

He sat up suddenly. Looked around. 'He knows where he's going,' Ben said. But he didn't sound convinced.

I said something that surprised me at the time, and still surprises me now. I said, 'Yeah, maybe twenty beers ago, he did.' Of course, I didn't say it loudly enough for my father to hear. But I was surprised I even said it to Ben. 'Look,' I said, and pointed to the big stand of trees that marked camp.

'Oh, shit,' he whispered. 'I think you're right.'

By this time we'd built up quite a head of steam. He had that boat flying over the lake at a good clip.

'Dad!' Ben and I both shouted it in exact unison.

He looked at us, to see what we were yelling about. But he never found out. Just in that moment the light of my big flashlight illuminated something huge and gray. Did I instinctively know it was the dam? Or did I just register that it was big and hard, and that we were about to hit it?

Just to give some idea of how far we could see by flashlight, by the time I saw the dam, my father did not have time to change the course of the boat. In fact, I didn't have time to tell him to. The dam was so close that I could only do what reflexes dictated, which was to jump out of the boat.

We'd been so close to the dam by the time we saw it that the boat hit the dam before I hit the water.

Everything I recall after this should be taken with a grain of salt. I remember flashes of it vividly, too vividly to possibly be wrong. But in some cases I can tell that time is compressed, while in other cases I'm stretching the sequence out without meaning to. More to the point, some of my vivid memories conflict with others just as vivid.

But I'm doing my best here.

I plunged into the surprisingly warm water and watched the flashlight sink, turning end over end, its light illuminating spooky tentacles of lake vegetation, and, at one point, a broken beer bottle as it, too, sank. In that sort of disconnected crisis 'thinking', I remember marveling that a flashlight could be built so well as to sink to the bottom of a lake without going out.

My face broke the surface and I saw only two things floating at the crash site. A life jacket. And a hand.

At first I had a horrible jolt of fear that the hand was only that. A hand. All by itself and attached to nothing. But I dog-paddled closer to it, and the angle of the hand in the water made it clear that it was attached to a body below the surface. By the time I got to the hand, it had sunk just out of sight. I grabbed the arm under the water and pulled hard, and Ben bobbed to the surface. He was unconscious, and his head was banged up just above his hairline. There was a lot of blood, diluted with lake water.

That part is painfully clear.

This next part is sketchy, but I know it happened. I got Ben into a life vest. I don't remember doing most of it, but I have a nagging sense that it was panicky-hard. I just remember wrapping my legs around his waist from behind to zip it up.

After I let go, and his head stayed above the water, I know I screamed for my father. A lot. Enough that I had no voice the next day. But I can't remember if I swam around and looked for him or just treaded water and screamed.

Then I was lifted into a boat by a man who

said, 'Take it easy, son, you're OK.'

Part of me thinks that was the first I knew a boat or a man was even there with me. But I also remember seeing the flashing red light approaching on the water, like the light on the top of a police car, only in this case, of course, it was on a boat. So that's where it gets contradictory.

I remember sitting on the boat, wrapped in a stiff blanket and watching two men receive Ben from a man in the water. They took off his life vest and turned him around and bent him over — the way you would if he were choking on his food. One of the men held Ben from behind and gave a big yank upward underneath his ribs, and what looked like a whole bucketful of water splashed up out of Ben's lungs and splattered on to the bottom of the boat.

That's the clearest and most haunting image. That was my moment of truth. Though I didn't think it out in such precise terms, I knew in my gut that the one accomplishment I was so proud of — getting Ben into that life vest, keeping his head above water — had been of no use to him at all. His lungs had been filled with water the whole time. I could have left him with one hand floating on the water and looked for my dad, and it wouldn't have affected his situation in the slightest — that is, if I could somehow have trusted him not to finish sinking.

It had never occurred to me to try to get the water out of his lungs.

So. Do I feel guilty for that? Do I blame myself?

No. Absolutely not. Except to the extent that I do.

The bottom line is this: even if I'd known enough to try to get the water out of his lungs, I would never have succeeded. There was no way I could have bent him forward, and even if I could have, it just would have put his head right back under the water again. I couldn't have done it.

But I didn't even try. I never even thought to try.

If I'd thought to try, that would have felt so different. I could have cried to the rescuers, and said, 'I couldn't do it, no matter how hard I tried. I wanted so much to get that water out of his lungs, but I couldn't get him bent forward.'

And they would have said, 'Hey. Hey. Son. Stop beating yourself up. It was impossible. But at least you tried.'

But I hadn't tried. It hadn't even occurred to me to try.

I yelped, 'My father!' for about the thirtieth time as the boat took off for shore, and a very patient rescuer told me for about the twentieth time that there was a diver in the water looking for him. This time he added that we'd best hurry up and get my brother someplace where he could get help.

The whole way back, I watched them work on Ben. One man gave him CPR while another held pressure on his head wound to slow the bleeding. More than once I saw them make eye contact with each other in a questioning way, and I knew instinctively that they weren't sure whether or not there was any point continuing.

181

Here's the last thing I remember, and I remember it very, very clearly.

I looked up at the patient man. He was sitting beside me with his arm around my shoulder.

I asked, 'Is my brother gonna be OK?'

He said, 'I'm not gonna lie to you, son, it's not looking good for his situation, but you never know. They're just going to keep trying to bring him back. Because you never know.'

He didn't offer any comment on *which* Ben they were trying to bring back. Or *how much* of Ben. He didn't point out that the answer to my question depended on your definition of the concept of 'OK'.

Looking back, I realize that I really did save Ben with my actions that night. Because if I hadn't put on his life jacket, he would have ended up at the bottom of the lake. Like my father. And by the time they found him, it would have been way too late to bring him back.

Ben's survival is squarely on me.

So now the key question is, do I feel guilty about *that*?

Part Four

Melting

12 October 2001

Anat looked up at me, one triangle of dough hanging limply from her hand, stretching slightly from gravity.

'Did they ever find your father's body?'

'They brought it back the next morning.'

'Ouch.'

It was nearly a month later. I'd thought I was anxious to talk about all this, but I was wrong. I hadn't been as ready as I'd thought.

It took her a minute to notice the dough stretching out in her hand. To notice that she wasn't moving. She always moved when she was making the morning donuts. Whether she was talking or not. Whether there was something else on her mind or not.

When she finally noticed it in her hand, she threw it on a pile of scrap dough, turned fully to me, and looked into my face. My heart pounded harder. My heart always pounded hard, whenever I was around her. But if she looked straight into my face, or moved closer, it pounded as though it might burst out on to the table.

'That's an awful lot of tragedy for one family,' she said. 'Especially now, with your mother dying young, and all. And the office where you worked, with everyone you knew in it . . . Don't you wonder sometimes why so much gets heaped on certain people?'

I almost told the truth. That truth being, 'I wouldn't dare.' I wouldn't dare dwell on a thing like that. I try to look forward in my life. Because what's behind me is a little hard to take.

Instead I passed it off to lighten the mood.

'That question has been raised about our family,' I said. 'More than once. But never satisfactorily answered.'

It didn't work. It didn't lighten the mood at all. It was more as though my being a brave little soldier and trying to laugh it off only increased the bounds of her sympathy for me.

She took two steps closer and placed one of her hands on mine. I had my hand on her wooden baker's table. Just kind of leaning on it. Talking to her. And suddenly her hand was on top of mine, and my heart tried to kill me.

'I'm getting flour all over you,' she said, looking straight into my eyes.

'I don't mind,' I said, revealing far too clearly, with my tone, *how much* I didn't mind.

She backpedaled fast. Took her hand back, moved away, looked away. Buried herself in her work again.

'So, I guess, then, Ben was in the hospital a long time.' She didn't make it sound like a question.

I tried to breathe, to calm myself, so I could speak normally. It took longer than I would have liked.

'Yeah. I can't really remember how long, but I remember he had to do all kinds of physical therapy before he came home. And after, of course. He had a lot of motor-skill issues. But I remember it was five days before he was even conscious. I remember getting to the hospital with my mom about seven in the morning one day, just like we'd done every day, only this time the doctor came out and told us Ben was awake and talking, and he wanted to take us in to see him. Not that we hadn't seen him already, but . . . '

I wasn't sure where I'd been headed with that last sentence. My brain was still feeling a little bit like corned-beef hash.

'He — the doctor, I mean — kept saying it was a miracle. So I guess my mom and I were expecting . . . you know . . . like . . . a full-on miracle. And maybe it was, but . . . I mean . . . What do I mean? I don't know about my mom, but I expected to walk in there and have Ben sneer at me and call me Wussy Boy and tell the doctor he needed better company if he was ever going to recover. And that wasn't exactly how it happened.'

I stopped, to see if she would look up at me. But no matter how long I paused, she just kept cutting dough. I think she'd scared herself. I looked down and saw I still had flour on the back of my right hand. I wasn't anxious to wipe it off again. Maybe ever.

'So we walk in, and Ben looks up. I was walking a step or two behind my mom. And Ben looks at her, and then at me. And his face just lights up. Lights up to see her, lights up maybe even more to see me. And his speech was bad, a little slurred, but you could make out what he said. He said, 'My mom and my buddy! Look, it's my mom and my buddy!' I'm not lying to you, Anat, I swear to God I'm not exaggerating and I'm not kidding: I turned around to see who was standing behind me. Literally. And there was nobody there. The doctors had been warning us for days that lots of things could be missing. Anything, really. That his memory might be hugely impaired. He might not know who we were. He might not know who *he* was. And that it might come back, or it might partially come back, or it might not come back at all. So I'm just standing there, staring at him, and he's so elated to see me. And I thought, Oh, my God. Ben forgot that he hates me. We think he started calling me 'Buddy' because he couldn't remember my name at first. He got better for about six months. Mostly physically. Mostly motor-skills stuff. Walking and talking. But then he hit a plateau. And nothing's really changed since then.'

I waited. But Anat continued to work in silence.

'So here's what I wanted to ask you,' I said.

Her eyes flicked up toward my face, but never quite made it. I waited. Then I went on. What else could I do?

'I want somebody to explain to me how brain damage can make a person nicer.'

'It can't,' she said.

'You wouldn't think so.'

'The nice had to be in there already.'

188

'But that's why I told you all that. So you'd know — '

Her eyes came up, but not to me. She looked up at the door.

'We have a customer.' Her voice was quiet. Almost conspiratorial. As if to tip me that I should not be alone in the kitchen with her when we had a customer.

But it was a little late by then.

I wondered who comprised 'we'. Did Anat and I have a customer, even though it wasn't my bakery? Or did Anat and Nazir have a customer, even though Nazir was home sleeping?

I picked up my uneaten donut on its little paper plate, and carried it out to the front seating area.

The customer was a woman whose name I didn't know, or at least didn't remember, but she was the mother of a girl I'd gone to school with.

'Good morning,' I said, about three notches too loud and cheerful. 'I had to get my donut straight from the source today. She hasn't had time to load them into the display cases yet.'

I turned and indicated the cases, as if to prove my point.

I was doing badly. I was way overdoing it. But I had no idea how to fix that.

I poured myself a coffee and sat, eating my donut and watching Anat wait on this woman. Waiting for the woman to leave again, so I could have my conversation with Anat back.

But by the time the woman had paid and left, before I could even open my mouth, 'we' had another customer, an old man.

189

People were getting over their fear of the name Nazir. People get over things.

I looked out the window and saw it was light. And people were driving to work. And I knew I really *shouldn't* be seen hanging around the kitchen with her. People would talk. People talk in a small town.

I waved goodbye to her just as she was making change for the old man. I think I purposely timed it so she couldn't argue.

I drove back feeling like I had wet concrete setting up in my stomach. And it definitely wasn't the donut. The donut had been lighter than fog.

★　★　★

Anat showed up at my door a few minutes after noon.

I answered the door in sweat pants and a white tee-shirt, both freshly purchased and ridiculously stiff and weird. I'd been napping, and I'm sure my hair was a disaster.

I just stood there blinking at her. I couldn't believe what I was seeing.

I'd never seen her outside the bakery before. I'd never seen her in full light. And yet all I could focus on were her eyes. Her black eyes shone with something. I just couldn't say what. There was affection in there somewhere. Also fear. It looked as though the fear was winning.

'I woke you,' she said. 'I'm so sorry.'

'No, it's fine. Really. Come in.'

'I can't.'

We stood like that for an awkward length of time. I wanted to ask why she was even here if she couldn't be here, but I couldn't find the right way to phrase a question like that. Probably there is no right way to phrase a question like that.

'You're a single man,' she said. 'And I'm a woman unaccompanied by any male family member. Like my father. Well, who else but my father? But anyway, I can't come into your house. It wouldn't be proper.'

I nodded twice, still a bit confused, and pointed to the two white wicker chairs on the front porch.

We sat. The front door of the house was still hanging wide open. I don't know why I left it that way. Maybe it seemed more proper.

I looked up to see Mark from next door walking out to get the mail. He glanced over his shoulder at us seven times. Seven. I counted.

'I didn't get to tell you what I thought,' she said. 'You know. About your question.'

'Right. But for such a good reason, though. It's nice to see the customers starting to come back.'

'Yes, and very suddenly. As though a little bird told them to do it.'

'I didn't. I might've mentioned it to McCaskill from Ben's store. Like, a month ago. But nobody else. So what do you think? About my question?'

'Oh,' she said. 'That.' As if it had been the furthest thing from her mind.

It definitely wasn't just me. This was a nervous conversation. Mark wasn't helping. He was on his way back up his driveway now, staring at us so hard that he tripped once.

'Have you ever met an evil baby?' she asked.

I wasn't sure, initially, how to place the question in the context of . . . well . . . anything.

'Um. Hmm. No. I don't think so. Then again, I haven't met many babies. But it doesn't sound like anything too common. Except in a few old horror movies.'

'I think you know that killing brain cells can't put something into the brain that wasn't there to begin with. I think you're convinced that somehow Ben was born bad and mean. But I don't think anybody is ever born that way. You didn't know Ben when he was little. He was six when you met him, and even then you were too young to understand. By the time you knew him, he'd already been twisted by thinking he wasn't loved the way he needed to be. But that's not his true nature. I think if you hit somebody on the head or starve their brain of oxygen, you don't get a false nature. You get a true one. I think maybe it's just hard for you to accept how much Ben loves you.'

I did nothing but blink for what could have been nearly a full minute.

'Ben loves me?' I muttered, nicely proving her point.

'Of course he does. You're all he can talk about. Everybody who knows Ben knows how much he adores you. Except maybe you.'

I looked into the open garage next door and saw Mark setting up to use his weight bench.

Right where he could keep an eye on us.

'I guess maybe he could've learned to see me differently during those years after his accident. Before I left home.'

'Russell,' she said, the way you speak to a child when you're feeling impatient but still want to be kind. 'When you walked into his hospital room, his eyes lit up. And he said you were his buddy.'

'Right.'

'He loved you all along.'

'He sure didn't act like it.'

'You have another explanation?'

I just sat there, thinking, for a long time. Watching how the sun hit my bare feet, which were stretched out in front of me, without hitting any other parts of us. The porch roof shielded the rest. I didn't dare look at Anat.

When I glanced at her peripherally, I saw she was staring into Mark's garage, watching him bench-press what looked like the approximate heft of a car, but in the form of a weight bar. His head was half-up, watching her watch.

Then, quite suddenly, Mark hoisted the bar back up on to its rack, swung into an upright position, marched to the door of the garage and punched — literally punched — the automatic door button.

Anat and I openly watched as his garage door rumbled down, obliterating him.

'What's with him?' she asked.

'Butthole-dom, as far as I can tell.'

'You know him?'

'Oh, yes. We've known each other all our lives.'

'He has a problem with me?'

193

'No. I don't think so. I think he has a problem with *me*.'

'I should go.'

'Don't go just because of Mark.'

'No, I need to. I should. For more reasons than that. If my father knew I was here, it would be big trouble. He's very traditional, my father. Especially when it comes to me. It's a cultural thing. It's different in my culture.'

'I know. He told me all about it. Quite some time ago.'

A long silence. It took me several seconds to find the guts to look at her face. She looked stunned. Horrified.

'What did he say to you?'

'Oh, just that American girls are different. You know. They hook up with guys. Egyptian girls don't hook up. That sort of thing.'

I watched her drop her face into her hands.

'Oh, good God,' she said. 'That's so incredibly embarrassing.'

'I don't see why. He's just taking good care of you.'

Anat shook her head. And shook it, and shook it, and shook it. And shook it.

'I have to go,' she said.

She sprang out of her chair and made it down the porch steps before I could argue. And even then I couldn't think what to say to make her stay.

'See you tomorrow,' I called to her.

But she never answered or turned around.

★   ★   ★

194

I tried to go back to bed, but that was a joke. Of course I couldn't sleep.

I just lay there, on my mother's bed, shaken through and through.

I stared at my cell phone, sitting on the bedside table. For five or ten minutes, I just stared at it. Then I grabbed it up and flipped it open. And hit number three on my speed dial.

Number three was Kerry.

I guess I figured now was the time to do this. I guess I figured I couldn't possibly feel any more shaken up than I already did.

My heart pounded as it rang four times. Then I heard the shift as the call went to voicemail. I breathed as though I'd never breathed before, not once in my life. I can't remember when I'd felt so profoundly relieved.

'Kerry,' I said. 'It's me. Russell. I owe you a call. I know I owe you a call. I owe you the goddamn truth, I guess. Don't I? So . . . here goes. I know what happened isn't your fault. But I can't get over it. I can't get around it. I'm sorry. I can't. It's like all my post-traumatic stress is wrapped up with your voice and your name now. My God, Kerry, if you knew how many times I've thought of calling you. Just to tell you this,' I added. So she wouldn't think I meant something more. 'But every time I even think about calling, my heart starts hammering, and I get dizzy — almost to the point where it feels like I'm going to pass out. I don't know how to explain it. I'm sorry. I'm sorry it turned out like this, but it did. I'm sorry I didn't call you sooner. I'm just . . . sorry. I don't know what else to say.' I

195

paused. For way too long. Listening to the silence on the line. Then I said, 'I hope you're OK. I hope you find some support out there. I'm sorry it isn't me. I know it should be me, but I can't do it, and I can't change that. I'm sorry.'

Then I flipped the phone closed.

I curled up in a little ball and just lay there, doing nothing, thinking nothing, for an indeterminate length of time. If you'd asked me how long I lay there, I'd have guessed it was an hour.

The phone jangled me back into the world. At first I thought Kerry was calling me back, which made me dizzy. But it was my mom's home phone. The land line. It wasn't my cell. It wasn't even my phone.

I stumbled into the kitchen, the home of my mother's only phone, so far as I knew. I grabbed it up on the fifth ring.

'Oh, good, you're there,' a voice said. It was the voice of a female stranger. Before I could answer, or ask any questions, she said, 'Ben's really upset because you're late to pick him up.'

I looked at the clock over the kitchen stove. It was twenty-five minutes to four.

'Oh, shoot,' I said, quickly morphing the word 'shit' into something more socially acceptable. 'I fell asleep. Tell him I'm sorry. Tell him I accidentally fell asleep. Tell him I'll be right there.'

I hung up the phone and literally ran to the car. While I was running, I remember thinking I

196

was amassing an awful lot of sorry for one afternoon.

*   *   *

I found Ben box-pacing in front of Gerson's Market. I could tell he'd been crying.

When I honked the horn, it shocked him out of his pattern, and he stumbled, as if nothing was holding him up off the ground any more.

He shuffled over and climbed into the passenger's seat.

'You're late,' he said.

'I know. I'm sorry.'

'You shouldn't be late.'

'I fell asleep. I'm really sorry.'

'I don't like it when you're late.'

'I know. I feel terrible about it. But I'm here now. Can we move on?'

Obviously, I'd forgotten who I was talking to.

*   *   *

'I'm never late,' Ben said as I parked the car in the driveway.

'That's true,' I said. 'You never are.'

I was looking forward to getting into the house, but I'm not sure why, because going indoors was unlikely to stop him.

Mark was watering the lawn next door, and by the time I'd made it halfway up the driveway he'd dropped the hose and was standing on our front grass, not three steps away from me.

Mark Jespers was the last thing I needed on a day like this.

'Hey. Rusty. What's with you and the Arab girl?'

'Not now, Mark.'

'Is this, like, a new small-town romance?'

'That's the only thing you notice about her? That she's Egyptian? You look at her and that's all you see — how is that even relevant?'

'Well, she's a Muslim. Right? She worships *the Allah*?'

I sighed. I thought of just plunging through to my front door. But his energy felt tight and aggressive, and I was guessing this was not a problem I could walk away from.

'I don't know what religion she is. I never asked.'

'She is kinda good to look at, though. I mean, if you're into that sort of thing. You tapping that?'

I hit him.

I hit him before I even mentally registered that I was about to hit him. It's just something that did itself. I swung my fist hard and connected with his jaw, and he staggered backward but didn't fall.

It may sound like a scene from an action film, in which this would be a smooth and obvious reaction, and I would handle it as such. But I'd never punched anybody in my life. I had no idea that it hurts the puncher as much as the punchee. It was all I could do to stifle a howl as I grabbed my right hand.

Then he laid me out with a hard right that

landed on the bone outside my left eye. He crouched on top of me, and pulled back for another good wallop, but the impact I braced for never came to pass.

Instead I just heard Ben yelling, 'You don't do that!'

I sat up.

Mark was lying on his back on our front grass, with Ben kneeling on his chest, his finger in Mark's face. As if he were chastising a four-year-old.

'You don't hit Rusty! You never hit Rusty!'

Despite Ben's vertical size, Mark was a lot bigger and stronger. All he had to do was dig his elbows into the grass and push hard, and he succeeded in tossing Ben on to the lawn. But he didn't go after Ben. Or me. He just looked at me once over his shoulder, with exaggerated contempt. Then he marched back to his own yard and picked up the hose. I heard the hiss of the water when he squeezed the nozzle.

Ben stood over me, peering down into my face.

'Why did he hit you?'

'Let's just get inside. Give me a hand.'

He reached his huge hand down, and I pulled myself to my feet.

'Come on,' I said. 'Let's just go in.'

'But why did he hit you?'

'I hit him first.'

'Why did you hit him first?'

I struggled to get my key into the lock, but my hands were shaking. I got it on about the seventh try, and we stepped into the safety of the living room.

'Why did you hit him first?'

'Because he said something about Anat.'

'What did he say?'

'It's a long story, Ben.'

'Was it mean, what he said?'

'I thought it was mean, yes.'

'He shouldn't be mean.'

'But he is.'

'But even if he is. You shouldn't hit.'

'I know.'

'But you did.'

'Ben!' I barked. More harshly than I had intended.

'What?'

'I'm a little upset. Can we just have it quiet for a minute?'

'OK. What's for dinner?'

I sighed. 'You want macaroni and cheese?'

'Yeah.'

'Will you go watch TV till it's ready?'

'OK.'

I had twenty heavenly, silent moments in the kitchen. Nearly enough to pull myself together. Or, anyway, as together as I'd been in the first place. The beautiful silence was punctuated only by occasional throaty laughter from the TV room.

I held a paper towel full of ice to my eye as I worked. Now and then I shifted it to the knuckles of my right hand. I stopped once to swallow four aspirin.

Eventually I put two bowls of highly refined

flour and reconstituted cheese-related powder on the table with two glasses of milk.

Then I called Ben to come and get it.

The TV went silent.

What seemed like too much time later, he ambled in and sat at the table with me. He picked up his fork.

'Napkin,' I said.

'Oh, right.'

He shook out his paper napkin and spread it carefully on his lap.

Then he wolfed down a good half of his dinner in five or six big bites.

'Taste OK?'

He nodded. He looked lost in thought. Whatever 'thought' meant to Ben.

'What?' I asked. I can't imagine why I asked.

'You were really late,' he said.

13 October 2001

I let myself into the bakery at 6.51 a.m. But not through the kitchen door. With a distinct sadness, and a physical feeling of loss that seemed to be wedged up under my ribs, crowding my heart and making it hard to draw a full breath, I used the customer entrance.

Anat looked up from the kitchen. Waiting. Waiting, I suppose, for me to come back and talk to her. The way I always did.

I didn't.

I took a table in the darkened seating area up front.

A long moment passed, during which she did not cut any donuts.

Then she wiped her hands on her white apron, and came out and stood behind the counter and stared at me in silence for another moment, and I looked at her in the dim light.

'You're angry with me,' she said. Alarmingly, she sounded as if she was forcing back tears.

'No!' I said. Shouted, really. 'No, of course I'm not! Why would I be angry?'

'I shouldn't have come to your house.'

'No, it's fine. That was fine. It's not that at all.'

'What is it, then?'

I looked out the window for just a second or

202

two as a car cruised by, its headlights cutting through the civil twilight, half-necessary and half-not. I pointed to the car as I spoke.

'People will notice,' I said, 'if they haven't already. Which wouldn't bother me in the slightest. But it's obviously a problem for you. And I don't want to make problems for you. I want to be a good thing in your life. I don't want to bring you trouble.'

Then I just sat and breathed for a moment, unable to bring myself to look at her, to see how my words had been received. When curiosity overcame fear, I looked into her face.

What I saw there could only rightly be described as . . . it frightened me to use the word, but there's only one word that will finish that sentence. Love. She looked at me with love. Or, if not love, something that lived close by.

'You're sweet,' she said. 'No wonder . . . '

I waited for her to tell me no wonder what, but she never did. Too bad. I'm guessing I would've liked it.

We survived a long, awkward silence.

Then she said, 'Well, at least let me put the light on for you. Don't sit out here in the dark.'

'The dark is OK.'

'That will look as odd as anything, don't you think?' She marched around the counter as she asked this. 'You're my customer. I put the lights on for my customers.'

And she did.

And so, of course, she saw. Sooner or later she was going to see. I'd just somehow been hoping for later. Not enough to make me stay home. But some.

Her mouth fell open, and she stared at my face for what seemed like an eternity. I remember thinking I must have looked even worse than I'd thought. I'd brushed my teeth and combed my hair in the mirror that morning. But I purposely hadn't turned on the overhead light.

I just mostly knew my left eye was so swollen I could only open it halfway, and only that with great and painful effort.

'Russell, what happened to you? Did Ben do this?'

'Oh, no. Ben? No. Never.'

'I'm sorry. It's just that you said he has tantrums.'

'He has tantrums like a kid has tantrums. He cries and paces. And sometimes he even hurts himself. But not anybody else.' Silence. During which I knew I had to say it: if not Ben, then who? There was nothing else waiting to be filled in. 'This is about the butthole next door.'

'He attacked you?'

I cleared my throat and hesitated, and as I did I flexed my swollen right hand, feeling the pain in my bruised knuckles. I did it without thinking.

She noticed.

'I see you gave as good as you got,' she said.

'I don't want you to think I go around getting in fights. I never do. I'm twenty-four years old and I never punched anybody before. I always use my words. As my mom used to say. Or I just walk away. But there's something about Mark. He pulls my strings. And everybody's just more on edge right now. It's like everybody's nerves are raw. I don't know how to explain it.'

'You don't have to explain that part. I'm a member of everybody. I've noticed things are extra tense.'

She walked back into the kitchen, leaving me to wonder what part I did still have to explain. No, I take that back. I damn well knew.

'What will you have this morning?' she called out to me.

A second later she wheeled the first big rack of trays up front and began to load donuts into the display case.

I got up and walked to the counter and watched her, thinking I'd know my breakfast when I saw it.

'The almond Danish look good,' I said. 'I've never tried your almond Danish.' Somehow that came out sounding personal, though not for any logical reason. Still, it embarrassed me.

She used a piece of tissue paper to lift one on to a paper plate. It was glazed and covered with thinly sliced almonds, which had toasted to a nice golden brown in the oven. I could see the edges of the almond paste bulging out between the folds of crisp brown dough.

I reached out to take it from her, but she didn't hold it in my direction.

'Was it about me?' she asked.

I lied.

'No. Of course not. Not at all. Mark and I have a lot of old differences, that's all. And we have three mutual friends about to ship out to Afghanistan, if they're not there already, and

205

Mark might join up, and I guess it's bringing out our political problems. I'm not one of those 'rah-rah America' types. A few weeks ago that was fine, but now all of a sudden it causes big trouble. Every time I turn around.'

She handed me the Danish.

'Be careful what you say to people,' she said.

'I tell myself that all the time. But then the wrong things are out of my mouth before I can even question them.'

I sat and ate and watched her load the cases, and we didn't say more.

Then she had to go back into the kitchen to work, and it would have been too hard to talk much over that distance anyway. And besides, we had customers.

I only stayed another ten or fifteen minutes, but that feeling stayed much longer. The one I'd had when I first came through the customers' entrance. The one that seemed to be wedged up under my ribs, crowding my heart and making it hard to draw a full breath.

★   ★   ★

When I got back, I left the car in the driveway.

I stepped out to see Mark looking out his window at me.

Instead of heading for my own door, I cut kitty-corner across his lawn and headed straight for him. He dropped the curtain again and disappeared. But I didn't change my path.

I just stood there for a moment or two, outside the front windows of the Jesperses' house.

Predictably, Mark looked out again to see if I had gone away. And there I was.

I waved.

He didn't.

The curtain fell back into place again.

I walked across the lawn to the door and rang the bell.

First nothing. A long nothing.

Then, just as I raised my hand to hit the bell again, the door opened about a foot, and Mark stuck his head out.

'What?'

'I just wanted to say I was sorry. You know. For going straight to hitting. Without an intervening, 'Please speak respectfully about her.' Or, you know. Something along those lines.'

I looked at his face. The side of his jaw where I'd hit him. Nothing. I hadn't left any noticeable mark. I was half-relieved and half-disappointed.

'Oh,' he said. 'Well. I guess it was none of my business.'

'True. But saying, 'It's none of your business,' would also have been a better choice.'

'Yeah. Well. Whatever. Water under the bridge, you know?'

And the door eased shut again.

★   ★   ★

I picked Ben up at three fifteen. Needless to say, I was careful not to be late.

'You're on time,' he said, as he put on his seat belt.

'I'm almost always on time. Yesterday was the only day.'

'But yesterday you were late.'

'I *know* that, Ben. I just *said* that. Yesterday was the *only* day I was late. Every other day I've been on time.'

'But yesterday you were really late.'

'Ben! Drop it!' It was a full-on snap. I was on a short fuse. I hadn't slept well, and my morning had left me in a strange state of unfocused misery. And I really bit his poor head off.

'But you *were*,' he said, pitifully. As if to stress how justified he'd been in mentioning it.

Then he sulked quietly, and, much as I enjoyed the silence, I felt like shit for hurting his feelings.

'Let's talk about something different,' I said.

'OK. Like what?'

'Like . . . tell me about your day.'

'OK! It was good.'

'Tell me about it.'

'Like what?'

'Tell me something that happened at work today.'

'I bagged groceries.'

'Something more specific.'

'I bagged a lot of groceries.'

'OK. Never mind.'

'Wait! I know! I've got one. I know something. Mrs Durst came in. And she bought a great big giant-size thing of kitty litter. But she had it on that bottom thingy part of the cart, and so when Eddie walked her groceries out to the car he never put it in her trunk. And so then when he

208

brought the cart back in, there it was. This great big thing of kitty litter. So Mr McCaskill had to call her, and she had to drive all the way back, and I had to carry the kitty litter out to the parking lot so she wouldn't have to come in again. And then guess what happened?'

'I have no idea, Buddy.'

'It turned out it never got rung up, either. Cause it was down below. But Mr McCaskill said to just forget it. Because he was embarrassed that she already had to come back. But he really gave everybody a talking-to about being more careful.'

'There you go. See? It was a pretty eventful day after all.'

A silence. Then, as I turned the last corner toward the house, Ben said, 'Oh. Oh. And another thing, too. I saw Anat. She came in the store.'

A predictable pounding from my heart. Embarrassingly, no more than the mention of her name was required.

'Did she talk to you?'

'Yeah. She always talks to me. She's nice.'

'She is,' I said. 'What did you talk about?'

'You.'

I pulled into the driveway and cut the engine.

'What about me?'

I already had the instinctive sense that I wasn't going to like this.

'She said your eye looked really bad, and she felt bad for you. And I said yeah, I felt bad for you, too, but Mark wouldn't have hit you if you didn't hit him first. And I said I told you about how you shouldn't hit, but you said you sort of had to hit, because what Mark said about her was mean.'

I sat there for a moment, then dropped my head to the steering wheel.

'And then what did she say?'

'She wanted to know what he said about her, but I told her I couldn't really remember, because even though I was there, nothing Mark said sounded mean to me, but that he *was* talking about her, so probably I just missed something. Are you OK?'

'Not really,' I said, my forehead still pressed to the wheel.

'I wish you would be OK.'

'Me, too,' I said, and forced myself to rally. 'I wish I would be OK, too. Let's just go inside.'

14 October 2001

In the morning I stepped into the bakery at the usual time. Through my new choice of doors.

I noticed a bell that sounded as I opened the door, and I wondered if it was newly installed, or if I really could have missed that on previous days. I tended to be dazed and preoccupied on my way in, so anything was possible.

Anat looked up, then down at her work again. There was definitely something to be read in her reaction to me. But I had no idea what. Well. I had some idea. And it wasn't good. I was just short on specifics.

I stood on my side of the counter, staring at her, until she looked up again.

'What?' she said.

'I have something I need to tell you.'

At first she looked as though she didn't intend to stop working. But in time — too much time, really — she wiped her hands on a small towel and came and stood on the other side of the counter from me. When she looked at my eye, I saw her reaction. It wasn't literally a full-on flinch. But close.

'That looks even worse today.'

'I know. It hurts more, too.'

'What did you want to tell me?'

211

'I'm sorry I didn't tell you the truth yesterday.'

I paused, in case she wanted to comment. She didn't.

'I guess I thought it would only make you feel bad to know. But it's one of those decisions you make fast, on the spur of the moment, and then you look back later and realize it only works for the short term. In the long run I think it's always better if everybody knows the truth. But right at that moment, yesterday, when you asked me, I just felt like I couldn't handle seeing the look in your eyes if I told you. I guess it was more selfish than anything else. But I've been under so much pressure lately. I feel like I'm walking some sort of tightrope, and any little thing could unbalance me. So I ducked that moment when I should have told you the truth. And now I regret it.'

'Because you got caught?'

'I don't think so. I think I would have regretted it anyway.'

'And would you have come and told me?'

'Probably not. I would've wrestled with myself about it. Because I would've been afraid it was one of those things that would do more harm than good. But I'm glad things worked out the way they did. So I didn't have to leave it that way.'

'Wow,' she said, her eyes flickering up to mine and then away again.

'Wow what?'

'You're very honest for a big fat liar.'

I laughed a little. Happy to let off a puff of tension.

'I usually am pretty damn honest. Actually.

Sometimes too much so.' Silence. It stung. 'So . . . '

'So?'

'Am I forgiven?'

Anat sighed. 'It's not that big a deal,' she said. Not sounding like she meant it. 'Well, it is. It is, but it isn't. Next time I want the damn truth whether I'll like it or not.'

I reached my right hand over the counter and offered it to her to shake. It took her a long time to notice it, and a little while longer to figure out what she was supposed to do with it.

But then we shook on our new deal.

22 October 2001

It was two thirty in the morning, and I couldn't sleep.

Then it was three. Then it was three thirty.

Ever since I'd given up going into the kitchen to be alone with Anat in the morning, I'd had a miserable time sleeping at night. It was almost as though holding back the urge to enjoy that time with her was like capping steam. The pressure just kept building, making normal things impossible. Like living.

I'd even switched to decaf coffee in the morning. In case that was part of it. That wasn't part of it.

Then it was four, and I started wondering what time she came in. I started engaging in dangerous thinking. Because if she came in at four, there would likely be no one on the street at that hour. I could tell her I couldn't sleep, which, God knows, was true. And I could see her. Really see her.

And not like a customer.

And I could be back in plenty of time to drive Ben to work.

I wrestled with myself for a while. After all, she'd looked at me with such love when I said I didn't want to bring trouble into her life. I should stay here.

Then again, I could tell her with absolute honesty that I was in a bad way, and needed to be with someone. Talk to someone.

Well. Her. I needed to be with her.

By about twenty after four, I lost patience with the wrestling. I got up and got dressed, careful to put on the shirt I liked best. Of my three. Of course I had more clothes. But not locally.

I turned on the overhead bathroom light before brushing my hair and my teeth. The bruise around my eye was turning sickly shades of yellow and light purple, and the eye itself was shot through with blood.

There was no way around it. I looked a sight.

But I was going.

★   ★   ★

I parked the car around the corner, rather than right out front.

My heart hammered as I walked to the kitchen door, but I kept my stride even and brave. I stepped up to the bakery window and looked into the dimly lighted kitchen, already raising one hand to wave.

And there, inside, was . . . Nazir.

It hit me like a mule kick to the gut. This must be Monday. Had I known this was Monday? Obviously not, but why not? How could that have been a whole week? I couldn't make it all mesh in my brain.

Meanwhile Nazir was waving back. He shot me a broad smile and came to open the door. His smile flickered slightly when he got a look at

215

my new face. But he didn't comment or stare.

'Hey,' I said, not yet coming in. As if I had to apply for his permission first. Which was possible. 'I can't sleep. I'm having a hard time. With . . . I don't know . . . everything. I needed to talk. I thought maybe I could come talk to you.'

Thankfully, somewhere in the middle of that last sentence, the fog in my brain cleared and I understood the importance of giving the impression that I had known it was Monday all along. That I had come by at four thirty to talk to him. Not to Anat.

'Of course,' he said. 'Of course. You are my good friend. Well. New. But good. Please come in.'

He stepped back from the doorway to allow me to enter. The bakery kitchen seemed to be infused with a long-lost warmth. It looked the way home might look after you've been lost in a storm for days, thinking you might never see it again.

I stepped inside and breathed deeply.

'Pour yourself a coffee,' he said. 'I have a pot going.'

I did as directed, then rejoined him in the kitchen.

I leaned on a stool, and for the longest time I watched him scrape down the inside of the big industrial mixer as it turned. Without speaking.

In time he looked up at me.

'You don't do much talking for a man who needs to talk.'

'True. I guess I'm having trouble getting

216

started. Maybe you could get me going. Ask me what's wrong, or something.'

'I don't have to ask you what's wrong,' he said. He turned off the mixer and leveled his bold gaze on me. 'Your mother just died. The place where you worked was attacked, killing most of your colleagues and friends. No one can take care of your brother now but you, and he's not easy. And someone has apparently been beating on your face.'

I nodded three or four times.

'That sums it up surprisingly well. I wonder why I even need to talk about it now.'

Nazir shrugged. 'You tell *me*,' he said.

I watched him remove the mixer bowl and hoist it on to the table, turning and scraping the mountain of donut dough on to the floured surface.

I sipped the coffee. It almost blew the back of my head off.

'I make it strong,' Nazir said.

I hadn't known he was paying such close attention to me.

'I feel like I'm stuck in some kind of bad dream,' I said. I turned my gaze out the window. A streetlight illuminated the empty miniature intersection. Like a dollhouse. This town was sleeping. And possibly not real. 'I hitchhiked here with nothing but what I could fit in my big backpack. Because there were no planes. There was no transportation to be had, but I had to get here. And it's like I stepped into this dream, and now it won't let me go again. I wasted a month's rent on my apartment in New York.' I never said

217

Jersey City. New York sounded better. 'Because my stuff still lives there. Now I'm going to have to pay another, soon. For all intents and purposes right now I own like, two pairs of jeans and three shirts and four pairs of socks. And I don't even know when I can get to New York to get my stuff because Ben probably can't be left alone that long. I thought I'd go back there. To live. Or at least to make some arrangements to really move. But I don't see how I can. But everything I have is still there. Except me. It's like I don't even know where I live.' I dropped my head into my hands for a minute, and then made a sort of growling, angry noise. 'Listen to me. I'm pathetic. I should pull myself together.'

'You are too hard on yourself,' Nazir said.

'Am I?'

'Much too hard. Anyone would be having a hard time in your situation. And you would be patient with them. Why won't you be patient with you? If my mother had just died, I would be a mess. Even just that one thing. I would be a mess.'

'Is your mother alive?'

'No.'

'I'm sorry.'

'She died ten years ago. When Anat was only ten. I was a mess.'

My brain ran in circles, figuring out that Anat was only twenty. Somehow I'd thought she was my age. Or close, anyway.

'You have friends you can talk to?' Nazir asked, interrupting my brain.

'I guess not, or I wouldn't be here. I have Ben,

218

but I can hardly talk to him. There was a woman before I left New York — just a friend, nothing more — but I've broken that off. And there was one guy at my office who survived, but I don't really know him. Anat has been very nice. And you. You've both been very nice to me. But I've only known you for . . . '

I stopped to think how long I had know them. Had it been the fourteenth or fifteenth of September when I stumbled into town? This was the twenty-second of October. I had known Anat a little over five weeks. That didn't seem possible.

While I was trying to wrap my brain around this readjustment, we were startled by the sound of glass shattering. Nazir made it around the counter long before I did. I let the moment freeze me.

When I caught up with him, the dark seating area in the front of the bakery looked like a broken-glass sea. I could feel the cold of the wee hours of our Kansas morning pouring through. Nazir turned on the lights, and I was able to make out some of the bits of glass painted with what I knew were the letters of his name.

In the middle of it all was a rock about the size of an orange.

I threw open the bakery door and ran out on to the sidewalk. I heard the bell jingle, but vaguely. Like it was far away. Or I was. I looked in every direction. But the street was empty. Empty and unreal, still like an old unused movie set. Whoever it was had gone.

I stepped back inside.

Nazir's face looked too flushed. I couldn't tell

if he was about to release sorrow or rage. But I could see something trying to come out.

He kicked viciously at the glass once, but barely grazed the top of it. One piece flew across the floor and made a clinking sound when it landed.

'All right,' he said. His voice sounded deathly calm. Eerily calm. 'All right. I thought we were done with this, but all right. I will not go to pieces. I will just get a broom and sweep it up, and then at nine o'clock I will call some kind of glass company, and that's it.'

He looked up at me. Straight into my eyes. I was startled by the anger I saw in his. Not at me, of course. But still.

'Until next time, eh, my friend? That's it, until they decide to have some more fun with us.'

He clapped me on the shoulder before he moved off toward the kitchen.

'Shouldn't you call the police?'

'How can the police catch them? How can they know who did this? This could be anybody.'

'I was just thinking . . . you're insured, right? I mean, are you? If you're insured, you might need a police report before you can file a claim.'

Nazir stood like a statue for a weird length of time, halfway between me and the kitchen. I was starting to worry about him. Then the spell broke, and he hit himself in the forehead with the heel of one beefy hand.

'That is absolutely right,' he said. 'You are so right. Where is my brain? It's a good thing you were here with me, because I can't think with a thing like this. You probably just saved me a lot of money. Something I can't afford to lose any more of right now. Wait here. I will call.'

I don't know where the phone hid in that bakery. Maybe way back in the storeroom. Because I never heard him call. I never heard what he said to the police. But I know he called. Because less than ten minutes later, we received a visit from one of Nowhere-ville's finest.

Unless things had changed since I left town, that was one out of all two of Nowhere-ville's finest.

★　★　★

'I need to know you can make me safe!' Nazir roared.

Somehow, in the intervening ten minutes, he had found his voice.

'Sir — ' the cop said, but got no further. He was a guy, I swear, no older than me, with blond hair in an army-length buzz cut. His name badge said he was Officer N. Michelevsky.

'You are the police! If you can't keep us safe, who can keep us safe? What am I to do? I ask you this! Why can't I live in this town like anybody else? Why can't I live in peace? What have I done to anybody that I don't deserve to live in peace? I lead a quiet life. I hurt no one. Who do I hurt? Next time it will be a bomb.'

Michelevsky got a word in edgewise. 'I doubt that, sir. I don't think they're trying to hurt anybody. Maybe scare you. Maybe even get you to move.'

'This is my livelihood. I know there are those

who want us to pack up and move away, but how can I do that? Business is so bad I don't have the money to start again. I must know you can keep me safe.'

'I didn't say you should move. Just that it doesn't seem like they're out to hurt anybody.'

'My daughter. My daughter is only twenty, and she works by herself at night. And it's a small town, so everybody knows this.'

'If everybody knows this, did it ever occur to you that somebody purposely did this when *you* were here, not your daughter? Maybe it's easier to pick on a grown man than a young woman.'

'I'm surprised they have even that much honor. So what if you are wrong?'

'Here's what we can do for you, sir. We'll increase the patrols by here — drive by three or four times a day between four and seven in the morning. And, this being a small town and all, we got a pretty good idea who our small batch of miscreants are, so how about we put out the word that we're taking any vandalism against this shop very seriously. That we're watching, that we'll come down hard if we don't like what we see. That sort of thing. What do you say?'

I watched Nazir to see how he would react. He stared into the cop's face for a moment, proud and defiant.

Then he said, 'This is far from a guarantee.'

'There are no guarantees,' the cop said. 'I think you know that, sir.'

A long silence. I could feel a cool breeze on my neck.

'I have to go make the donuts,' Nazir said. 'I

can't afford not to go on with my work.'

Then he walked away. Marched into the kitchen, and that was that.

The cop turned to me, and motioned with his head to a table away from the direct cold of the broken window. We sat down across from each other.

'He seems a little upset,' N. Michelevsky said.

'I'd say.'

'Not that I blame him.'

'No.'

'So maybe just fill in a few details for my report.'

'Sure.'

'This happened right before he called? Or you came in and found it this way?'

'We were here when it happened. But we were in the kitchen.'

'You work here?'

'No. Just a family friend. I couldn't sleep, so I came down here to talk to Nazir.'

'And did you see anyone? A car, or someone on foot?'

'No. I ran out into the street, but I didn't see anybody. It was too late by then.'

'OK. Well. You know. I'm not going to lie and say the investigation will go much further than this.'

'I know. I think he just wanted the police report for insurance purposes.'

'Understood.'

'I worry about his daughter, too. You don't think they'll really throw a bomb next time, do you?'

'I doubt it,' he said, standing up. 'Your name, for my report?'

'Russell Ammiano.'

'Spell it?' he asked.

And I did.

'Anyway, I wouldn't worry about it too much. So far the crimes seem to be about expressing an opinion. Maybe costing them some money. Nobody seems to be out to hurt anybody. Things'll cool down after a while.'

'Hope you're right,' I said.

'Me, too.'

And he picked his way through the sea of glass to the door, and let himself out.

I walked back through the kitchen to get a broom.

I found Nazir standing with his head bent forward to the table, resting on his fists. I thought he was crying.

But when he looked up at me, I saw it was rage he was battling. Not tears.

'I'm going to get a broom and sweep it up,' I told him.

He nodded. Not as though nothing needed to be said, but as though his speech was not currently functioning.

I found a big push broom in the storeroom. I also found a gigantic roll of plastic wrap. I wasn't even looking for the plastic wrap. I just leaned in to get the broom, leaned over the big white buckets — the storeroom was a sea of those five-gallon white buckets with snap-on lids — and there it was, in front of my eyes.

Working slowly, being careful not to cut

myself, I swept up all the glass. I cut myself once, anyway. Then I shrink-wrapped the open window, stretching the plastic wrap from one side of the window frame to the other in several long strips, securing it to the frame with tape from a dispenser on the counter. For extra good measure. As I did, I noticed there was still a smudge of paint on the bricks under the window.

I looked up at the clock. It was well after five. Ben would be up. Ben always got up at five.

Back in the kitchen, I leaned the broom against Nazir's big refrigerator.

'I have to get back,' I said. 'Ben gets up at five. If he sees I'm not back he'll have a fit.'

Nazir nodded. Without looking at me.

'Funny, huh? I came in here to get some support from you, and you ended up having a night that made mine look happy.'

'Life turns on a dime,' he said, still not looking at me.

'Well . . . bye.'

I let myself out.

I walked halfway across the parking lot, then turned and walked back in.

'Got a pen and paper?' I asked him.

He flipped his chin in the direction of a small yellow pad adhered to the side of the refrigerator. Beside it, a pencil dangled on a string.

I picked up the pencil and wrote 'Russell's cell phone number. Call anytime.' And the number.

'I'm leaving my number,' I said to Nazir. 'In case you're ever here alone and you need me. Or Anat. If Anat was alone here and anything

225

happened, I'm literally less than two minutes away. I could beat you here by half an hour. But make sure she knows it doesn't matter if it's four o'clock in the morning. And it doesn't matter if she's not sure. Even if she hears something she can't identify. Or there's a car idling out front. Anything that doesn't seem right to her. She should call me. I mean, obviously if something really happens, she should call the police. But if there's just something she's not sure about, she should call me. And I'll come down here and sit with her.'

He looked at me then. Turned that searing gaze on me.

'Thank you, my friend,' he said.

There didn't seem to be more to say, so I just walked to my car and drove back to the house.

★ ★ ★

Ben was sitting at the kitchen table, eating cereal. He seemed surprised to see me walk through the door. But he obviously hadn't been upset. So apparently he'd had no idea I'd been gone.

'I thought you were asleep,' he said.

'Good.'

That was exactly what I'd hoped he'd thought.

'But you weren't. You were out.'

'True.'

'Why weren't you asleep?'

'I couldn't. I couldn't sleep. I tried, but I just couldn't.'

'Oh,' Ben said, around a mouthful of

half-chewed food. 'OK.'

Miraculously, he said nothing more about it.

★ ★ ★

On the way in to his work, Ben spotted the broken window from blocks away.

'Oh, no,' he said. 'Oh, no. Uh oh. That's bad. That's really bad.'

'It's pretty bad,' I said.

'You don't sound like you think it's as bad as I think it is.'

'No. I do. It's just that I already knew about it.'

'Oh. Who broke it?'

'We don't know.'

'Somebody broke it and ran away?'

'That's about the size of it, yeah.'

Ben whistled softly, obviously impressed by the scope of the crime. By small-town standards, it was quite a happening. By Ben standards, it was earth-shattering.

'I'm glad I didn't do a bad thing like that.'

'Me too, Buddy. I'm glad you didn't, too.'

23 October 2001

When Ben and I drove by the bakery the following morning on our way to Gerson's Market — it was a Tuesday but Ben had to cover another bagger's shift — we saw fresh new window glass already in place. Nazir must've gotten someone to come fix it in-between the time I drove Ben home and closing time.

Only problem was, it no longer said Nazir's Baked Goods on the window. That would take a little more time.

* * *

I stuck my head in the front area of the bakery. The lights were on. It was ten minutes to seven.

'It's only me, Nazir,' I called.

I heard nothing in return, so I walked to the end of the counter and looked back into the kitchen. Nazir was cutting donuts, intensely. It gave me a trace of sudden indigestion. That stress level of his. On top of my stress level. Well. Anything on top of my stress level would have been a problem.

'Good morning,' I said, and he waved without looking up.

'Get yourself a coffee,' he said. 'I have it

228

regular. Regular coffee. For customers. You can't strip paint with it, or anything such as that.'

I poured a big coffee into a to-go cup, black, and took it into the kitchen with Nazir. I stood with my back leaned up against the long bar handle of one of the two ovens. The warmth felt good against my back. I thought, I remember warmth. Whatever happened to warmth?

'Looks better,' I said.

He looked up for a fraction of a second. 'The window?'

'Yeah. That was fast.'

'Except it doesn't say what it is, this place. Could be a dry cleaner, like it used to be. Could be a florist. Who knows what it is unless you come and look in? You don't know if you will see flowers or bread.'

'I expect the locals have it pretty well memorized. You know. Which shop is which. Besides, you'll get it repainted.'

No answer.

'Right?'

'Will I? I don't know. I suppose I will have to. I think it must say 'bakery' or 'baked goods'. But must it say 'Nazir'? I don't know why that's so enraging to some. But I hesitate to pay to have that painted back on. It costs money to have someone come paint that, you know. I already have to pay five hundred dollars for the window. That's the deductible for my insurance. No matter what the window costs my bill is five hundred dollars. Then I pay a hundred or two more to have my name painted on. Then some wise guy drives by when I have it all back to

229

normal again. Throws another stone. I can't keep up. I am feeling tired, my friend.'

I just leaned and breathed for a moment. I knew tired. I could relate to tired. I had no cure for my own tiredness. What was I supposed to say to alleviate his?

I said, 'You want me to go by the hardware store and get a stencil? I could just stencil on the word 'bakery' if you want.'

Nazir slid a tray of Danish into the oven, the one I wasn't leaning on. Then he looked into my eyes. I could tell he was taking my offer seriously.

'What do you think it should say?' he asked.

'I think it should say your name.'

'You do.' It was a statement. It wasn't a question.

'It's what I would do. Otherwise I feel like I'd be letting them win.'

Nazir laughed soundlessly. 'I have news, my friend. They are winning. I am not letting them. They just are. But all right. I think you are correct. It should say 'Nazir'. I am not ashamed of my name.'

'I'll still stencil it on if you want.'

He didn't answer. Just grabbed his white china coffee mug and took it out into the customer area. When he came back with it full, he said, 'I have been thinking. And, also, talking to my daughter. And . . . maybe between Anat and myself, we could look after Ben.' I know my shock must have showed, because he said, 'Close your jaw, my friend. I don't mean for all of time. I mean for as long as you would need to go quickly and get your belongings. How much time would you need?'

'Wow,' I said. Truly impressed. 'That's a nice offer. That's a really nice offer. But I don't think you know how trying he is.'

'How much time would you need?'

'Oh. I don't know. Let me think. Two or three days to pack up the apartment. If I work fast. Most of a day each way to fly. Four days, at least. Maybe five.'

'I think maybe we could allow ourselves to be tried for four or five days.'

'You might want to compare notes with the Jesperses first.'

'The Jesperses? Who are they?'

'My next-door neighbors. They looked after Ben for most of three days while I tried to get back here. And they were just about at the end of their rope by the time I got back. Ben's a real creature of habit. I'm not sure how he'd do at anybody else's house.'

'Maybe we could come to yours.'

'Wow. It's a really nice offer. But . . . I'm just afraid you're going to be sorry you ever made it. But . . . You know what? I'll feel him out about it. I'll talk to him and let you know what I think of our chances.'

★   ★   ★

It was after dinner, and I was going through the mail. So far I'd done nothing with it except bring it in. Throw it on the table. After all, it wasn't my mail. It was clearly addressed to Margaret Ammiano. So, that was not my gas bill. That was my mother's gas bill. Surely no one expected me to pay it. Right?

Yes, I'm kidding. In a not-funny sort of way.

So there I was sorting through the bills, thinking I'd have to go to the bank and take over her account somehow. Thinking I'd have to find out when Ben got paid and how much, and whether he brought his check home or had it done as a direct deposit. And if there was any money in the account. And if there was — God forbid — a mortgage on the house. There hadn't been, when I left for college. But you never know what people might have to do to get by.

I'd have to find a way to assess what went out every month. And whether there was any other income. I had to start taking care of business. I'd been ignoring business as long as business could be safely ignored.

It sure would help not to have to pay another month's rent on my apartment in New York. Then again, there'd be the plane fare. Then again, if I didn't hurry up, there'd be both.

'Ben,' I called.

I suppose it goes without saying that Ben was in the TV room.

He stuck his head around the door frame.

'What?'

'I need to talk to you.'

'I'm watching.'

'It's important, Buddy.'

'Two more minutes.'

'Fine. Two more minutes.'

I sat there and stared at the bills for about another twenty minutes.

Finally I looked up, and there he was. Sitting down across from me.

'That was more than two minutes,' I said. My stress over the bills was looking to spill out. And of course Ben was the only available recipient.

'Sorry.'

'I need to talk to you about something.'

'You already said that.'

'I have to go back to New York to get my stuff. You know. And get it all packed up. And ship it out here. Or put it on a moving van. Or something.' Jokingly pretending for a moment that I could afford any of those options.

'OK,' he said.

I felt genuinely happy. For the first time in a long time. Then a little voice in the back of my head said, That was too easy. It said, Look out.

'You're OK with that?'

'Sure. As soon as Mom comes back.'

My heart fell. That was unexpected. I thought we'd at least gotten beyond that one.

'Buddy. I've told you and told you. Mom's not coming back. You told me you knew that.'

'Then don't go.'

'But I need to.'

A pause. About long enough to count to three. Then he began to sob quietly. He didn't pace, or repeat anything. It wasn't what you might call a tantrum. He just began to cry Muted. Pathetic. Heartbreaking.

'I won't leave you all alone, you know.'

'Who will I have?'

'Anat and Nazir will stay with you. You like Anat.'

'I don't know her.'

'You do know her. You told me she's nice.'

'I know her for coming in the store. She's nice for coming in the store. I don't know her for staying here. I don't have anybody who can stay here except you.'

His nose began to run, so I handed him a paper napkin left over from dinner.

'That's not true, Buddy.'

'It is true, Buddy!' he said, raising his voice for the first time that evening. 'You're my only buddy!'

'You stayed with the Jesperses.'

'And it was terrible! They don't like me.'

'They said they love you. Mrs Jespers said they love you.'

'But they don't like me.'

Whoa. A glimmer of an area in which Ben is not stupid. Mentally, I added that to the time he announced that I 'liked' Anat. Two rare random areas in which Ben is not stupid.

'It would only be for about four days.'

'Four days!' He wailed, stretching it out for ever and making it sound like four lifetimes. 'You can't go. Please don't go. Don't go, Buddy. They don't know what time I go to bed. What if they didn't drive me to work on time? Mr McCaskill wouldn't like it if they didn't drive me to work on time.'

'I'll tell them everything they need to know.'

I had been glancing briefly down at the bills as I said it. When I looked up, Ben was in the process of disappearing. He was sliding down off the chair and on to the rug. As if his bones had spontaneously dissolved. I got up and went to him. Got down on my knees beside him. I could hear the hitches between sobs. But barely. He must have been trying to sob as quietly as possible.

'Please don't go, Buddy,' he whispered.

I didn't know what to say, so I said nothing.

He whispered it again.

'Please don't go, Buddy.'

Thirty-one times. Before I gave up and left the room. After that, I couldn't say.

I know I shouldn't have left. I felt like shit for leaving him like that, on the rug, half under the table. I should have stayed with him and tried to make him feel better. But there was only one thing I could possibly have said to make him feel better. Nothing would do but that I promise him I'd never go away, ever, not even for one day. And I wasn't about to do it.

I took a long, hot bath, purposely soaking until I knew it must be almost eight o'clock.

Then I went back into the dining room. And there he was. Right where I'd left him. Still crying quietly.

'Come on, Buddy. Get up now. It's almost time for bed. And you have to wash your face. Your face is a mess.'

'OK,' he said, in a voice so small it broke my heart. He lumbered to his feet. 'Are you going away?'

'I don't know, Buddy. I don't know. Let's just get you to bed. We'll talk about it another time.'

'OK,' he said.

'You need a haircut, Buddy. You're looking a little seedy.'

'OK.'

'Where did Mom take you to get your hair cut?'

'She didn't.'

'She cut it?'

'Yeah.'

'I don't think I could do that. I think I'll have to take you to the barber.'

'No!' He wailed. 'Please don't. I don't know him. I know him for coming in the store, but I don't know him for cutting my hair. You do it. Please?'

'OK. Fine. I'll try.'

It was the only issue before us that I could afford to cede.

I watched him as he moved his uncooperative legs down the hall to his room, sobbing softly the whole way.

236

24 October 2001

This moment was unexpected. And somewhat inevitable. All at the same time. All rolled up into one key piece of my life.

It was the next morning. Wednesday, Anat's first day back from that unbearable chasm of her two days off. And again I hadn't been able to sleep.

I'd been developing dark circles under my eyes. I'd been feeling on edge. Even by the standards of my horrifying new normal.

I strode across the parking lot at about four fifteen in the morning, cruising like a heat-seeking missile. I can't say what I was thinking, because I know I wasn't. I'd flipped the off switch on my poor brain. It was such a relief.

I just remember feeling my heart pound. My heart was getting tired of pounding. Let me tell you.

You can only wrestle with something for just so long. Then you have to break in one direction or another. Just to end the wrestling. Something has to give.

Anat looked up and saw me through the glass of the kitchen door, and her eyes lit up. It fueled me, right at that moment when I might just as easily have lost my nerve.

I let myself in.

'Hey. You look like hell,' she said. But cheerfully. 'You look like you haven't slept in weeks.'

I walked right up to her. She took two steps back from the table. Maybe a bit unsure about my intentions. My intensity.

That made two of us.

I didn't stop when I got to her. I just kept walking. Which gave her no real option except to back up.

I backed her all the way into the storeroom. My heart pounding, pounding. Pounding.

'What are we doing?' she asked. Laughing.

I kissed her.

It was short but intense. Enthusiastic. Then I knew I needed to check in. Because, well, I mean . . . finally being sure of yourself is a good thing as far as that goes. But consent is still hugely important in situations like these.

I pulled back and looked into her face. She looked surprised. But not unhappy. That's when it hit me. My heart had finally stopped pounding. I thought, Oh, thank God. I don't know how much more of that hammering I could have taken. But, I noticed retroactively, when my lips finally touched hers, it stopped. Well, I don't mean my heart stopped. Well, nearly. Nearly stopped. But it mellowed. It turned into a sort of warm, oozing liquid, like gelatin that never set up correctly. Viscous but pourable. And it just started to drip.

It was a major step in the right direction.

'If I shouldn't have done that . . . ' I said,

barely over a whisper. But there was really no way to finish that sentence. Unless I was willing to tell her I was sorry.

I wasn't sorry. Not at all.

Maybe I needed to say, If I shouldn't have done that, then I won't do it again. No matter how badly I want to. No matter how sorry I'm not.

But, before I could say any such thing, I felt her hand weave into the back of my hair, and she pulled my face in close and kissed me in return. It was slower this time. Gentler. More heartfelt. This time we both knew it was in no danger of getting away.

She pulled back, and frowned. As if from a distance, I heard her say, 'Oh, Russell. What am I going to do about you?' In a way that did not sound entirely affectionate.

I sat down on a sealed bucket of maple icing. Fortunately there was a bucket of maple icing there for me.

I looked at the linoleum for a moment.

My heart had a long way to fall. It was up at the end of a long kite string. In uncharted territory. And when she said that, it felt like it hit the bakery linoleum so hard I thought it would never be of any use to me, or anybody else, ever again.

I didn't think I'd be able to talk. But I managed.

'You make me sound like a disease.'

I sounded like Ben to myself. Like Ben saying, 'Please don't go, Buddy.' Abject heartbreak. Unfiltered.

She sat on a bucket of cherry filling, right next to me, her hip touching up against mine.

'I didn't mean it like that. You know I didn't.'

She stroked my hair. Just one stroke, but it helped. Then she took her hand back.

'What did you mean it like?'

I heard her sigh. I couldn't bring myself to look at her.

'I feel like I'm already halfway down a street I know I can't go down. But here I am. And I don't know what to do. Things seem to be doing themselves.'

'Yeah, things are like that,' I said, far from occupying my own brain or body. Then I shifted suddenly into a different tack. 'Explain that to me. Tell me why you can't go down this street. In your culture, you just have to be alone for ever?'

'No, of course not. But there's a right way to do things.'

'And that is . . . ?'

'How do I explain? It's just . . . different. It isn't up to only you and me. You would get to know me and my father at the same time. Well. My family. But my father is the only family I have. So . . . you would ask us over for a meal or to tea. And we would host you in return. Many times, until we all knew each other well. And then . . . '

I waited. Anxious to hear the end of that sentence. But she never finished.

'And then . . . what?'

'I can't say that.'

'But I need to know.'

'Let me start over. I shouldn't have started like

that. You know. Saying 'you' and 'me'. So let's just say, 'One would . . . ' Hypothetically. Let's say the man gets to know the woman and her family for at least a couple of months. Maybe more. There's no set rule about that. And then, if he still wants to take it to the next level . . . '

'Sooner or later you have to say this, you know.'

'He asks her father for her hand in marriage.'

'Oh, hell, is that all? I thought it was something terrible.'

'Russell, we've only known each other — '

'Fine,' I said, and blasted to my feet, my knees cured. 'We'll do it right.'

'You make it sound easy, Russell. But you don't know my father.'

'Your father likes me.'

'That's because he didn't see what just happened.'

I stood a minute, trying that on. Trying to make it fit. Anat stood up and gave me a small, chaste hug.

'We'll do it right,' I said. 'He wants you to be happy.'

'Yes.'

'So in time he'll understand.'

'I hope so.'

I grabbed the handle of my bucket and slid it out of the storeroom. Hard. It stopped sliding near the baker's table. Right about where I wanted it. I ducked my head down going by the window. And I sat on the bucket again.

'What are you doing?' she asked. As if the whole moment were somehow amusing.

'This way if someone comes by, they won't see me in here with you.'

'Ah,' she said.

She went back to her work, measuring flour into the mixer.

We were both silent for a long time. I know you can never speak for anybody else, but I believe the same thought was dawning on both of us.

'Another good thing about that,' I said, talking over the obvious. My own personal filibuster. 'Ben would get to know you two a lot better. And maybe he could even get comfortable enough that I could go to New York. You know. In, like . . . a decade.'

'I take it he's not big on the idea so far.'

'He cried for hours.'

'Oh.'

Another few seconds, and then I stood.

'This is not the right way,' I said. 'Is it?'

'You don't have to go.'

'Yes, I do. We're going to do this right. I'll see you at seven. Or a few minutes before. But I won't be back in the kitchen.'

I forced myself to walk out without looking back. Otherwise I doubt I would have walked out at all.

Halfway across the parking lot I heard her call my name.

'Russell.'

I turned. I was relieved. Because she'd asked me to turn. I'd wanted to turn. But I hadn't been able to give myself permission.

'I already miss you,' she said.

Her voice had changed into something soft. Something I'd never heard before. I wondered if this was the first moment the softness had existed. Or if she'd just never allowed it in front of me until now.

My heart did that thing again. That drippy thing. It was a funny feeling. Pleasant, yet not. Still, I couldn't help being relieved that my heart had finally stopped pounding around inside my chest. And started to melt instead. So much less violent. So smooth and quiet. Like resting.

Like finally getting to rest.

Part Five

Too Soon

9 November 2001

'You're not holding still enough, Buddy.'

'But it tickles.'

I was standing behind Ben in the TV room, trying to cut his hair. He was sitting on a kitchen chair, a towel wrapped loosely around his neck. I'd tried to wrap it more tightly, so he wouldn't get hair down his collar. But he'd complained, and said it choked him.

I looked up at the TV just in time to see a rerun of an old 1950s sitcom come on. It was hard to be with Ben in the TV room because of the quality — or lack of same — of the programs he found amusing.

'It's getting all down into my collar,' he said, sounding whiny.

'Then you should have let me wrap the towel tighter.'

'I don't want to choke. *And* I don't want hair down my back. I don't want both. And I don't see why I have to get my hair cut just because there's company coming.'

'That's not the only reason. I told you days ago you needed a haircut.'

'Maybe you already knew company was coming.'

Again, whoa. Was that another odd little bit of

knowing on his part? Or just a shot in the dark?

'You need your hair cut for everything. For any place you go.'

'I don't go any place. Except work.'

'You need to look good for work.'

'Nobody at work ever said I didn't look good.'

'Sooner or later they would have.'

'One of the guys at the store has long hair.'

'I'm not saying you shouldn't let it get long. If you really want to grow it out, fine. But it still needs to look like you take care of it. Right now it's all shaggy and . . . '

I looked up at the TV. A plane was headed for the South Tower. The voice-over had something to do with that night's evening newscast.

I froze. I couldn't move or speak. I wanted to scream to Ben to turn it off, but nothing came out. I couldn't thaw in time.

I just stood there, mute. And watched the plane slice in. The heat and pain in my body matched perfectly with the collision. As though the plane had sliced into me. It was the first time I'd watched it since I'd actually watched it. I must have been the only human being on the face of the planet who hadn't been glued to the TV in the days since. The only time I'd even gotten near a TV was during Ben's cartoons. I hadn't stayed long. I didn't know if I'd had any conscious idea of what I was avoiding. I knew now.

Fire, papers, smoke billowed out the far corner. I stood like a statue, as horrified as if it were happening for the first time, right in front of my eyes. Maybe more so.

Then the scene changed . . . to the plane heading for the building again. Apparently they planned to loop that footage for as long as the promotional text lasted. The fear of having to see it again shocked me out of my paralysis.

'Turn it off!' I screamed.

It startled Ben so much that he fell off the chair.

I watched him fumble for the remote, but he was too upset to remember where he'd left it. He was too upset to function.

I lunged for it, thinking I was somehow in a race for my sanity. If I couldn't turn it off before the tower got hit again, that would be that. I got my hand on the remote. But not in time. The terrorists won. Again.

Fire. Papers. A tickertape parade, ninety-some floors up. In my old world. In a few minutes, people would begin to jump.

My knees buckled, and I hit the rug. And I turned it off.

I leaned forward, pressing my forehead to the carpet. For a minute or two, I wrestled with whether I was about to be physically ill. In time, the feeling subsided.

I straightened up, still on my knees.

Ben was staring at me in abject horror.

'Sorry,' I said. I could hear my voice shaking. I know Ben could, too.

'What happened?'

'That upset me.'

'Why?'

'Why? It was thousands of people dying.'

'But everybody's seen that. A lot.'

'It's different for me.'

'Why?'

'Because I was there.'

'You were? You're not burned up.'

'I was close enough to see it, but not close enough to get burned up. I told you that. I told you the first day I was back. You don't remember?'

He shook his head, still wide-eyed.

'I was supposed to have been in one of those buildings. If I had been, I'd be dead.'

With the shift of my mood, the draining away of the most violent upset, Ben got up and came over. He dropped to his knees beside me, and draped an arm around my shoulders.

'Why weren't you where you were supposed to be?'

'I was late, that's all.'

'I'm never late.'

'I know. Sometimes I am.'

'You would have been dead?'

'Yes.'

'Then what would I have done?'

'I don't know, Buddy.'

'Poor Buddy,' he said, and threw the other arm around me. And held me tightly. Almost too tightly. But I didn't argue.

'You talking about you or me?' I asked.

'You, Buddy. I'm sorry the TV made you upset.'

I opened my mouth to explain to him that it wasn't really the TV. It was the actual events of that day, relived. Retriggered. Then I decided that would be a colossal waste of time.

So I just stayed there on my knees, and let my brother Ben embrace me.

★ ★ ★

A few minutes later we tried to get right back to the haircut, but my knees wouldn't seem to hold. I had to spend an hour in my room — well, my mom's room — just pulling myself together. And, even then, I was hardly together. I was merely able to stand.

The El Sayeds were coming at five thirty. And I was officially an hour behind schedule.

★ ★ ★

'I don't know what you're so worried about,' Ben said, shouting to be heard over the sound of the vacuum cleaner. He was following me around, dust rag in hand, as I vacuumed the living room rug.

'Just dust, Ben,' I shouted. 'We're late.'

'Why are you acting so nervous?'

'I'm not nervous.'

'You sure act like you are.'

'I just want Nazir to like me.'

'You said he already likes you.'

'I just don't want him to stop.'

'Why would he stop?'

I turned off the vacuum. The silence felt stunning.

'Please, Ben. They're coming in less than three hours. I haven't picked up the food yet. I haven't made the mashed potatoes. Or the salad. The

251

cleaning is going too slow . . . '

'You wasted too much time finishing the haircut. I told you not to waste time finishing.'

'I wanted you to look like someone takes care of you.' Truthfully, I'd tried to leave it half-done, but Ben had looked actually laughable, like a kindergartner who took construction scissors to his own hair. I had to clean it up as best I could. 'Now please, Ben. Go dust.'

★   ★   ★

It was 5.29 p.m. The El Sayeds would be ringing the doorbell any minute. And Ben was in a state of total meltdown because the hair under his collar made him itch.

'Take off your shirt,' I said.

'That won't help. It's on my back.'

'Ben! Please do as I say!'

He sulked. But he took off the shirt.

I ran into the bathroom and soaked the end of a towel, wrung it out as best I could, and then brought it back into Ben's room. He was standing in front of the full-length mirror in just his good slacks. I could see every one of his ribs. His skin was painfully white, as though it hadn't seen the sun in decades.

'Hold still,' I said, somehow knocked out of my irritation.

I used the wet towel to clean as much hair as I could off his shoulders and back. His shoulders were freckled. There was something childlike about them. Which may sound like a strange thing to say, when I had to stand on my tiptoes

252

to see them. But his bare skin looked so completely helpless.

The doorbell rang, freezing my heart.

'Put on your shirt,' I said, and then ran to get the door. But three steps out of his room, I realized my mistake. I stuck my head back in. Sure enough, Ben was threading one arm into the same hairy shirt. 'Not that shirt, Ben. That one has hair on it. A clean one.'

'Oh. You didn't say that. Which one?'

'Any one. I have to get the door.'

★ ★ ★

Nazir, Anat and I had been sitting in the living room, making nervous small talk, for a good three or four minutes when Ben came lumbering in. How he could take so long to put on a shirt, I have no idea. Plus, he was still buttoning it when he arrived. Plus, he was buttoning it wrong. He was a full two buttons off from one side to the other.

I found this perplexing, since he dressed himself with reasonable success every day. Must have been the stress.

Oh. One more plus that was actually a minus. It was the most ridiculous shirt in the history of clothing. Pink and purple plaid. I had no idea he even owned a shirt so grotesque, not to mention why he chose it. But he had very specifically asked me which shirt to put on. And I had very specifically given him permission to choose for himself. So I said nothing. About that, at least.

'Ben,' I said.

'What?' He already knew he wasn't going to like it. I could tell.

'It's not polite to come greet your guests until you're finished dressing.'

'I just have one more button.'

'But you have it buttoned wrong.'

'I do?'

He took the shirt by its tail, raised it as high as he could, and looked closely at the buttons, exposing his pasty white stomach. I didn't dare look at Nazir and Anat for their reactions. It would just be too sad if they found my brother sad. I knew they did. How could they not? I just didn't want to see it.

'Oh,' he said. 'Yeah. How'd that happen?'

And he began to unbutton the shirt again.

'Ben!' I shouted, louder than I'd meant to.

'What?'

'In your room.'

'OK, OK. Fine.'

He ambled away, clearly hurt.

I turned to Nazir to speak, to apologize for Ben's behavior. But he raised a hand to stop me.

'No, don't say anything,' he said. 'You don't have to apologize for your brother. He is as he is. He is doing his best, I'm sure.'

'Probably so. He's usually better at taking care of himself than this. I think he's nervous about having people over.'

At that moment Ben appeared again. This time he was far ahead of schedule. This time I had no idea how he'd managed so fast. His shirt was buttoned correctly, but not tucked in. I chose to let that slide.

His hair looked ridiculous. I was a very bad hairdresser.

'I'm not nervous,' he said. 'You're the one that's nervous.' He sat on the couch, so close to me that our hips almost bumped. 'Rusty got really nervous today. I thought he was gonna die.'

A painful silence.

'Ben was watching TV,' I said. 'And I was in the room with him. All of a sudden they showed that footage of the plane hitting one of the towers. I'd only seen it once before, and that was out my window. You know. Real time. While it was actually happening. I hadn't seen the footage of it since then. I really did take it hard. It's amazing how much I don't think about that on a day-to-day basis. But when it got triggered, it was quite a shock.'

'Poor Russell,' Anat said.

Nazir said, 'I can't stand to watch it, either, and it has nothing to do with me personally. It's very upsetting.'

'No,' Ben said. 'Not that. He was already nervous.'

'Well,' I said, leaping to my feet. 'Not to rush you to the table, but everything's pretty much ready. Ben, come help me in the kitchen.'

'OK,' he said.

I stood watching as he slowly pulled himself to his feet.

'I'll be in,' he said.

'I'll wait.'

I wasn't taking a chance on leaving him alone with my guests. Not even for a few seconds.

255

I followed him into the kitchen.

'Don't talk about that,' I whispered.

'Why not?'

'Just talk about something else.'

★ ★ ★

Ben followed my advice to the letter. He not only talked about something else, he talked about everything else. Through most of the first half of dinner.

Mostly he talked about his haircut. Primarily, how it itched. Every time I thought he'd gone off on a new tangent, the one hair I'd missed with the damp towel would tickle him again, and we'd be right back to haircut complaints.

I couldn't decide which would be more embarrassing, to stop him or let him ramble. Then I realized the answer lay in whether he'd be hurt if I stopped him. And whether he'd react to that hurt by making a scene.

I let him ramble.

Anat was seated to my right. The table was small and square, with one of us on each side, and I couldn't stop looking right. Well, I suppose I could have. But I was doing a bad job of trying. I was desperate to look at her. Every glimpse was like a glass of water in the desert. The way tendrils of her jet-black hair curled around her cheeks. I'd never seen it any way but back. The smooth narrowness of her fine shoulders and upper arms in that sleeveless dress. How could I look at something else? Anything else? But I knew I was being too conspicuous. But then I let myself get awkward about my efforts to stop. I tried to forcibly focus on not looking right, and found it to be much the same as trying not to think about elephants. My brain locked up in its inability to stop focusing on looking right, and the next thing I knew I had done it again.

When I finally got a word in edgewise, I said, 'I really think I did a bad job on that haircut. More so than I realized at the time. I might have to take him to a barber to get it fixed up, if I can get him to agree to that.'

'I could probably fix it up for him,' Anat said. 'If that would be OK with Ben. Would that be OK with you, Ben?'

I said, 'You wouldn't mind if Anat cut your hair, would you?'

'It's not how it looks,' he said. 'I don't even care about that. It's how it itches.'

And he was off to the races again, basically repeating the same set of complaints.

Meanwhile my heart was inching down a series of cliffs, falling the way a person might tumble from one rock down to the next, until they've fallen down the whole mountain. Anat was getting her first good look at what it would be like to have Ben around full-time and long haul. She would never come out of this dinner wanting to be with me. How could she? It was all too new between us, and Ben would be too big a shock. What could I possibly have that was so wonderful that she'd be willing to put up with a lifetime of this? How could I offset such a handicap?

I cut him off again.

'Sorry to interrupt, Ben, but there was something I wanted to say to our guests. Something like . . . well, a little bit of an apology. I probably don't have to, I know. But I've just been on this kick of being completely honest lately. Even more honest than usual.'

I glanced right. At her. Then I looked across the table at Nazir. He'd noticed. He was keeping count.

'Anyway, it's a simple apology. I didn't make most of this dinner we're eating. I probably should have tried to make my own dinner for you, but I really don't know much about cooking. I figured I had two choices. Serve something that I could proudly say I made myself. Or serve something you'd enjoy eating. So I picked up the two roast chickens from Ben's store. And the cold bean dish was from their deli. I made the mashed potatoes. I can proudly say that. I used to always make the mashed potatoes . . . ' I stopped myself from saying 'for my mom'. In case that would upset Ben. ' . . . when I lived at home. So that's one dish I can handle. And I made the salad. And thank goodness you folks brought the dessert, or that would have been store-bought as well.'

'The mashed potatoes are the best part of the whole meal,' Anat said, and gently rested her hand on my arm.

It was a mistake. A misstep. Possibly her version of looking right. She'd probably told herself to be sure not to touch me so many times that she eventually touched me.

I watched her stare at her own hand in alarm.

258

The thing to do would have been to remove it casually. As though nothing had happened.

She didn't. She froze, and left it there, then removed it awkwardly. Guiltily. With a glance at her father.

Then she tried to talk over the moment.

'So. Ben. Did you go along and help pick up the food?'

And I thought, Oh, good God. Don't get him started again.

'No,' he said with his mouth full. 'I didn't want to.'

I decided it would be more awkward to correct him for that lack of etiquette, so I didn't.

Of course, he didn't stop.

'I thought it would be weird to go in after work. You know. When I'm not supposed to be there. Because . . . well . . . I don't know. It just would be. Because I'd get up to the check-out with Rusty. And there'd be all this stuff to bag. All these groceries. Ours and other people's, too. And I'd feel like I had to bag them. I mean, how could I just leave them there? Even though I knew Matt would be there — Matt, he's the guy who takes over after I go home. But I never watched Matt bag groceries before. So what if I watched him, and he didn't do it right? There's more to bagging groceries than you think. It's not as easy as it looks. There's a lot to know. You can't put too many glass bottles and jars together or they'll hit against each other and break. And no eggs or bread on the bottom. You can put fruit on the bottom, but only if it's hard like a coconut, not if it's soft fruit like bananas. Even if they're not very ripe bananas. And it all has to balance, otherwise it'll be too hard for people to carry. And it can't be too heavy, or it might break right through the bottom of the bag. I bet you didn't know there was so much to know about it.'

Ben was directing his diatribe at Anat. Probably because he knew her better.

'I didn't,' she said. 'I just know you're very good at it. Everybody thinks so.'

'Maybe we should let the guests talk a little,' I said.

'Do they want to?' Ben asked.

'I don't know. Let's find out. I was hoping we'd learn a little bit more about them.'

'Like what?' Ben asked.

Suddenly, alarmingly, I found myself fighting the urge to strike him. My frustration over the gap between Ben and acceptable social behavior had reached breaking point. And there was so much at stake. Love. My life. My future. Happiness. If only he could make a good initial impression.

Then I shook it off, and kicked myself for setting my expectations of him unrealistically high.

I'm pretty sure none of this showed on the outside.

'I was hoping they'd tell us where they're from — '

'Egypt,' Ben said.

'I meant more specifically. Like we're from the US. But we're also from Norville, Kansas. And maybe how long they've lived here. What made them move so far from home. That sort of thing.'

I already knew. All that. I had asked Anat endless questions about herself. When we were all alone in the mornings. But I had to pretend none of that had ever happened. I had to act like she was almost a stranger.

'Fine,' Ben said. 'OK.'

We both looked up at our guests. It was immediately clear that Nazir did not plan to speak. His head was bent slightly downward, toward his plate, as if the sawing of a slice of roast chicken were some type of life-or-death surgical procedure.

With a physical jolt to my gut, I knew he was upset. I didn't know why, exactly. But I had a couple of ideas.

Then it was Anat's turn to talk too much, with a brand of nervousness similar to Ben's. But I heard only that they were from Kafr Dawar and that, when her mother died, her father had wanted to leave everything behind. Beyond that, I was totally distracted wondering what exactly was bothering Nazir, how soon I'd find out, and how much of a bad omen it would prove to be for my future.

★ ★ ★

'I'll gather up the dishes,' Anat said.

'No. Absolutely not. You're our guest.'

'I don't mind at all. Ben will help me. Won't you, Ben?'

'OK,' Ben said.

'No, Ben and I can — '

Anat turned and shot me a look that I knew was significant. In fact, it stunned me a little. I froze, and awaited further instructions.

'My father will want to smoke a cigar after dinner. He always does. So I thought it would be a good chance for you men to get to know each other better.'

I nodded carefully. Message received.

Then I wondered if Ben had caught his lack of inclusion in the category of men. Apparently not, no.

Nazir rose and patted the pocket of his sports jacket, as if to assure himself that the protruding cigar hadn't been stolen.

'Where do we do such things?' he asked. 'Inside your house, or out of it?'

I had a choice to make. Nazir was obviously perched at the border of The Land of the Offended anyway. Should I tell him he could not smoke in my house?

Yes. That's what I decided. I'd promised Anat I'd tell the truth.

'The front porch would be nice,' I said. 'I'll see if I can find an ashtray. And I'll join you out there.'

I rummaged through kitchen drawers, already pretty sure this hunt would turn up nothing.

'Ben,' I said. He was halfway into the kitchen with a precarious stack of dishes. 'Did Mom have ashtrays?'

He stopped in his tracks. 'Ashtrays?'

'Never mind.'

I grabbed a saucer instead.

I ran into Anat on my way out of the kitchen.

I looked full-on into her face for an extended moment. For the first time since she'd arrived. It made my heart melt again, but there was nothing hot or even warm about it. It felt cool, in a good way, like ice on a burn. She seemed OK. She didn't look ready to call the whole thing off.

'Am I in trouble with him?' I whispered.

'It's a hard adjustment for him. Go and talk to him. Please.'

★ ★ ★

I found Nazir sitting up rigidly straight in one of our porch chairs. He had that odd little cigar smoker's tool. I've never understood those. Somehow they nip off the ends and drill little holes or something. Something I always thought the cigar manufacturer should probably do for its customers. Instead of forcing them to buy accessories.

I placed the saucer on the porch rail in front of him, suddenly embarrassed by the condition of the paint on my mom's house. The paint was peeling. And I'd never noticed. Somehow I'd have to find a way to paint the house.

I watched out of the corner of my eye as Nazir lit the end of his cigar with the equivalent of a blowtorch. He puffed and puffed until it drew, then clicked the flame off.

Then, with nothing to trim or light, the silence felt more awkward.

We sat in the dusk and watched a car go by, and a neighbor walking her basset hound. She waved to us. As if we both lived here, like a couple, and she completely expected to see us sitting out on the porch together. I waved back. Nazir didn't.

A minute or two passed.

Then I said, 'You're awfully quiet.'

For a terrible thirty seconds or so, I thought he didn't intend to answer.

Then he did.

'It's a little different than I thought, with you and my daughter. It's a little different than what you told me.'

'What I told you?' I asked, stupidly. What would I have dared tell him about my feelings for his daughter?

'You said you didn't feel that way about her.'

'No. I didn't. I said I had no dishonorable intentions toward her. And look at me. Look at us. I'm bringing the families together. To get to know each other. I stand by what I said.'

'Hmm.'

He puffed a few more times. The air around his head filled with a cloud of smoke that didn't seem to want to move or dissipate. The smell made me a little bit sick. Well. Something did. Maybe I was scapegoating a smell.

'All right,' he said. 'I will grant you that.'

It took a little courage to say the next thing. But I said it. 'I sense a 'but' coming.'

Nazir sighed. 'She is my little girl. My only family. Yes, of course I knew she would grow up and meet someone. That she would want to settle down and start a family of her own. Yes, I know this. I accept this. But I cannot say I am pleased that the moment seems to have arrived. I feel like I'm losing my little girl.'

'You're not,' I said. 'Just . . . ' Then I couldn't think how to put it.

'Right, I know. I'm not losing a daughter. I'm gaining you.' He turned to me and leveled me with that frighteningly intense gaze. 'And him,' he added, with a flip of his head toward the inside of the house. 'He comes with the deal, you know. And that's a bit of a disadvantage.'

Nazir was nothing if not direct.

'I know.'

'Maybe Anat won't want that responsibility for all of her life.'

'Maybe she won't.' I felt numb as I said it. Beyond feeling. Willing to accept anything that came along, including the guillotine. As if it was too late to affect my own fate. I was just a limp dishrag, moving forward through one of the most important junctures of my own life.

'Don't get me wrong. I like Ben, as far as that goes. He is a good boy. And it's not his fault what happened to him. But you said it yourself. He can be trying. He is a lot to take on.'

'A lot of families have something like that, though. You know. Something — someone — who comes along for the ride. A horrible in-law. Or children. Lots of people have to deal with ready-made children when they meet someone. So this is not so different from that.'

'It is and it isn't,' he said. 'In-laws die while you are still fairly young. While you still have some life left. Children grow up to be self-sufficient. Ben is for ever.'

We sat quietly for a while longer. It was getting

dark. I was wishing I'd turned on the porch lights. But then I thought, No. I'm glad I didn't. Maybe it was better to air these thoughts without a strong light, like the one the cops turn on you when they want the truth.

'Ben can be more self-sufficient,' I said. 'I've had a lot of thoughts about that.' This was not entirely true. I mostly had the thoughts right then, as I spoke them, in response to Nazir's candor. 'I was thinking maybe he could be enrolled in some kind of school or program that would help him be more independent. And I'm going to start teaching him to ride the bus to work and back. I think our mother might have given up on that too soon.'

'And how independent do you think he can learn to be?' It wasn't so much a request for information. More a request for realistic thinking on my part.

My heart fell. I sat still, feeling its descent, for a long moment.

'I think he can do better than he's doing now,' I said.

He smoked. I sat.

Mark came out of his house and walked down his driveway and back for no reason I could see. I marveled at his choice not to bother pretending he had some purpose in doing so.

'I realize Ben's a big strike against me . . .'

'It's some of each, actually,' Nazir said. 'On the one hand, I hate to think of my daughter using up so much of her life on his needs. On the other hand, it says a good thing about you. That you can be relied upon. That you don't give up on your family. Young people in America today are not always so good about this. Mother gets old, they stick her in a facility. Dad gets sick, none of the children will even come home. 'We have our own lives,' they say. They show no responsibility. At least you show responsibility.'

'Thank you.' Then, before I realized I was even going to say it, I said, 'What if there were no Ben? What would you feel about me and Anat then?'

Long pause. As if he were truly trying this new thought on for size.

'It will sound terrible.'

My stomach cramped in rhythm with his words.

'Go ahead.'

'It's foolish on my part. But always when I thought about my daughter meeting a man, in my head, in the picture in my head, I see now that always the man was Egyptian. So what was I thinking with that, right? How far would you have to drive from here to find a marriageable Egyptian man? I'm not talking about interfaith marriage, mind you, because we are not that religious anyway. I'm not saying I insist she marry within Islam. I just pictured someone who looks more like us. The mind is a funny thing, isn't it?'

I refused to answer the question.

'Well,' he said, when he'd given up waiting for a comment, 'I guess we all have our little prejudices.'

'Guess so,' I said.

'I apologize for mine. You have done a lot for

267

us. You have been kind. I don't know why I have said all these things to you.'

'Because they're the truth?'

Nazir puffed furiously, then said, 'Yes. I suppose. Because they're the truth.'

★ ★ ★

When we arrived back inside, the dishes were done. Drying in a rack beside the sink. Ben was seated on a kitchen chair, getting his hair cut. Properly, this time.

'Look!' Ben said. 'Look what Anat did! It's so much better than what you did! She put wet paper towels all around my neck. And the hair's wet, and it sticks to the paper towels, and it doesn't go down my shirt. And it doesn't choke me.'

'You're supposed to wet the hair first?' I asked Anat.

'It helps. Why don't you make some coffee or tea, and then go ahead and cut the cake? And by the time dessert is ready, we should be all done here.'

So I wandered in and out of the kitchen, fetching dessert forks and cups and plates and clean napkins, and setting the table for a second round. Nazir sat quietly in the living room by himself. I listened to Anat small-talking with Ben, and thought maybe he really would stay with them while I flew back to New York. Given time.

'Got a hair dryer?' Anat asked.

I fetched her one from my mom's bathroom.

268

Then I sat at the dining room table, feeling the cracks and fissures between individuals, until the dryer turned off and Ben proudly emerged.

'No itches!' he shouted, as if that were the only criteria for a good haircut.

But it was a good haircut. For the first time since arriving back here, I looked at Ben and thought he looked just like anybody else's brother.

'Ben,' I said. 'You look so respectable.'

Then I looked past Ben and into the kitchen at Anat. Our eyes met, and caught. And stayed. And played. And communicated. And promised. And healed.

And I thought, She's not gone. She hasn't run screaming into the night.

I thought, It's a goddamn miracle.

10 November 2001

Anat called me at two in the morning. The phone blasted me out of sleep. It froze my blood. I could only think that something was wrong down at the bakery. Then I looked at the clock again, and realized she wouldn't even be down at the bakery this early. Something wrong at home?

I grabbed up the phone.

'What? Are you OK?'

'I'm fine,' she said. Her voice was soft. Familiar. Affectionate. 'I know I woke you up, and I know I scared you. I'm sorry. I just wanted to talk to you. And your number was right there on the refrigerator . . . '

'You're at the shop already?'

'I never went home. We took two cars. Because we figured it was silly for me to drive all the way back out to our house at about eight or nine at night, and then all the way back here at four in the morning. So I stayed in the room over the shop. But now I can't sleep. I miss you.'

I lay still, feeling my blood and organs rapidly thaw.

'I miss you, too,' I said.

Then nobody said anything for a long time. And it hit me that we might both be thinking the exact same thing: that we were only two minutes apart.

'I should stay here,' I said. 'Shouldn't I?'

'I don't know,' she said, her voice small. Almost a whisper. 'Should you?'

'I'll be right there.'

★ ★ ★

She met me at the kitchen door of the bakery, grabbed my hand, and led me upstairs. Her face looked tight and frenzied.

'I have been doing nothing but worry since we talked on the phone.' Before I could open my mouth to ask why, she said, 'I hope you don't think — '

'No,' I said. 'I don't think that. I didn't think that.'

'Oh. Thank goodness.'

I sat on the edge of the bed, because there was nowhere else to sit. I looked around. The room was small, maybe six feet by ten feet. No bathroom that I could see. Probably she had to use the one downstairs. There was just a bed, and a bedside table with a lamp, a drinking glass, and a bottle of water. On the other side of the bed was a small set of shelves, with a few folded clothes. It reminded me of a room in a monastery. Not that I've ever been to a monastery.

She came and sat beside me, but not too close. She offered me her hand, and I took it, and held it. My heart didn't pound, and it didn't melt. It just felt warm. Full. For the first time in my life, I felt full.

'I'm glad you understand,' she said. 'I have to be a virgin. Until I'm married. At least I have to meet my father that much of the way. I know probably you're thinking he won't know. But I will. I'll know.'

I put one finger to her lips. 'It's fine.'

She leaned forward and kissed me. Gently. Tenderly. Almost tentatively, but not quite. More like thoughtfully. She pulled back, and we looked at each other for a moment, then broke into a spontaneous, incurable, embarrassing attack of the smiles.

I looked at her hair. Brushed it back from her shoulder.

'I thought you'd never want to talk to me again after last night,' I said.

'Why do you say that?'

'Because of Ben.'

'Oh, no. It was just the opposite. It was so sweet to watch you with him. If I hadn't already been so taken with you, I would have been after last night.'

'Really? Am I good with him? I don't feel like I am.'

'You're too hard on yourself. You correct him when he needs it. But then other times you make allowances for him. And you're so patient. Like a good parent. You'll be a good father.'

'Think so?'

'I know so. You want children, don't you?'

'Sure I do.'

'How many?'

'I've always thought two,' I said. But then I

added, 'But I'm completely flexible.' In case she had other thoughts. 'What about you? What's the right number for you?'

'Two. That is a perfect number. Two. And Ben will be a good uncle, I think, to two children.'

'Well, they'll all have a lot in common.'

She laughed. And everything in the world was right. Everything. Even Ben.

Then she lay back on the bed, and I lay down beside her. We stared at the ceiling together. There were cracks in the plaster of the ceiling. It made me feel better about the paint on my mother's house. I remember thinking I would always love those cracks. Not because they got me off the hook for my own peeling paint, but because I was so happy on the night I memorized them.

After a while she rolled closer and rested her head on my collarbone.

We lay there together for what seemed like ten or fifteen minutes, and then she raised her left hand and looked at her watch.

'I'm late,' she said. 'I have to start the donuts.'

I sat up. Took hold of her left arm. Looked at the watch myself. It was almost four thirty. Our ten or fifteen minutes had, in reality, lasted well over two hours.

★ ★ ★

'OK, Buddy,' I said. 'Come on.'

Ben stood at the end of the garage, as though waiting for me to pull the car out. Even though I'd told him we were taking the bus today. Even

273

though I was standing near the end of the driveway.

'Why again?'

'To show you that you can do it.'

'But the car's right there. You could just drive me.'

'But if I just drive you, you'll never know you can do it.'

'I pretty much don't think I can.'

I sighed. And walked to where he was standing.

'You know you can ride the bus to work *with me*, right? With me right there telling you where to get off and all?'

'Yeah.'

'Well, that's all we're doing today. Let's go.'

'Why again?'

'Ben. I said let's go.'

We walked side by side together, two and a half blocks to the bus stop. I had to slow my pace over and over again to match his. I had to breathe, and think consciously about going easy on him.

A woman in a bathrobe was letting her dog out to pee in the yard. She waved as if we were long-lost friends. 'Hi, Ben!' she called. 'Hi, Rusty! Welcome home, Rusty!'

I waved, but said nothing.

Ben called back, 'Good morning, Mrs Givington.'

'Where are you two going so early?'

Ben called, 'My buddy is teaching me to ride the bus to work.'

Her face fell. 'Oh,' she said. 'Well. Good luck.'

I knew the universe wanted me to see it as an omen. But I refused to.

⋆ ⋆ ⋆

'So, are you here every morning?' I asked the driver, as I helped Ben count out the change I'd given him.

'Beg pardon?'

'Are you on this route at this time every morning?'

He still seemed confused by, or suspicious of, the question. 'Five days a week,' he said.

'You'll be here tomorrow?'

'Should be.'

'Good. Tomorrow I'll bring my brother down here to the bus stop, but I won't get on with him. And I'd appreciate it if you'd remind him to get off at Ridgewood.'

'Tomorrow might be too soon,' Ben said, tugging at my sleeve.

The engine roared as the driver pulled away from the curb, and Ben spoke loudly to be heard over the drone of it. 'What if I forget Ridgewood between now and tomorrow?'

'I'll be standing at the bus stop. I'll remind you.'

'Oh. Right.'

I led Ben to a seat right up front and across the aisle from the driver.

'Always sit right here,' I said. 'So you can watch the driver and hear what he tells you.'

'What if someone else is sitting there?'

'Then just sit as close to the driver as you can.'

'Oh. OK. I think tomorrow's too soon, though.'

'Let's just focus on today.'

'Oh. OK.'

★ ★ ★

We got off at Ridgewood, and I stopped a minute to help him orient himself. It was only about six thirty.

'See where you are?'

'No.'

'What do you mean, no? How can you not see where you are?'

'Well. I see what's around me. But I don't know where I am.'

'You're only two blocks from the market.'

'But I don't know where it is.'

'Ben. You've lived in this town all your life.'

'Don't yell at me, Buddy. Sometimes I get confused.'

I hadn't yelled, actually. But I'd spoken from a lack of tolerance, and it had shown through.

'Sorry. Just stand here a minute and look where you are.'

'OK.'

'You get off the bus . . . '

'I did.'

'I know that, Ben. Just listen.'

'OK.'

'And you go left. You know which way left is, don't you?'

'Sometimes,' he said.

I just stood a minute, trying to find the

patience that had made such a positive impression on Anat.

'Let's try this, then. You see that pet shop?'

'Yeah.'

'Turn toward the pet shop and walk to that corner.'

'Aren't you coming with me?'

'Yes, I'm coming with you.'

'Then why are you telling me this? Why can't I just follow you?'

'I'm trying to teach you what to do tomorrow.'

'I think tomorrow is too soon.'

'Yeah,' I said. I started to walk, and he followed me. 'I'm beginning to see your point about that.'

★   ★   ★

'You're so late,' Anat said. 'I was just getting ready to worry about you. I thought you weren't coming in.'

It was twenty minutes after seven. And she had other customers. Three of them. So we had to speak in a different way. A different tone. As if none of these words had any weight behind them. As if we were nothing to each other. As if she were only teasingly commenting on a customer's routine.

Frankly, I don't think we were doing well. I think that, after our early morning happenings, there was no turning back.

I looked around to see all three of her customers staring at us. We must have been shedding an energy that stuck to them. They

277

must have felt an overspill of our emotion.

'Today was my first day trying to teach Ben to ride the bus to work. So then I had to wait for the bus myself. To come back. And then I had to get off at Whitley and walk four blocks. It's not a speedy process.'

'How did it go with Ben?'

'Badly. But I intend to keep at it.'

'Good. Well . . . ' And behind that 'well' was an evaporation of all of our options. We had reached the end of our tether, like a couple of chained dogs. All we could do now was strain until we choked. Or accept our limitations. 'What will you have?'

'Cinnamon twist,' I said. And I reached into my jeans pocket to pull out a few folded bills.

I saw her start to shake her head, but I stopped her with a look. And she caught it and understood it. I needed to pay for the cinnamon twist. This was the first time I had ever been beaten into the shop by other customers. And it would be the first time I'd paid for my food. Otherwise it would leave a bad impression.

She took my money and rang me up. Handed me change. The tips of her fingers brushed my palm lightly. Maybe purposely. Other than that, I found the whole moment profoundly depressing.

I felt like we were paying for our impetuous morning. Suddenly we had something to hide.

I ate the cinnamon twist and drank coffee and watched her putter in the kitchen for ten or fifteen minutes. Watched her glance at me far too often.

Then I waved goodbye and walked the nearly

two miles back to the house, hoping to catch up on at least some of the sleep I'd missed.

★ ★ ★

The doorbell jolted me out of sleep. I'd been deep into a REM cycle, dreaming something dark and convoluted and a little disturbing. And the sound was like a bomb going off under my bed. I woke up on my feet, standing beside the bed, with no memory of how I'd gotten there. My heart hammered so hard I felt like it might be dangerous to my health.

I looked at the clock beside my mother's bed. Ten thirty. Too early to be Anat.

I put on a shirt, and combed my hair as best I could with my fingers. The bell rang again before I could get to it.

'I'm coming as fast as I can,' I called, trying not to sound pissed.

I threw the door open wide.

It was Mrs Jespers from next door. Mark's mom. She looked like she'd been crying.

'Oh, honey, I got some bad news,' she said. 'Mark wanted to tell you, but I said, 'No, let me.' Because of how you two haven't been getting along so good. Anyway, sit down. You should be sitting down.'

'Did something happen to Ben?'

'No, it's not Ben, honey, sit down.'

She barged into the house. Just walked right around me and sat down on our living room couch. Then she patted the couch next to her thigh. But I didn't feel like sitting.

'I'm fine,' I said. 'Just tell me.'

'It's Vince, honey.'

I must've still been half-asleep. Because I made no immediate connection with knowing someone named Vince.

'Vince?'

'Vince Buck. I just got done talking to his mother. Oh, dear God, she's a mess. She was on her way out the door this morning to go to the hospital because her husband — Vince's father — just had a quadruple bypass. Yesterday! And just as she's walking out her front door she sees them. Coming up her walkway. Those two uniformed soldiers they send to tell you. She said she knew right away, before they even said anything. She said her knees just went right out from under her, and she took a tumble down her three stone steps. Banged herself up good.'

With that image, Mrs Jespers began to cry again. I excused myself and found a box of tissues in the TV room, and brought them back to her. I held them out for a long time before she looked up and saw what I was offering.

'Oh, thanks, honey.' She took them from me, yanked out one tissue, and used it to delicately wipe under her eyes without smudging her make-up.

I watched her, wondering why, when a person is crying and you hand them tissues, they always wipe their eyes. They never blow their nose. I always think the nasal stuff is more to the point. But maybe we're only worried about the part that shows. I guess I'm famous for disjointed thinking in times of stress. As if there were any other times these days.

'She says she didn't even ask why they were there, because she knew. She just asked them, 'Where did it happen, and how?' They said his unit was trying to secure this prison in Kandahar . . . Oh, Lord, honey, it's so sad. Now she has to go to the hospital and ask the doctors when they think her husband can take the bad news, and then she has to break it to him and hope it doesn't kill him. Can you think of anything sadder than that?'

My brain did a fast scan of fallen towers and mothers dying suddenly and young. Well, not just any old mothers. My mother. This news had stiff competition.

Plus, it could have been Larry, the guy with three kids; but even so, it was bad enough.

'It's very sad,' I said, not wanting to play games with sadness ratings.

'I just knew you'd want to know, seeing how you two went to school together and all. And Ben. You've got to be the one to tell Ben, OK? Those two were pretty close. Vince was nice with Ben. Nicer than most. He and Larry even came by after your mother died, just to see how Ben was doing.'

Just for a flash of a moment I entertained the idea that this might all be part of my discordant dream. Then, failing with that theory, I grilled myself regarding what I felt. No doubt it was a shame. And yes, Vince and Larry and Paul had been there for the first eighteen years of my life. But had I known them? And had they known me? Or were we just semi-strangers operating in the same small piece of real estate? This is not to say I didn't care. I'd very much wanted Vince to come home from Afghanistan in one piece. And not in a flag-draped coffin. But it wasn't a heavy personal loss. He was just a guy I knew. But not really. I was very sorry for his family, but only a little bit for myself.

'Thank you for telling me,' I said. 'I'll tell Ben.'

'I thought maybe it was something you needed to hear. You know. So you could . . . kind of . . . ' I felt the pressure of subtext. Heavy agenda. I could feel it rise. ' . . . reexamine some of your choices.'

Blessedly, at this point, I had no idea what she was talking about.

'My choices?'

'You have to be careful who you let into your home, Rusty. Your life. You know. Not everybody is suitable friend material.'

And then I knew.

I leaned down a little, so my face would be closer to hers.

'Get out,' I said. I didn't raise my voice. I didn't need to. Those words spoke volumes for themselves.

She recoiled as if I'd slapped her.

'Beg pardon?'

'Get out. What part of 'get out' don't you understand?'

She dove off my couch and practically ran for the door.

'Mark was right,' she said, stopping with her hand on the knob. 'He was right all along. He said you've gone downright un-American, and I wouldn't listen, but now I see it with my own eyes. Choosing those people over the good people who knew you all your life.'

'You're not getting out yet.'

This time she did.

The door drifted open behind her, letting in a blast of cool air. I closed it, and stood a moment with my forehead leaned on the door.

'So that's where Mark gets it,' I said out loud to the empty room.

I walked back to my mom's bedroom. Not because I thought I could possibly get back to sleep, but because I wanted a shower. Needed one. I felt as though I needed to scrub off Mrs Jespers's world view. Like part of it had stuck to me, and could infect me if I didn't wash myself. I felt dirty.

Before I could even get there, I heard my cell phone ringing on the bedside table. I walked into the bedroom and stared at it for another two rings. Wondering if it could hurt me. It felt like it wanted to hurt me.

I took two steps closer and picked it up. It was Anat.

'Hey,' I said, all the weight of the morning sliding off me. 'It's you.'

'Oh, Russell,' she said. And it was not good. It was not a good 'Oh, Russell.'

'What? What's wrong?'

'My father is very upset. As upset as I've ever seen him, and I've seen him pretty upset. Someone called him and told him they saw you come in at two in the morning, and that your car was here until four thirty.'

'Wait,' I said. 'Wait. I need to sit down.'

I plunked into a sit on the bed. Hard enough to bounce a little. Which I could have done while she was talking. But I needed her to stop for a moment. I needed the world to stop pelting me with more and more bad news.

I had a sudden weird image that those two planes had hit the towers with such impetus that they'd knocked the world, or at least the country, just slightly off its axis. And that we still hadn't managed to get balanced again. It felt like nothing had gone right since that morning. Except Anat. And now even that was in peril.

'Who called him?'

'I don't know. He doesn't know. Someone just called and said this. They didn't say their name.'

'And he believed it? From an anonymous stranger?'

'Russell. It's true.'

'Oh,' I said. 'Right.'

'He asked me. I think he wanted not to believe it, but he came into the shop and he just asked me right to my face. Is this true? Maybe I should have lied to him. But I've never lied to my father. Well. Not about anything important. Childish lies, maybe, when I was younger.'

'Did you tell him nothing happened?'

'Of course I did. And I think he believes me. I hope so. But somewhere in his mind he must wonder. Plus, our nothing and his nothing are two very different things, Russell. In his culture . . . our culture . . . if a man and a woman are alone in a bedroom in the middle of the night,

284

this is very much something. No matter what they do.'

'I'll talk to him.'

'No!' She literally shouted it. It made me jump. 'No, you must leave him alone. Give him time with this. That's the main reason I called, to warn you to stay away from him. Even I wouldn't try to talk with him now. Not until he calms down. If you want me, I'll be at the shop. I'll be in the room upstairs. I won't be going home for a while. If you want to call. But don't come in when he's around.'

My head swam. I pressed my forehead into my palm. Hard. As if I could physically steady my thinking. I couldn't think what to ask first.

'Are you afraid of him? Would he hurt you?'

'Yes. And no. Yes, I am afraid of him. No, he would never hurt me. But I can't be around him right now. I have a temper, too, you know. And he brings it out in me. We both said some things we can never take back. I need to stay away until things calm down.'

Speaking of calming down . . . I counted breaths. I tried to pull them in deeply.

'I'm so sorry,' I said.

'No. Please. It was every bit as much my idea as yours.'

'Should I not come in at all for a while?'

'You can come in, but on my days only. Not when he's here.'

I breathed some more. I wanted to ask a dozen more questions about our future. If indeed we still had one. But I was afraid that, if I did, she might answer them. I decided to go with her idea

285

of giving everything time to settle.

'I have a customer,' she said. 'I'll talk to you as soon as I can.'

And she clicked off the line. Before I even had time to say goodbye.

★ ★ ★

'You look bad,' Ben said. 'You look really upset.'

'Walk with me,' I said. 'I have to tell you some news.' We stood together just outside the sliding doors of Gerson's Market. Close enough to hold them open with our presence as we spoke.

'Bad news?'

'Yeah. Pretty bad. But pay attention to where we're going, anyway. OK? The bus stop is that way. You look that way. And, see the stoplight? You walk to the corner with the stoplight.'

'OK. But I think tomorrow — '

'Right. I know. Too soon. I won't ask you to do it by yourself tomorrow. But pay attention anyway, OK?'

We set off walking.

'What's the news?' he asked, struggling to keep up.

I was too agitated to match my pace to his. So I just kept gaining. I stopped at the corner and waited for him to catch up.

'Maybe it should wait till we get home,' I said.

Maybe you don't tell Ben bad news in public. What if he collapsed or had a tantrum right in the middle of Conner Avenue?

'No, you have to tell me now,' he said. 'Or I'll be scared for too long.'

'Yeah. OK. But first . . . do you see which way you're supposed to turn?'

'No.'

'You don't know which way the bus stop is?'

'No.'

'It's right.'

'Right.'

'That way.'

'Oh. That way. OK. I can see the pet store way down there. Walk to the pet store, right? What's the bad news?'

I started off walking.

'It's Vince. Vince Buck. He was killed in Afghanistan.'

No response. I looked over my shoulder to see Ben a good six paces back.

'Could you slow down, Buddy?'

'Sorry.' I stopped and waited for him. 'Did you hear what I said?'

'Yeah. Vince. What's Afghanistan?'

'It's a country where we're fighting a war.'

'Oh.'

'Do you know what it means when someone gets killed?'

'I think it means I don't see them any more.'

'Right. That's what it means.'

'I like Vince.'

'Yeah. Me, too. You ready to walk some more?'

This time I tried to breathe, and to slow down. We walked, more or less together, to the corner.

'Pet store there, bus stop there,' I said. Pointing. 'That's pretty easy. Right?'

'Well. I was just following you.'

'But we talked about which way to go. Which

287

way do you go when you come out of the store?'

'I don't remember.'

'Toward the stoplight.'

'The stoplight! Right!'

'Then which way?'

'I don't remember.'

'How can you not remember? You love pets, right?'

'Oh! The pet store!'

'Right. Now. Again. Which way when you come out of the store?'

No answer. We stood there on the corner for a good minute. Well, not a *good* minute. But a minute. Ben had no answer.

I sighed, and walked to the bus stop, and he followed me.

We sat with our backs up against the cool bench, covering up an ad for a funeral home. Looking off in the direction of the bus. Assuming there would be a bus. At some point.

Ben spoke first. 'Are you mad at me, Buddy?'

'No.'

'Oh. Good.'

'But I'm not giving up on you, either. We're going to keep after this.'

'Oh,' he said.

It sounded far less optimistic than his previous 'oh.'

22 November 2001

It was twelve miserable days later, at 7.05 a.m., when I got the call that Ben hadn't shown up at work on time. I was standing at Anat's counter, picking out a powdered sugar donut. And dying a thousand deaths. From the look on her face, she was dying in similar numbers.

My cell phone went off in my pocket. I fished it out, and recognized the number as Gerson's Market. And I knew this could not be good. But, to put it as bluntly as possible, I didn't even expect good news any more. I just hunkered down as best I could and waited for the bad news I assumed was stacked up waiting.

Anat looked up at me expectantly. I think she saw my concern.

We were alone in the shop. But, though we'd never discussed it, I think we had both toyed with the idea that Nazir might be watching us, or having us watched. We were behaving. In an exaggerated display. Thus the numerous deaths.

'Problem with Ben?' I asked, in place of hello.

It was McCaskill. 'I'm thinking so. He's not here. He's twenty minutes late. And you know how Ben is. Ben's never late. I'm thinking maybe he forgot to get off the bus.'

'I don't think so. He had a note for the bus

driver, asking for a reminder to get off at Ridgewood.'

'Maybe he forgot to show it to him.'

'No, that driver knows him. I made sure that driver would be on today. He knows Ben now. He would've asked. He must have gotten off the bus and walked the wrong way. I made him a map, but . . . '

'I just know he's not here. We're all a little concerned.'

'I'm sorry. I'll go out and look for him. Right now. And from now on I'll drive him in and we'll practice on the bus home. I know you want him in on time.'

'That's not the problem,' he said. 'That's not what we're worried about. It's Ben we're worried about.'

A pause, during which I had a flash of knowing. It told me to hang up quickly, before he said more. It told me he was gathering up to say more. But my reflexes let me down.

He said more.

'You know, your mom tried this. And it never did work out.'

'I know that. I was just thinking maybe she gave up too soon.'

'She tried for an awful long time.'

I sighed deeply, moving the phone away first, so he wouldn't hear. I looked up at Anat, snagged on her worried gaze. I covered the phone with one hand.

'I have to go look for him,' I said, realizing as I spoke that there was nothing I could tell her that she hadn't already gathered. I uncovered the phone and turned my attention back to McCaskill. 'Give me a little more time with him,' I said.

'I guess it's up to you. I guess you know best. I just want to make sure you know — '

I cut him off. I was tired of knowing things. Everybody wanted me to know things. All things I'd be happier not knowing.

'I have to go look for Ben. I'll get back to you.'

And I hung up on him.

I sighed. And looked right into her eyes. We just locked into that moment for a long time.

Then I said, 'I guess I'll be taking that powdered sugar donut to go.'

★   ★   ★

I drove around until twenty after seven, dropping powdered sugar on to my jeans, and on to the driver's seat of the car. I almost ran a stop sign brushing powdered sugar off my lap. I almost sideswiped a parked Lexus craning my neck to follow a man who turned out not to be Ben.

Finally, just by luck, I saw him. In the back seat of a station wagon as it drove by, heading in the opposite direction. I swung a dangerous U-turn and followed the car. Not surprisingly, my chase led me into the parking lot of Gerson's Market.

I parked right behind the station wagon and jumped out, leaving the engine still running.

Ben was just opening the door. Untangling his endless legs.

He looked up at me. 'Hey, Buddy,' he said. 'Don't be mad.'

291

'Ben, what happened?'

'I don't know.'

I looked up at the driver, who had gotten out of the car. An old man, maybe eighty. His face looked familiar, but only in that small-town way. He definitely wasn't new around here, though. We'd grown up somewhere near him. His wife stayed in the passenger seat.

'We picked him up over on Randall,' the man said.

'*Randall?*'

'Yeah. He was a good mile and a half from work. First we saw him, but we just went by. But then we went around the block. My wife said, 'Ben should be in to work by now. What's Ben doing wandering around all by his lonesome?' So I drove around again, and we stopped and asked him where he was going. 'Gerson's Market,' he says. But he was walking in the exact opposite direction.'

I looked to Ben, but it was too late. All I saw was his back disappearing through the automatic door of the market.

'Well, I appreciate your help. I appreciate your stopping for him.'

'You know, your mom tried to teach him to ride the bus. Never did work out.'

Small towns. I had an overwhelming flash of longing for New York, where the person who offers assistance is nearly guaranteed not to know your entire family history

'Thanks again,' I said, and followed Ben inside.

He was already at his station, bagging groceries.

'Don't be mad at me, Buddy,' he said.

'I'm not mad at you. I was just going to see if there's anyone at your work who could walk you to the bus stop.'

'I could walk him,' the checker said. She looked about fifteen, with braces and problem skin. 'I can take my break around the time he gets off.'

'Thank you. That would be really helpful. Ben. Don't forget to show the driver your note.'

'OK. But I have to think about work now. I'm late. And there's a lot to bagging groceries. More than you think.'

I just stood rooted to the spot for a moment. Then I looked at the checker, who smiled shyly at me. As though she thought I was dreamy.

'Bye, Rusty,' she said.

I didn't bother to correct her. I just drove back to the house.

★ ★ ★

I left the house at three thirty to walk to the bus stop. I sat on the bus bench for nearly an hour. Three buses came by. Ben wasn't on any of them.

★ ★ ★

At about six o'clock, after nearly two hours of driving around looking for him, I came home to check the answering machine. In case somebody had called on the land line to say they had him, or had seen him.

I saw the red message-light blinking, and prayed this would be good news for a change.

I played the message. It was hard to make out. Someone calling from a crowded room. Like a party, or a bar. A guy. I didn't get his name.

'Just want to let you know we have Ben. Found him wandering over by the railroad tracks, a few miles out of town. So we took him to the funeral with us. I was gonna bring him home right after, but Mark said let him come with us. And that was OK with Ben. All the guys are out getting drunk. You know. In honor of Vince. Anyway, I'll make sure Ben gets home tonight. I'll drive him home myself.'

Click.

'Oh, shit,' I said out loud.

Then I pulled up the caller ID and called . . . whoever it was . . . back.

'Yeah?' I heard. And the same rush of background noise. Voices, and the unmistakable clink of bottles and glasses.

'Who's this, again?'

'Rusty?'

'Yeah. Who am I talking to?'

'It's Chris, man. Chris Kerricker. You know. From track? Norville High?'

'Oh, Chris. Right. I didn't understand your name on the message.'

'Yeah, it's noisy in here, man.'

'What was the thing about a funeral?'

'Vince, man. His funeral was today. Full military funeral at sunset, you know, with the gun salute, and the flag they fold up and give to his mother. The whole nine yards.'

Right. Vince. I didn't even know they'd shipped his body home.

'Nobody told me Vince's funeral was today. I would've wanted to go.'

A long, ugly silence. Freighted with something.

'Sorry, man.'

But he wasn't. Well, maybe he was now. I don't know. But it was clear, in the way he said it, that I was not left off the guest list by accident.

Unless I was being paranoid. Reading something in.

No. I wasn't. What I heard is what was there.

'Wait . . . where was this funeral? Around here?'

'Fort Scott.'

'Fort Scott?' I shouted. 'That's like a hundred miles from here!'

'No way, man. Sixty. Sixty-five tops. We made it in a little over forty-five minutes with Mark driving, but he was booking it pretty good.'

Great, I thought. It's OK that you took Ben sixty-five miles out of town, because Mark drives like a maniac. Perfect. But it was water under the bridge now.

'How did Ben do with the gun salute?'

'Freaked him out. But he's OK now.'

'Look. Chris. This is not acceptable. I'm coming to pick up Ben. I don't want Ben drinking. Are you back in town?'

'Yeah. We're back. But he's not drinking, man. He's just with us.'

'Is Mark there?'

'Yeah. Mark's here. Everybody's here.'

'Just tell me where you are. I'll come pick up Ben.'

'No, let him stay, man. He knew Vince. He loved Vince. It's like an extra private memorial. Just for us guys. We're honoring Vince. Ben wants to be a part of this. He's having a good time. It's his life, man. Let him have a life.'

That one hit me below the belt. Because that *is* the idea. The goal.

'Chris, I . . .'

'I won't let him get sloshed, man. But let him be with us. Vince was our brother. It's what brothers do.'

I knew better. There was a very clear place in my gut that knew better.

But all I said was, 'OK, but no booze. And not too late.'

★ ★ ★

By eight o'clock I knew all was not as it should be. I'd fully expected Ben to walk in the door by 7.58 p.m. So he could be in bed by eight. Not a moment sooner. Not a moment later.

I sat by the window, steaming up the glass with my breath. Looking out into the darkness. Every time I heard a car engine, I sat up straighter. But the car always drove by without stopping.

At eight thirty, I called Chris's cell phone again. And every ten minutes after that.

All I got was his voicemail every time.

★ ★ ★

At nearly eleven, the phone rang. I grabbed it up on the first ring.

'Ben?'

'Ben's not there with you? Where's Ben?'

Anat.

'Oh. Hi. He's out with some of the guys.'

'I didn't know Ben ever went out with some of the guys.'

'No, neither did I.'

A long silence. I wondered how much I should tell her about it. I didn't want to talk about Ben. I didn't want there even to be a Ben to have to talk about. I had Anat on the phone. I had my own needs. My own life. I was already tired of being Ben's constant manager.

'Where did they go?' she asked.

'I didn't really mean to let him go out. At all. I went to meet him at the bus stop, but he must've gotten on the wrong bus or something. I don't know what he did. But this guy I know from high school picked him up out by the railroad tracks. They're all out drinking and mourning this friend of ours who got killed in Afghanistan.'

'Vince, yes. Vince. I heard. His funeral was today. Out at Fort Scott. You didn't tell me he was a friend of yours.'

'Didn't I? I thought I did. Well. I probably tried. There's been a lot going on.'

'Are you worried about Ben?'

'Closer to frantic at this point. Chris promised me he wouldn't give Ben any alcohol. But it's eleven o'clock. I can't imagine what would be going on with Ben that he would miss his bedtime. He's fanatical about it.'

297

'Maybe he just got caught up in the moment. They'll bring him home. If you have to sober him up, you will. Life will go on.'

I looked out the window for another moment, letting her last sentence percolate. Does life really know enough to go on? Even after all of this? Is there life after Nazir's disapproval? Would we get beyond that someday? Look back at it and laugh? Or at least not cry? I hadn't been able to bring myself to ask her if she would ever consider marrying me against his wishes, or even without his blessing. What a question to ask a woman you've known just over two months.

'Where did you just go?' she asked. Quietly. Intimately.

'Sorry. Talk to me about something that isn't Ben. Tell me why you called.'

A long silence.

Then she said, barely over a whisper, 'I was having an imagining.'

'Oh. Tell me about it. Please.'

'I was imagining I called you and said, 'Unlock your front door.' And then I came over and climbed into bed with you, and we held each other all night.'

'I should get to bed, then. I'm sitting up waiting for Ben.'

'I can't, really,' she said. 'You know I can't.'

'Afraid he'll find out?'

'Maybe. Maybe he would, maybe he wouldn't. That's not why.'

'Why?'

'Because I think if I were to go through with this idea I might not be a virgin any more.'

298

I felt tiny hairs standing up on my forearms, and the back of my neck.

'I wouldn't do anything you didn't want. You know that. I promise.'

'But I don't. I don't promise that.'

No one said anything for close to a minute. A literal minute. I was too aware of my breathing, and I wondered if she could hear it.

Then she said, 'Take the phone and go into your bed.'

'OK.'

I did as I was told. Except I really didn't have a bed. Not in this part of the country. My mother's bed would have to do.

I slid in under the covers.

'OK. Now what?'

'Just put the phone right beside your face. Right where you would want my face to be.'

'OK.'

'Now tell me anything you want to tell me. Anything that's true. Tell me what you would say if I were there with you.'

I froze. I couldn't say anything. What if I told her I loved her and she thought I was out of my mind? What if she said I couldn't possibly after so little time?

The silence dragged on.

'Russell,' she whispered. 'If you're ever going to go out on a limb, make this the night.'

'What about you? How are you at going out on limbs?'

'I'm going to be with you whether my father objects or not. Can you think of any scarier limbs than that?'

I lay under the covers, feeling the news warm every nerve synapse, every muscle, every brain cell. I wasn't frozen any more. But I still couldn't speak.

'All right. You're very bad at this,' she said teasingly. 'I'll go first. The very first day you ever walked into the shop, I looked up at you, and I said to myself, There he is.'

'There he is?' I parroted. Stupidly.

'Yes. There he is. You know, you think about who you might meet and when they might come. You always know that someday a door will open and in will come the one you've waited for. And then the waiting is done. And the rest of your life can begin. And the minute I looked up and saw you there, I thought, There he is.'

More silence. I just could not pull it together to speak.

'Did you know anything special the first time you saw me?'

'No,' I said. 'It was the second time.'

'Oh. That's not bad.'

'Remember when we were talking about my mother, and I started to cry? And you handed me paper towels because you didn't have tissues? And a minute later you said I was looking at you strangely? I was looking at you strangely because I'd just fallen in love with you. At the time I wasn't sure if it was fair to call it love. But now I know it really was.'

'Just like that?'

'Just like that.'

'I know it seems too soon, doesn't it, Russell?

If someone were listening, they'd say it was too soon.'

'What do they know?'

'Right. What do they know?'

'Things change so fast. Life turns on a dime. Someone said that to me. Recently. Who said that to me? Oh. Right. Your father. I'm sorry. I probably shouldn't have mentioned him.'

'It's OK. I haven't forgotten him or anything.'

'You sound sleepy,' I said.

'I haven't slept in days. I mean, barely. Ever since the trouble with my father. Tonight I broke down and took a sleeping pill. Stay with me until I fall asleep, OK?'

'Sure. Should I talk?'

'I don't know. Do you want to talk? What would you do if I were there?'

'Probably just listen to your breathing.'

'OK. We'll just listen to each other's breathing.'

★ ★ ★

I have no idea who fell asleep first.

I just know I woke to a noisy thump against the living room door. Then the doorbell rang one long blast. I stared down at the phone on the bed beside me. I checked to see if the line was still open. But sometime in the night the call had been dropped.

I heard tires squealing on the street out front as a car spun away.

I turned on the light, squinted, and checked the clock. It was after two thirty.

I made my way to the front door.

When I opened it, Ben fell into the living room. I looked down at him, sprawled on the carpet, and honestly thought he was dead. Then his eyes flickered open, and he looked up at me.

'Hey, Buddy,' he said.

'Oh, God. Ben. You're drunk.'

'I had a bad dream,' he said.

I got him into a cold shower. I didn't ask him about his dream.

I should have asked him about his dream.

23 November 2001

I woke up again at a few minutes after six. Woke up from a nap that had probably lasted all of forty-five minutes.

I sat up, and listened for Ben in the kitchen.

Then I got up and climbed into my jeans.

I found Ben still in bed.

'Buddy. You're going to be late to work.'

'I threw up,' he said.

'Oh. In the bed?'

'No. In the toilet.'

'Oh. Good.'

'I had a bad dream.'

'Another one?'

'No. The same one. Before I got home. That one.'

'When were you even asleep before you got home?'

'I don't know.'

'You sure you weren't just drunk?'

'I don't know.'

'I'm going to kill Chris. Would you excuse me for a minute?'

I stomped back into my mom's bedroom and grabbed up my cell phone. It would be a great pleasure to wake the son of a bitch at six in the morning to tell him I was going to kill him.

I got his voicemail.

I froze briefly, then hung up without leaving a message. I hadn't seen this guy since high school. If I left a message saying I was going to kill him, he might think I was going to kill him. He might call the police and tell them his days were numbered. That he needed protection.

I made my way into the kitchen, but Ben still wasn't up. I guess I shouldn't have been surprised. I don't know why I hadn't seen that coming.

I found him still in bed.

'I think I'm going to throw up again,' he said. I stepped out of his way. But nothing happened. 'You have to go tell Mr McCaskill I'm sick and I can't come in.'

'Yeah. I guess. But I'm going to kill Chris.'

I stomped back into the bedroom. Picked up my cell phone again. Redialed Chris. This time I was going to leave a message saying how sick Ben was. How he was missing a day of work over this. How in the course of the evening he'd somehow had a nightmare that might have involved more drunkenness than actual sleep.

I hung up again.

Why was I trying to change this guy when I could just make sure Ben never got anywhere near him again? Why bother telling someone he's an asshole? He's not likely to hear you, take your advice to heart, and improve his character immediately.

I stuck my head into Ben's room one more time.

'You OK while I'm gone?'

'I guess. Can I tell you my dream?'

'Can I pick you up something? Ginger ale or something?'

'No, I'd just throw it up. It was a very bad dream. I dreamed there was a fire.'

'What kind of fire?'

'A big one. Real fast.'

'Fast?'

'Yeah. Like there was just this tiny little bit of fire in my hand, and then it was really fast. Everything burned really fast.'

'Our house?'

'No, not our house.'

'Was it like a forest fire?'

'No. It wasn't in the forest. It was in the bakery.'

'Oh, God. Don't even say that, Buddy. Don't even tell me any more about it. That's too weird.'

'Told you it was bad.'

'I'll be back in a few minutes.'

'OK.'

'You'll be OK?'

'No. But I can throw up even if you're not here.'

★   ★   ★

I warmed up the car for a long time. It was a cold morning.

I thought about Anat. Would I stop on the way back and see her? Get a donut? Talk? Or would I feel I had to get straight back to Ben?

This would be the first time I'd seen her since she told me her 'There he is' story. I drove down

305

the street toward the bakery, looking forward to just getting a look at her through the bakery window. Maybe she would look different to me, now that I knew what I knew.

But there was no bakery window.

There was no bakery.

Just a pile of black. Blackened beams, buckled. Only one corner of the building standing as high as a single story. Two firefighters still training the arc of their hoses on the rubble, which steamed in the morning air.

I slammed on the brakes, and looked all around, desperately, somehow trying to believe I was looking at the wrong corner.

I put the car in park, right in the middle of the street, and stepped out.

It's hard to sum up what was going on inside me, because it was disjointed, overlapping, and out of my reach. The clearest message I can pull out was this: a new desire to kill someone. I wanted to pull God down from wherever God lives, if God lives, and tear him limb from limb with my bare hands. I wanted to force him to stop hitting me. To stop taking things away. I wanted to strong-arm him into submission. This was simply getting out of hand.

And that was all before I remembered that Anat had been in the building all night. Next thing I knew, I was holding a firefighter by his waterproof coveralls. He was trying to tell me I couldn't park in the middle of the street. I was trying to tell him there had been a woman sleeping in the room above the store. He knew, he said. 'She got out,' he said.

'She's OK? Tell me she's OK!' I kept asking that, screaming it, over and over. I screamed it both before and after he said she was 'stable'. I screamed it the whole time he kept trying to tell me I had to be family. That he wasn't supposed to give me more information on her condition if I wasn't family.

Then I was holding him more tightly, and our faces were very close together, and I remember him telling me I needed to pull myself together.

I think I said I was her fiancé. I know for a fact that I asked him if he'd ever been in love.

He sighed. He sighed when I asked him that. So I don't know who he was, that firefighter, but I know he'd been in love.

He called to another fireman, by name. Ricky. He said, 'Ricky, you were there when the girl came out, right? How was she?'

'Third degree,' Ricky called. Holding his palms straight out toward us. As if we would want to see them. 'Hands and knees. Nothing life-threatening.'

Then I remember I breathed. Maybe I breathed before that, but I don't remember. Then again, maybe not.

'You better move your car,' the fireman who was not Ricky said.

'Where is she?'

'County General.'

So, yeah. I would move my car. I would damn well move my car all the way to County General. And not slowly.

I jumped into the car, shifted into drive, and squealed my tires taking off.

I drove less than one block, and stopped. My foot hit the brake by itself, as if it had an independent brain system. I pulled over and shifted into park.

Ben dreamed that the bakery burned.

What did that mean?

I won't say my brain was working well, or even that it was working. But I could think of two reasonable inferences.

One, my brother Ben is an oracle. He knows what's going to happen before it even manifests. He fell asleep in the car on the way home last night, and had a prophetic dream.

Two, my brother Ben was there when the bakery caught fire. And, in his unfamiliarity with drunkenness, interpreted what he saw as something other than reality. Like a bad dream.

My brain, my intentions, tried to go two directions at once. They raced to the hospital, and back to Ben, shearing painfully.

I had no idea what to do first.

Then I decided that the firemen were on top of fighting the fire and the hospital was good at treating burns, but the police likely had nothing to go on so far. I needed to ask Ben who did this. Suddenly nothing was more important than that. Not even getting to see Anat fifteen minutes sooner.

I swung a wide U, during which I was nearly T-boned by a pickup truck I hadn't bothered to see coming. And I got myself back to the house.

And not slowly.

★   ★   ★

'Tell me about your dream!' I screamed. 'Everything! Every detail!'

I had him by the collar of his pajamas.

'Ow!' he said. 'Ow! Let go! You're scaring me! Why are you yelling at me?'

'Tell me everything you can remember!'

'I did! I told you everything!'

'Who was there with you? Tell me who else was there! Was Mark there?'

'Mark was there, yeah.'

I thought briefly about letting go of Ben, marching next door, and dragging Mark out of his house. Only problem was, I might kill him. Literally. Kill him.

'Who else? Was anyone else there? Was Chris there?'

'Maybe,' he said.

'Maybe? What the hell does maybe mean?'

'It means you're scaring me! Let me go! I need to throw up!'

He pulled away from me and stumbled for the bathroom. I stood, shaking uncontrollably, as if it were below zero in Ben's room, and listened to the horrible sound of his retching. It seemed as though he never planned to stop.

Then I walked to the kitchen phone, called directory assistance, and was connected to the Norville Police Department.

Michelevsky picked up, and identified himself.

'Russell Ammiano. Remember me?'

'I do. I was just about to call you. Your friends are having a bad morning.'

I brushed over why he'd been about to call me. It made no sense. Or I had no time for it.

Or, more likely, both.

'I have some information for you. About the fire. You need to talk to Mark Jespers. And Chris Kerricker.'

'Oh, we're all over Mark Jespers,' he said. 'We just happen to have him in custody. Picked him up in the middle of the night staggering down the middle of Conner Avenue. Seems he'd smashed his car into a lamp pole about a block and a half from the bakery and set off on foot. Left an empty gas can on the seat. Drunk criminals are bad criminals, I always like to say. So we're all over talking to him. Now we need to talk to Ben. You need to bring Ben down here.'

'And Chris Kerricker.'

'We'll get to him. You need to bring Ben in.'

'Sure. I will. I just need to get to the hospital . . . '

'No. I mean *now*. Or we'll come over and get him.'

'I have to go see Anat. I have to see how she is.'

'We've been in to see her. We took a statement from her. She's hurting, but she'll be OK. Maybe not good as new, but OK. She can wait a while to see you. She's not going anywhere. But we can't wait to see Ben. You need to get him in here pronto.'

I held still, forcing myself to breathe. It sounded like an order. In fact, it sounded like an order repeated several times, with exponentially increasing gravity.

And, maybe he was right. Anat was getting good care. And the investigation was important.

310

And Ben was a witness. He could help.

'Right. Fine. I'll pour him into the car and we'll get right down there.'

'Good,' he said. 'No detours. No visits. No changing your mind. No nothing. I'm holding you responsible.'

I stared at the phone for a moment. Trying to read a subtext that might just as well have been written in an alien language.

'OK,' I said. 'Bye.'

Sometimes we have no immediate option but to ignore what we can't yet understand.

★ ★ ★

I found Ben wandering unsteadily out of the bathroom. He looked pale and miserable. I've never understood why people do that to themselves on purpose.

'How much did you have to drink?'

'Just one beer. Two.'

'That's all? Two beers?'

'And something that was sweet, but I don't know what it was.'

'We're going to the police station.'

His eyes bulged. Opened wide, like an exaggerated painting of a street waif.

'I don't want to go.'

'Doesn't matter. You have to go.'

'Why?' He made the one syllable stretch into the length of maybe twelve.

'Because, Ben,' I said, probably too harshly. 'It wasn't a dream. The bakery really did burn down.'

My brother Ben has never reminded me more of a deer on the highway, frozen in my car headlights. Eyes wide, knowing it's about to be hit, caring very much, yet unable to change the course of events. And the scary thing is, he's often reminded me of a deer on the highway. Usually, in fact. But never more than this.

He turned suddenly, lunged for the toilet again, and dry-heaved for a painful length of time.

I waited.

★ ★ ★

Ben said nothing on the way down to the police station. Nothing. Not one thing.

I'd been prepared for almost anything he might have said. I was only unprepared for nothing.

I looked over at him several times on the drive. His face was ghostly white, and he hunkered over his own knees, hugging them, rocking softly.

I didn't go by the bakery. I took the long way around. I didn't tell him Anat had been sleeping over the shop. Sooner or later I would have to tell him. Right now he was scaring me. Even without the added information.

Once, about six blocks from the station, he made a noise that sounded like something trying to come up. So I pulled over. Reached over him and pushed his door open. Then I looked the other way until he was done.

★ ★ ★

312

Michelevsky asked if I wanted my brother to have an attorney present during questioning.

I said no.

I said, 'Ben has nothing to hide. He's just going to tell you what he saw. But be patient with him. Please. Because he gets confused and has trouble remembering. And the more he thinks you're mad at him, the more confused he gets. I might be able to help with that.'

'You'll be waiting out here,' he said.

He didn't elaborate. And I didn't ask any questions. Sometimes I wonder if I should have asked questions. Made demands. But none of it seemed terribly important. At the time.

They'd take Ben into a room. Ask a lot of questions to establish that he'd really been there. He'd implicate Mark and Chris. He'd come out of the room. We'd go to the hospital and see Anat. We'd survive this day. We would. Life would go on. Maybe not smoothly, certainly not as if nothing had ever happened. But life would know enough to go on.

This day would be over.

I had to keep talking to myself like that. I had to keep telling myself those simple, comforting lies. It was survival one minute at a time.

I'll never forget the look on Ben's face as they led him into that room. Never. He looked over his shoulder at me the whole time. They had to more or less drag him. Lead him along by one arm.

Meanwhile Ben looked at me the way your dog looks at you when you give him over to the vet assistant for surgery. That awful moment

313

when they have to drag him by the collar, his legs spread for traction. Looking to you for salvation. No capacity for words, but his eyes clearly saying, 'Don't let them take me. I want to be with you.' And you can't even explain that part about how it's all for the best.

'Go with them,' I said. 'It's going to be OK.'

It didn't sound like the kind of statement that would come back to haunt me. So I guess you never know.

★ ★ ★

I looked at my watch. Ben had been in that room with three cops — did Norville really have three cops? — for half an hour.

Now what had I been doing wrong? All I ever got was two sentences of information at a time out of Ben. The third usually being, 'I told you already.'

I paced. I needed to get to the hospital. I needed to ask somebody if I could just go. Just go to the hospital. Pick Ben up later. But there was nobody in the outer office. There was nobody to ask. So I had to stay. And pace.

At forty minutes, Michelevsky emerged, walked straight to a water cooler, and poured himself — or somebody — a paper cup of water.

'Are we done?' I asked. 'Can we go?'

'*You* can,' he said. 'You can go any time you want. Your brother will not be accompanying you. Your brother is in custody.'

I sat down on a wooden bench, sorting through all the things I could potentially think,

314

say, feel. All of some merit. But sometimes you just have to weed things down. Not everything makes the cut.

I didn't panic, though. It was a mistake, and we'd get to the bottom of it. My best guess was that Mark had lied and put the whole thing off on Ben. But it would never stick. How could the crime have been masterminded by a guy who couldn't learn to walk two blocks to work from the bus stop?

'What did Mark say about him?'

I was calm. I was proud of myself for that. Why bait the cops? Be the voice of reason. Work with them. Be somebody they can talk to. That's best for Ben in the long run.

'It's not what Mark said. It's what Ben said. Your brother confessed to throwing the match.'

I opened my mouth to argue. To tell him how ridiculous that was. How he must have confused Ben, or not understood him. How easy it is to put words into his mouth. How he'll say anything when he's scared.

But I didn't.

Sometimes a photographic memory is not such a good thing. Sometimes I'll remember something someone said to me word for word, and I'll wish to hell I didn't.

'Like there was just this tiny little bit of fire in my hand, and then it was really fast. Everything burned really fast.'

That's what Ben had told me about his 'dream'.

This tiny little bit of fire. In my hand. Now, how had I forgotten that so completely? I can remember anything I want. Then I realized. It was so obvious. It has to be something I want.

'Can I see him?' I asked. Or, anyway, somebody asked. Must have been me. Michelevsky didn't. And there was nobody else who could have.

'We're taking him over to the county jail this afternoon. You'll want to call and get visiting hours from them.'

★ ★ ★

The hospital building was a long rectangle. Long on one side, short on the other. When I got off the elevator and looked down the hall, it looked like it stretched to infinity. Like I could walk all day and never get there. When I finally reached the end of the hall, following the room numbers, I turned left, the only way I could turn, and the hall ahead of me was very short. At the end of it was a sort of informal waiting area, a corner with two couches and two lamps.

And Nazir.

He was standing, pacing, talking to someone on his cell phone.

He looked up and saw me. I forced myself to keep walking. Two steps later, he reared back and hurled the phone, which whizzed by my ear, so close I could feel the displaced air of it. If I hadn't ducked to my right, it would have hit me, as I'm sure he intended. I heard it shatter against the wall behind me, and someone, maybe a nurse, say, 'Hey!'

I never turned around.

I just kept walking.

'You have a nerve,' he said. He spoke to me quietly. With a measured calm. It was unsettling. I remember wishing he would just yell. I had no idea how soon I would get my wish. 'You have a nerve to show up here. After what you did. After what your brother did. First you ruin her reputation in this town. Then your brother tries to kill her. And you think she will want to see you? And you think I will let you go in there and see her? Think again, my friend.'

'Ben would never do anything to hurt Anat.'

'He already did!' Nazir roared. Roared. There was no other way to describe such an outburst. Nazir had found his inner lion. 'And I hold you responsible! He is no more than a child! He has a mind like a four-year-old! You are responsible for all that he does! You should have kept your brother on a leash!'

At no point did he temper his volume.

I stood and took it in the face, blinking, as if being hit by a hurricane. Which wasn't much of an exaggeration.

By the time he finished his diatribe, three white-uniformed employees — a nurse and two orderlies — had arrived to try to tell him he couldn't make so much noise in a hospital. But when they saw the look on his face, they stopped cold. They did not attempt to approach him. Nor did I blame them.

I heard the nurse say, 'Call security.'

Nazir heard her, too.

'Yes, call security,' he said, 'and have this man

317

escorted out. He is not family. And he may not see my daughter.'

'I am her fiancé!' I shouted. I tried for the lion roar. I tried to be strong like Nazir. But I fell well short. I just didn't have his capacity for rage.

'You are not! You are not her fiancé! You are only her fiancé if you ask me for her hand in marriage and *I* say you are her fiancé!'

I wondered if Anat could hear us from wherever she was. I listened for her in the brief silence, but heard nothing. And Nazir wasn't done.

'I brought Anat here to be safe. People say, go to a small American town. You will be safe in a small American town. They just forgot to tell me that a small American town is only safe if you are a small American.'

He looked right into my eyes as he bit off those last two words.

I opened my mouth to speak, and was tapped on the shoulder by security.

'Come with me, sir,' a youngish man said. Not much older than me.

'I'm not the one causing the trouble. I just want to see her.'

'He's family, sir. You're not family.'

He put one hand on my arm. As if he was about to eject me. Physically escort me out. I shook him off. Violently. So violently that he reached for his nightstick. Placed one hand on it.

I raised both hands in a gesture of peace.

'I'm not looking for a fight,' I said.

His hand relaxed to his side again.

318

'Sir,' he said. More firmly this time. 'Come with me, please.'

I looked past Nazir. Thought briefly about making a run for it. But what good would that do? They'd catch me before I could even find her room.

'I just want to see her. I just want to know she's OK.'

'She is not OK!' Nazir roared. 'She is hurt! She is burned!'

'Sir!' the security guard said, this time to Nazir. 'You need to keep your voice down.'

'Why should she want to see you again?' he asked, only about a notch lower. 'What has come to her from knowing you, except trouble? She will never want to see you. Not after what has happened.'

Humiliatingly, I had to put almost all of my energy into fighting back tears. I couldn't say much of anything without running the risk of crying.

'This *is* not over,' I said, clamping down hard on my own frazzled emotions.

'This *is* over,' he said.

But more quietly. And to my back. Because the guard was already escorting me toward the elevator.

★   ★   ★

I sat for a time in my car, wrestling with myself over what he'd said. My mind tumbling over and over itself, trying to know whether to believe it. Or whether it was a lie. Had she told him she

319

never wanted to see me again? Would she decide that? Could she?

No. It wasn't possible. Not after what we'd shared. All that emotion couldn't disappear. She couldn't just unfeel everything.

Then, for the second time in one day, I had a moment in which I regretted my photographic memory.

It was sudden. It hit me suddenly. The full text of the message I left on Kerry's phone. Every word. But there were a few relevant sentences that went through my head a good three or four times. I just sat there, gripping and ungripping the steering wheel, pressing my back up against the seat, watching them go by in my brain.

I'd said, 'I know what happened isn't your fault. But I can't get over it. I can't get around it. I'm sorry. I can't. It's like all my post-traumatic stress is wrapped up with your voice and your name now.'

And then, so long as I was torturing myself, I also remembered what I'd said to the older man who had given me a ride through Illinois. The one who'd overheard my conversation with Kerry.

'I just have this . . . aversion . . . to her. Since . . . you know. After what happened. It feels like one of those places you go to stop smoking, and every time you reach for a cigarette, they zap you with electricity. No. That's not a good analogy. Because that's a lot of little things. This is one big thing. It feels like when you eat a whole bunch of a certain kind of food and then get sick. And maybe the food didn't even make you

320

sick. Maybe you ate three plates of fettuccini Alfredo, and then got the stomach flu. And all night you're up, throwing up fettuccini Alfredo. You'll never eat it again. Guaranteed. It's knee-jerk.'

So maybe it *was* possible. To unfeel. Just about anything.

I got out of the car and walked back toward the hospital entrance. But the guard was waiting just inside the first set of sliding doors. He shook his head at me.

So I drove back to the house.

What else could I do?

24 November 2001

I was let into a room with about ten small wooden tables.

Ben was on the other side of one.

He sat curled over himself on a chair, arms locked around his knees, rocking. Rocking.

The guard indicated the chair across from him, and I sat.

'Hey, Buddy,' I said.

A long silence. Maybe more than two minutes. I thought maybe Ben had gone fully mute. Maybe permanently.

Then a tiny, thin Ben voice. 'You lied to me, Buddy.'

'When did I lie?'

'You said everything would be OK.'

'I didn't lie. I was wrong. I thought everything *would* be OK.'

'Well, it's not. So you lied.'

'Look. Ben. I was going on the assumption that you didn't do anything wrong. But if you threw the match that started that fire, there's nothing I can do to help you.'

He raised his head as if to look at me. But, in typical Ben fashion, his gaze missed my face by about thirty degrees.

He didn't answer.

'Tell me what happened, Buddy.'

'I did tell you.'

'You told the police you threw the match. You didn't tell me that.'

'You were yelling at me. I couldn't think.'

'Who gave you matches?'

'Mark.'

'Mark gave you a book of matches?'

'No. One.'

'He just handed you one match?'

'Yeah.'

'What did you light it on?'

'What?'

'How did you get the match to light?'

'I didn't.'

'It got lighted somehow, Ben.'

'It was already on fire when he gave it to me.'

I looked down at myself, vaguely noting that I'd gotten to my feet without any real awareness of it.

'Mark handed you a lighted match?'

'Yeah.'

'Did he tell you to throw it?'

'I don't remember if he said that.'

'Ben. You have to try to remember. This is huge. This is really important.'

'He was being weird. He kept saying everything would be OK if I did. The whole country. He said everything would be OK again. I could fix everything.'

A long, cold tingle started at the back of my neck and ran down my spine.

'Did you tell the police all this?'

'Maybe. I don't remember.'

'I have to go talk to them again.'

I spun on my heels and headed for the door, surprising the guard, who had to open it for me.

Behind me, I kept hearing Ben calling to me. Over and over.

'No! Don't leave me here! Take me with you, Buddy! I want to go home!'

Sometimes you have to close yourself up. Shut the portals into the places inside you that still know how to feel. Because there's just nothing you can do.

★ ★ ★

I paced in front of Michelevsky's cluttered desk. He kept indicating a chair. But I never sat in it.

'How can you even consider charging Ben with a crime? He's brain-damaged. He has the mind of a child. Mark handed him a lighted match and told him to throw it. He's easily manipulated. He gets confused when you yell at him. He didn't know what he was doing.'

'So he says now. Jespers tells a different story. And Ben didn't say any of that when we questioned him yesterday.'

'He gets scared. He has trouble remembering details.'

'Or he just wants to get out and go home.'

I stopped pacing.

'Look. Based on what I know about my brother . . . I seriously don't think he lies. I don't think he has enough brain to think up a lie. He can't even learn how to find his way from the bus stop to work. Two blocks. And you think he can figure out what to say to shift more of the legal blame on to Mark Jespers?'

'He'll be evaluated,' Michelevsky said. As though that should be the end of things.

'I've had a talk with a lawyer. You were never supposed to question him without a guardian present. He's like a child.'

'How was I supposed to know he was like a child?'

'Everybody in town knows that about Ben.'

Michelevsky sat back, his chair squeaking. 'I'm new around here.'

Just as I was about to call him out as a liar, which he may or may not have been, he said, 'You knew. Why didn't you say something? Why didn't you say you wanted to be present?'

'You said I couldn't be.'

'And you never said your brother was mentally incompetent.'

I sighed, and sat down hard on a wooden bench. He was right. It was my fault. Why hadn't I insisted? Stubborn, pig-headed refusal to accept that Ben could have been a suspect. I knew he wasn't involved, and expected everyone else to know it, too.

'Okay,' I said, 'he'll be evaluated. Meaning . . .'

'There'll probably be a competency hearing.'

'And if . . . I mean, *when* he's found incompetent?'

'Probably he'll be transferred to the state hospital.'

'For how long?'

'That could go a lot of different ways. Worst

325

case . . . for him . . . until they decide he's not a danger to himself or others.'

I'm not sure how long I stood there, taking that in. Wrapping my brain around this entirely new set of future obstacles on the obstacle course that was now my life.

'But . . . Ben's never going to change. He's always going to be just like this.'

'True,' Michelevsky said.

And that appeared to be the dead end of . . . well, many things. The least of which being that conversation.

Part Six

Someplace Cheery

10 December 2001

I parked my mom's old Buick half a block from the automotive shop and walked. I'm not entirely sure why. Maybe to make it harder for Chris Kerricker to see me coming. Not that he shouldn't have damn well known to expect me by then.

He was working inside the service bay, his head under the hood of a BMW.

I walked around to where he could see me, and his face fell.

'I had no idea Kansans drove BMWs,' I said.

He straightened up and hurled the wrench he'd been holding, bouncing it off the far wall of the shop. I remember thinking it must be a bad sign when people regularly hurl whatever they're holding in their hand when they see you coming. Especially if it's something of value, something they're going to need again.

At least he didn't throw the wrench at my head.

I still think it might be a sign that it's time to reexamine your life.

'I can't take much more of you,' he said.

'I can think of a way to solve that.'

'Fuck you.'

Oscar, long-time owner of Oscar's Automotive, stuck his head out of the office and into the service bay, his eyes narrow. He took me in, then looked at Chris. He must have known by then that my daily visits weren't happy ones. But he never asked. Maybe he didn't want to know. Maybe good mechanics are hard to find in a town the size of Nowhere-ville.

'What just happened?'

'Sorry, Oscar. Dropped a wrench.'

My guess is that Oscar had been around this business long enough to know the sound of a wrench slipping out of a hand and falling to the concrete floor, without force. If so, he chose not to pursue it.

His face disappeared again.

Looking back, I can't help noting the significance of a thing dropped as opposed to a thing thrown. How they are two very different animals. I didn't know enough to note it at the time.

'I wasn't there, man,' Chris said. 'I wasn't there, I wasn't there, I wasn't there. How many times do I have to keep telling you I wasn't there?'

'Maybe until you can make it morph into the truth?'

'I'm busy here. This is my livelihood. If you don't mind.'

'My brother Ben used to have a livelihood. Did I mention that? He loved his job. You know. The one he can't go to now. Because he's locked up in the state hospital. Doing time that rightly belongs to you and Mark.'

'Mark is doing plenty of time!' he snapped.

'Mark could get out in as little as twenty months.'

'That's a lot of time!'

'For nearly killing a woman?'

'We didn't know she was up there, man!'

Then silence. Embarrassed on his part, triumphant on mine.

Sounds like a key moment, right? Like I'd just cracked the case. But the truth is, Chris often committed little slips like that. If I pressed him hard enough. Then he'd look me in the eye, defiantly, and say he'd never said it, that it was his word against mine, that he'd deny it to the grave. Then I'd go back to Nowhere-ville's finest, who would pull him in for questioning. Again. His father would call the family attorney to go in with him. Again. And somehow he would get his story straight. With them.

Again.

If I could get another round of questioning out of this one, that would make four full rounds. But I think everyone was getting tired of going over this same old territory. Except me.

'That doesn't mean anything,' he said. 'I'm just saying none of us could possibly have known. Whether we were there or not, we didn't know. That doesn't mean that every single person who didn't know was there.'

'But you were.'

'How do you know I was?' he shouted. It wasn't hard to make Chris lose his temper. I did it almost every day. 'How the hell would you know?' Then he lowered his voice to a tense whisper. 'Even if you did see my car drive away from your house that night, which I have my doubts about, it doesn't mean shit. I could've

331

caught up with Ben later and brought him home. If you'd really seen me, and seeing me really proved I was there, I'd be in jail right now.'

Oscar stuck his head out again. 'I got customers in here,' he said.

'Sorry, Oscar.'

We waited for him to disappear again. But he lingered. As though a little extra staring might be just what the problem needed. Then he shook his head and withdrew it.

'You're gonna lose me my job, man. Right, I know, we lost Ben his. I know everything you're gonna say before you say it, man. Why don't you give it up? I'm not volunteering to go to jail. I got a life. In case you hadn't noticed.'

'And Ben doesn't?'

'No. Ben doesn't.'

And with that pronouncement, he crossed the shop, fetched the wrench, and stuck his head back under the hood of the BMW. As if ignoring me would solve everything. But, damn . . . that's a big everything.

'You have no right to say that. Just because it didn't look like a life *you'd* want. Ben had a job. He loved that job. He saw just about everybody in town, every day. He liked everybody and everybody liked him. And he loves his home. You know, the one he's lived in since he was six years old. And now he'll probably never get to see it again. You have any idea how much he hates being away from home? He's more miserable in that state hospital than you'd be in prison.'

'I doubt *that*,' Chris muttered.

'Plus *you'd* get out after a year or two.'

He drew his head back out from under the hood. Looked right into my eyes. Pointed at a spot at the bridge of my nose with the wrench. I tried not to go cross-eyed.

'Fuck you, Rusty. I'm not doing that to myself. I'm not doing that to my family. I'm not doing that to my girlfriend. I'm not doing it to Mark, either. You think I want to be responsible for Mark doing even more time?'

Bingo. Oh, snap.

'Nice one,' I said. 'Two in one day.'

He rolled his eyes and ducked under the hood again.

'So, basically, what you just slipped and told me is that if you were to tell the actual story of what happened that night, Mark would be charged with additional crimes. Like, and this is just a wild guess here, but . . . maybe the ones that are sitting on Ben right now?'

I remember thinking Chris must be a fundamentally stupid man. A smart one would have taken an oath of silence in my presence long ago.

For several minutes — or at least it seemed like several minutes — he just worked at loosening the bolts around the BMW's fan. He didn't look at me or speak. Then he stopped, and held very still. He continued to stare at the engine.

'You can ride me like this till the fucking cows come home, man. I'm not doing it. Why are you even fighting this? I don't get you at all. Great, you're a fucking hero because you didn't come right home and stick your brother in a mental institution first thing. But there must've been part of you that wanted to. Because I spent less than a day with that guy, and I nearly lost my mind. So now he's away, and it's not your fault. You can always say you did your best for him. Nobody can blame you after all you did. You're better off. You can have your life back, man. Maybe the Muslim girl'll even come back. You know. If she's sure Ben's locked up for ever. Because she sure as hell won't want to spend her life with the guy who set her business on fire. Right under her hands and knees. You could have your life again. I don't get why things aren't OK just the way they are.'

I winced at the mention of her, but only inwardly. It was something I wasn't prepared to let anybody see. I'd built strong armor around the fact that I still hadn't heard from her. I dealt with it when I was alone, to the extent I dealt with it at all. In the shower. On the drive out to the state hospital. In bed at night, waiting for the sleep that first wouldn't come, then wouldn't stay.

I did not deal with it in the presence of Chris Kerricker.

He finished. And waited. He still didn't move. He still didn't stop staring at the engine. As though the engine were about to argue with him. Not me.

'All good points,' I said.

I watched him closely. He shifted his head as though he might look at me. But he didn't. I guess he thought better of it. He didn't speak.

'There's not one thing you just said that I

haven't thought of myself. And I'm not going to say you're flat-out wrong about any of it. There's just one problem with the whole damn package.'

I waited for input. I'm not sure why.

'Fine,' he said. 'Tell me the problem. You will, anyway.'

'I don't think Ben did anything wrong.'

I waited a while longer, in case there was more he wanted to say. Apparently not. He finished unbolting the fan, and unhooked it from the three or four belts that circled it.

'Well, then,' I said. 'See you tomorrow.'

He dropped the fan. Which I'm guessing was an expensive mistake.

'Oh, bloody fucking hell!' he bellowed. 'When are you gonna leave me alone, man?'

'When you tell me what happened that night.'

But nothing moved for a long time. So I decided to call it a day.

'Well. Till tomorrow, then.'

I glanced over my shoulder to see Chris flipping me his middle finger as I walked away.

★ ★ ★

I arrived at the state hospital at twenty after eleven. Just like I did every Monday, Wednesday and Friday. With a ten-minute cushion to sign in before visiting hours. Maybe I had learned promptness from Ben.

I stood in front of the window, listening to the woman behind the desk snap her chewing gum. I hate it when people snap their gum. It puts me on edge.

335

Or maybe I'd been on edge lately anyway.

'Dr Bosco wants to talk to you today,' she said.

'Before or after I see Ben?'

'Before. Lemme call her.'

She had hot-pink fingernails so long that she had to dial the phone with the eraser end of a pencil. Looking back, that's another connection I make now that I couldn't have made at the time. Because the other half of that connection hadn't surfaced yet.

'Dr Bosco?' I heard her say. 'Yeah. He's here. OK.'

She hung up. Dialed again in the same weird manner.

'John? You want to come up front? Get Ben Ammiano's brother and see him back to Bosco's office? OK. Thanks.'

She hung up again.

'Have a seat,' she said, pointing with the dialing pencil. As if I wouldn't know from experience where a seat could be found.

I didn't sit. I was too off-balance to sit. I didn't like the dangling sword of knowing the doctor wanted to talk to me.

The big door buzzed, then popped open. John nodded at me. Big John, they called him. The go-to psych tech when a patient gets out of hand.

We walked side by side down the bright hallway. I tried to remind myself I was not going to the gallows. Probably. He opened the door to Dr Bosco's office and motioned me in, then closed the door behind me.

Dr Bosco was on the phone. She held up one

finger, then pointed it toward a chair.

I forced myself.

She wore her unusually long gray hair in an intricate braid that morning. She wore red. A bright-red wool blazer.

'I'm going to have to get back to you,' she said into the phone. 'I've got somebody here.'

She hung up the phone and leveled me with her friendly — yet somehow intimidating — gaze.

'Problem?' I asked. Then I attempted to swallow, with mixed success.

'We have a problem every visiting day, Russell. We've just gotten him settled down. And then he sees you. And then he falls apart again. And he wants to go home. And it takes him a long time to settle again. Just about as long as it takes for the next visiting day to come around. It's gotten to be a bad pattern. I'm going to make a suggestion. And I have no idea how it's going to strike you.'

She allowed a pause.

'You're not going to suggest I don't visit.'

More silence.

She was. She *was* suggesting that.

I looked her right in the eye. I didn't do that often. With anybody. Not lately.

I asked, 'Is this one of those things like loading kids up with Ritalin because it makes it easier for the teachers to deal with them?'

I expected her to avert her gaze. She didn't.

'Russell, if it was, I wouldn't be suggesting it. It's just starting to seem cruel. For whatever reason, Ben is incapable of remembering that

337

you haven't come to get him and take him home. Whether this is courtesy of his brain damage, or a function of how much he doesn't want to know the truth, I couldn't tell you. I just know that every time you walk out of here without him it breaks his heart. He cries for the rest of the day. He says, 'My buddy left without me.' A hundred times. Every Monday, Wednesday and Friday.'

'Please. Don't tell me that.'

'How can I not tell you, Russell? It's the damn truth.'

'I'm getting tired of the damn truth.'

'I imagine you are, my friend.'

A little ripple of electricity ran through me when she called me 'my friend'. It was as though she were channeling Nazir.

'He'll think I forgot him.'

Then we both took a long breath. A moment to poke our heads up above the sludge of the damn truth.

'Maybe we could just try it for a couple of months,' she said. 'See if we like the effect on his mood better than what we've got now.'

'All right. Here's some damn truth for you, too, doctor. I'm not in any position for experiments. I have to choose. I have to make a move. Make up my damn mind. I've got nothing keeping me in Kansas except Ben. I still pay rent on my apartment in New York. My stuff is still there. My mail is still dropping there. My utilities are probably about to be turned off. Any chance I have at continuing my career path is there. If I'm not going to see Ben, I need to make a full break. I'm not just going to sit here in Nowhere-ville for a couple of months while we wait and see.'

Bosco rocked back in her big leather chair until she hit the back of it with a little cushiony 'whump'.

'Oh, Russell. I had no idea. Russell, go get your life back. I had no idea you were staying here for Ben, and Ben only. And if it's doing him more harm than good . . . Just go. Let us take care of Ben. If it breaks his heart because he thinks you've forgotten him, you can fly out once or twice a year and tell him you haven't. You need a life. You need time to process everything that's happened to you. Don't you ever feel tired? Like you're pushing a river?'

'Always.'

'So maybe stop pushing?'

'Don't hit me with all the psychological crap,' I said. But in a tone that made it clear I didn't mean it as a genuine complaint.

'I have to,' she said. 'I'm a crappy psychologist.'

'No, I think you're a decent one.'

'If I was, I wouldn't be here. I'd be in private practice. Earning a mint. Get yourself someplace cheery for the holidays, young man.'

'Sure. Good idea. I'll go back to my apartment in Jersey City, overlooking lower Manhattan. I can spend the holidays looking at the empty space where my office used to be. Maybe the rubble is still smoking. That would be cheery.'

'Might be more fun than this.'

I rose to my feet. A little unsteady.

'You going in to see Ben now?' As though she

fully expected me to ignore her warnings.

'No. I'm going home.'

As I was walking out of her office, it struck me as ironic. Maybe even funny. I finally broke the strangle-hold of Nowhere-ville. After the better part of three months, I finally got it to let me go. Right at the same moment I accidentally let down and called it home.

★ ★ ★

I checked my cell phone when I got back to the car. Just like I always did. Nobody had called.

I drove home, or back to my mother's house, or whatever you want to call it, and checked the message machine there, too. Like I always did.

Nothing.

I sat for while with my head in my hands. I'm not sure how long.

Then I pulled out the comically thin local phone book and looked up that real-estate agent who'd been friends with my mom for ever. Cheryl Baker-Keene.

I dialed her cell phone. Told her who I was. Told her it was time to unload my mother's house.

She said she understood completely. She said she'd be over in less than an hour.

★ ★ ★

'I have no idea how long it'll take me to go through all my mom's stuff,' I told Cheryl.

I was re-experiencing how perky she always

340

looked. And, in reality, was. It was a nearly oppressive amount of perk.

'May I make a suggestion?'

'Please.'

'There are services that'll do it for you. For a fee, of course. There's one I recommend all the time. Two local sisters. They haul away everything that isn't worth selling and sell everything that is. Then they clean the house all up for sale. They're fast. And they send you whatever money's left over after their fee.'

'Sold. I didn't know there were people who do that.'

'Lots of people lose their parents, Rusty. And then they have to deal with the estate. I see it all the time. It's too overwhelming. Partly because their parents accumulated a lifetime's worth of stuff. Partly because it's a shared history. Too much emotion.'

'So let me see if I have this straight. I could basically pack a few things and walk out of here. Almost anytime. And you would handle the rest.'

'That's my job. What you would have to do is make sure you're taking anything you might possibly want. Because anything you don't take will be disposed of. One way or the other.'

I looked around. What did I want? I could think of a couple of wants, but they would not be filled by anything under this roof.

'Just photos, I guess. The photos on the mantel. And the big album.'

'Financial records.'

'Right. I'm glad you said that. I have to tie up a lot of loose ends of Mom's business. I've been letting things slide.'

'That's how I earn my percentage. May I make another suggestion?'

'OK.'

'I know you're probably not feeling very sentimental right now. But check the attic. The attic is always where the memories live. Holiday decorations that're a family tradition by now, but you won't think of them if it's off-season. The ashtray you made for your mom at summer camp.'

I almost said, So that's where you find an ashtray around here. I didn't.

'I have to ask you a weird favor,' I said.

'I've probably heard weirder.'

'I keep thinking . . . ' Then I stopped. And seriously questioned if I could go on. But I had to. I had no choice. 'I keep thinking maybe my friend Anat lost my phone number. Maybe it was in the bakery and got burned up. Maybe she can't get it from information because she doesn't know my cell phone is listed in Jersey City, not New York. But she knows where this house is . . . '

I waited. Silence. I looked up, hoping Cheryl Baker-Keene wouldn't have heard about me and Anat, that her eyes wouldn't be full of pathetic sympathy. I lost. They were.

'Did you ever try to call her? Or go out to their house?'

'The only phone number I ever had was the bakery phone. It took me two weeks to find out where they lived — it wasn't listed — and by the time I got out there, they'd packed up and gone.

342

I have no idea where they went. Never mind. It's stupid.' I knew Anat probably hadn't even tried to call.

I dropped my head into my hands. Thinking, I will not cry. I will not cry. I will not cry. And crying. Just a little bit.

Cheryl came close and sat on the couch beside me. I willed her not to touch me. She put her hand on my arm.

'What did you think I could do to help?'

'I was thinking maybe I could write a note. In case she came by the house. Later. After it's sold. Do you think whoever buys the house would give her a note if they had one?'

'I'd be willing to ask.'

I kept my head in my hands. It was the closest thing to a dark cave I could find.

'It's stupid. I know it is. But I feel like otherwise I'll always wonder. You know. If her father's keeping her from getting in touch with me. Or if she lost my number. Or . . . '

Needless to say, I was headed for my most likely option. That Anat didn't *want* to get in touch with me. I decided to stall. I decided not to get there. Ever.

'Write the note,' Cheryl said. 'It might make you feel better. And call me when you're headed back to New York. We can do most of the rest of our business by phone.'

She might have waited for a minute or two. I'm not sure why. Maybe to see if I would ever unbury my head.

Finally I heard the door click closed behind her.

★ ★ ★

Here's what I found in the attic, other than old furniture: three cardboard cartons. They were each the same size. All former paper-towel cartons from the supermarket. Probably from Gerson's. Carefully labeled. Carefully taped.

I was unprepared for this level of sparse organization. Why was the house so cluttered compared to this? Somehow my mother had exerted more control over her ancient memories than over her everyday life. Maybe there was some logic to that. I couldn't decide.

One box said CHRISTMAS. One said RUSTY. One said BEN.

I opened the Christmas box. Also very organized. On the bottom she'd packed the strings of lights for the tree, thoughtfully wound into a circle and secured with twist ties. No tangles. On top she'd packed the ornaments, each carefully wrapped in a full sheet of newspaper.

In the middle, the Christmas village. Fresh unused cotton batting, still in plastic. The houses. The horse-drawn sled. The mirror lake. The ice-skating skunk. The family of deer, perpetually bent to drink.

I taped it back up and brought it downstairs.

I remembered Dr Bosco telling me to get myself someplace cheery for the holidays. I'd pack this in the car with a few boxes of finance stuff, and drive it back to New Jersey. And I'd cheery up the apartment with the Christmas village. I didn't have a mantel. But maybe I could rig a table-top. It was worth a try.

I opened my box. But I didn't rummage around in there long. It was mostly what I would've expected. Report cards full of As. Handmade Mother's Day and Valentine's Day cards. Pictures I'd drawn in kindergarten. I opened Ben's. The same. Nothing of any intrinsic value. Stuff only a mother could love.

I taped up my box again and carted it down to the car.

Then, as an afterthought, I went back up for Ben's carton, and loaded that into the car as well.

Not that I really wanted all his memorabilia, or even mine. More because my mother obviously had wanted them. And because, if she wasn't around to hoard these memories, I'd have to hoard them on her behalf.

And maybe, just maybe, so that if Ben ever accused me of forgetting all about him, I could tell him, 'How can you say that, Ben, when I still have the Mother's Day card you made when you were six?'

★   ★   ★

I didn't exactly write a note for Anat. Because I had no idea what to say. Because I had no idea what had happened.

Instead I just wrote down all my contact info — cell number, land line in Jersey City, address in Jersey City, email — folded it up, put it in an envelope, wrote her name on the front, and left it on the kitchen table.

345

14 December 2001

It was Friday. Four days from the moment I'd done a complete turnaround on where I intended to be. Geographically and otherwise.

I was eighty-eight floors above Manhattan. More than halfway through interviewing for a new ad job. It would be a great job, if I ever got it. But it wasn't likely that I would. Because too many other people wanted it just as badly.

I sat in a leather chair, trying not to slouch, yet trying not to sit too stiffly, either. Which meant I was losing. Once you misplace the ability to be yourself without thinking about it, without second-guessing it, you're pretty well cooked.

And there was another problem I couldn't overcome. Or maybe they were intertwined. Sitting in the well-appointed offices of an ad firm in a Manhattan high rise was causing my post-traumatic stress to flare. There are only just so many times you can wipe sweat off your forehead before it gets conspicuous.

I watched my interviewer glancing over my application. Nodding here and there. He didn't seem to be paying full attention. Almost as if actually sitting down with each of these applicants was a burdensome formality. I took that to mean I wasn't high on his list. His head was tilted downward, exposing the thinness of the top of his hair. I guessed he was in his mid-forties. I guessed he was a nice guy at heart. But fundamentally tired. On the inside.

He sat back and looked up at me. Set my application down on his oak desk.

'What do you want for yourself in five years? Where do you see yourself? What do you want your life to be?'

'I just want to be happy.'

He cocked his head slightly. 'Happy?'

I thought, Yeah. Happy. You've heard of it. Right?

'I don't mean to make it sound like I don't have ambition. I have plenty of ambition. But I'm not one of those people who always wants more, no matter how much I get. The idea of drive is all wrapped up with the drive to be happy, right? I want to work at a job I'm good at, and that's good at me. I want to contribute. I want to live a good life. Now. In five years. Whenever.'

He blinked three or four times in quick succession. 'That's an unusual answer.'

'In a good way or a bad way?'

'I liked it. Actually. But, anyway. Let me just get this said. We've got over a hundred qualified applicants. So it'll be a long process, deciding. I'm not saying you're not still in the running. But don't pull back from your job search just yet. If you know what I mean.'

347

'Yes, sir.'

'Greg. Sir makes me feel old.'

'Greg.'

'Let me just make sure I've seen everything you . . . '

He reached for my application again. Flipped it over to the back. Ran one finger down it. Stopped. Stopped cold. Looked up at me. Looked down at the place he held with his finger. Looked up again. Looked down again.

'Is this a joke? No. Nobody would joke about that. Would they?'

'Sir? Greg?'

'Hatcher, Swift & Dallaire? You were with Hatcher, Swift & Dallaire? Through the tenth of September this year?'

I nodded, my forehead sweating again.

'Then what are you doing sitting on the other side of my desk? Or anywhere else, for that matter?'

The silence seemed to nearly echo. Like a ringing in my ears.

'Well. Greg. It's like this. My mother died on the morning of the eleventh. Unexpectedly. I got the call just as I was leaving for work. I have a brother who's . . . who can't take care of himself. And I was told I had to drop everything and get home. And that threw off the timing on my morning.'

'Jesus.'

Silence. I looked out the window and saw a plane, thousands of feet above the city. The size of a toy. Still, it made my chest constrict.

I didn't answer. What answer is there to 'Jesus' anyway?

'You know, I know the only other Hatcher survivor,' he said.

'Stan Harbaugh.'

'Stan's an old colleague of mine. We actually started out in the same mail room in the same ad firm out of college. He told me there was only one other guy who wasn't in the office that day. He must've meant you.'

'Must have. I'm having lunch with him after this interview.'

'Tell him Greg Wasserman says hello.'

'Will do.'

He stood, so I stood, too. He reached out his hand and I shook it.

'I just moved you up a tier in the running. Still a big field, so keep looking. If you haven't heard from us in four weeks, that's that.'

'Thanks.'

He shook his head as he walked me to the door. 'It's like interviewing a ghost. You're lucky to be alive.'

That was one way to look at it. But I didn't editorialize.

I'm learning.

★ ★ ★

I glanced at Stan again, over my menu. He caught it, and looked back. We smiled just the tiniest bit. Awkwardly.

Then we went back to studying our lunch options.

In a few minutes, when we'd closed the menus and set them on the table, he said, 'I couldn't have been more surprised when you called.'

'Took me long enough.'

'I figured you didn't want anything to do with me or the whole thing.'

'Just different coping mechanisms,' I said.

'Understood.'

We looked out the window for a while. I think we were still feeling unbalanced. I know I was.

'I was such an emotional mess,' he said. 'I figured I'd put you off.'

'Don't even take that on. We were both a mess. Everybody was a mess. You just tackle things more head-on than I do. You just got off to a better start. You know. Letting it all move through you.'

More awkward silence. A waiter came and took our orders. I was partially grateful for the distraction.

'You still talk to Kerry?' he asked. With something tentative in his voice.

'No. I haven't talked to her.'

'Oh. Not my business. Didn't mean to pry.' Silence. 'Seemed like you two might've been . . . close. You know. Something there. But I don't mean it like . . . '

'We didn't do anything behind Jeff's back. If that's what you mean.'

'Affair of the heart. That was the consensus. That's what most people thought. Anyway. I'm getting off on the wrong foot here. Like I'm trying to get all into your business, and actually I'm just trying to get a feel for whether I should tell you she's with somebody.'

I looked up. Into his face. Interested. But . . . did I feel anything about that? I stopped and put an ear to my own feelings for a moment. Nothing. Well. Not much.

So I just said, 'That was quick.'

'Yeah. Like, three weeks out.'

'Well. I hope she's happy.'

'Really? That's the most charitable take I've heard on it yet. Everybody else thinks it's scandalous. She hadn't even had a memorial for Jeff yet.'

An inward flinch at the mention of memorials. I'd brought my mom's ashes home with me from Kansas, but hadn't done anything respectful with them yet. At first I'd been waiting for Ben to adjust. And then . . .

'Wait a minute,' I said. 'Everybody? I thought everybody was gone.'

'I'm talking about the SO club. The close network of surviving significant others. Maybe too close. Too much fertile ground for rumors. And opinions. Especially about how other people should grieve. I'm half in that and half out of it. I mean, yeah, it was fast, but who's to say? Maybe she found somebody to help her with her grief. It doesn't necessarily mean she didn't love Jeff.'

'She loved Jeff,' I said. I'd been in a position to know.

'Things just happen, I guess.'

'Life turns on a dime.'

'I'll say.'

'Oh. I almost forgot. Greg Wasserman says to

351

say hello. I interviewed for a position with him this morning.'

'Oh, that would be a great firm for you. I really hope you get that. I'll see if I can put in a good word for you. Greg and I go way back.'

'So he says.'

After the food came, I told him everything. I told him all about my time in Kansas. I don't know why. Or, I don't know . . . then again, why not?

I said, 'It's like things took a turn for the horrible that morning, and I just couldn't get them to turn back again. Everything just kept going wrong.'

'I've been thinking about that a lot,' he said. 'You know there are some really ancient theories about that, right? It's like the same theory as to how the rich get richer and the poor get poorer. It's like my mom used to say, 'Bad luck comes in threes.' '

'Any theories on how to break the pattern?'

'I guess we just have to set our sights on being OK again. I think we just have to believe it's possible to get there from here.'

'Do you believe that?'

'I'm working on it,' he said.

'Well, then you're doing better than I am. See, that's the thing about people who hit emotion head-on. They have a head start over people like me. I just keep thinking about what happened. And it's like . . . I just don't know about this world. I don't know what we're supposed to make of a world like this.'

'Unless you've got another one in your

pocket,' he said, 'we're going to have to make our way in this one.'

'See? I'll just have to hang around you more. See if it rubs off.'

'Anytime, Russell.'

That's when we promised we'd do it again. Soon. And, all things considered, I figured it was possible that we actually might.

15 December 2001

I woke up and cleaned the place. Literally top to bottom. I even took down all the draperies and carried them to the dry cleaner's. I paid all my outstanding bills with a credit-card advance. I found a storage spot in the hall closet for my box and Ben's box. I found a spot on the dresser for my mother's ashes. For now.

How could I have a memorial for my mother that Ben couldn't attend?

I forced the thought away again.

I set up the Christmas village on the top of my bookshelf in the living room. I was hoping it would be cheery.

I knew exactly what I was doing. I was trying to force a change. I was trying to reset life, in any way I could. Send it off in a new direction.

By three thirty in the afternoon, I was exhausted. I sat staring at the lighted village, realizing that, without the drapes, I had no real choice but to see the changed skyline of lower Manhattan.

Reset, I thought. Reset. But how do you reset the skyline of lower Manhattan?

I don't know if it was a dodge or just inevitable hunger, but I decided I couldn't live without Pad Thai another hour. I set out on foot to a Thai restaurant, even though it was snowing, and the closest good one was twenty-two blocks away.

Then I caught a cab home so my food wouldn't get stone cold.

I emptied my mailbox on my way through the lobby, and took my mail and my Pad Thai upstairs. I knew I didn't really want to be in my apartment, but it was cold out. And I had to be somewhere.

I changed into sweatpants and sat cross-legged on my couch, staring at the Christmas village and eating with disposable chopsticks. Halfway through dinner, I opened my mail. Despite the fact that it was only my second foray to the mailbox since arriving home, there were only two things. One was a final turn-off notice on the electricity. But I'd paid it online that morning, so I figured it could be safely ignored. The other was a plain envelope, no return address, made out by hand, and postmarked Wichita. Which probably really meant Norville. All Norville mail was shipped overnight to Wichita for postmarking.

My heart began drumming in my chest, an old and unwelcome feeling, and I slaughtered the envelope ripping it open. But it was not a letter from Anat.

In fact, it was not a letter. And I had . . . have . . . no idea who it was from.

Inside was nothing but a clipping from the *Norville Weekly Leader*, Nowhere-ville's thin excuse for a local paper. The title of the article was 'Army National Guard Admits Norville

Soldier Killed by Friendly Fire.'

I unfolded it. And Vince Buck the soldier smiled at me from the page.

I began to read.

When two soldiers came to notify Betsy Buck of her son Vincent's death, the first thing she asked was how it happened. The soldiers said Buck, 25, had been killed by sniper fire while trying to secure a prison in Kandahar on 9 November. Later, the 58-year-old Norville native said, she called the local National Guard for more details and was told the unarmored Humvee in which Buck was traveling hit an improvised explosive device en route to the prison battle, in which five soldiers — four American and one British — were killed.

'I knew it had to be one or the other,' she said. 'I don't like to think this way about my own government, but I got the impression that somebody was trying to blanket over the truth.'

Today, nearly four weeks and dozens of phone calls later, the official story has changed. The deaths of all five soldiers are now being attributed to 'friendly fire', the army's term for a harmful or fatal mistake on the part of non-enemy troops. In this case, the troops who made the mistake of firing a missile at an Allied convoy were American.

I looked away from the text of the article for a moment. Into the photo of Vince's smiling face.

And I remembered offending Larry by telling him going to war would be pointless. In a weird way, I'd been right. Righter than I ever meant — or wanted — to be. But it turned out more pointless for Vince than for Larry.

I hated to even remember that. Suddenly I wanted to think like everyone else seemed to think. That military retaliation was honorable and just. But that's only wanting. War is always pointless. That's what I think.

I continued to read. For a moment. Mrs Buck was quoted as saying, 'I'm as American as anybody, but — '

My cell phone rang. And I didn't want to stop reading to answer it.

I figured it was Cheryl Baker-Keene. My real-estate agent. She'd called yesterday to deliver an offer on the house, which I'd authorized her to accept. Not as much money as we were asking, but it was fast, and fast was what I wanted.

Slightly irritated by the distraction, I grabbed up the phone and clicked it on.

'I'm going to have to call you back,' I said.

Silence on the line.

'Oh,' a small voice said.

It froze me, through and through. It hit me in a way I didn't even know I could be hit any more. I thought I'd armored up better than that. It felt sad to fail at something so basic.

'Anat?'

'Yes. Me.'

Disjointedly, I thought: Note to self, just say hello. Don't assume it's not Anat.

A long, long . . . long silence.

I looked out the window. It was nearly dark already. At not even five thirty. It was coming on to winter. This horrible year was nearly over. I took the phone to my drapeless window. There was no furniture by the window, so I sat on the freshly vacuumed rug. And I did what I'd been avoiding doing, at least as much as humanly possible, since arriving home. I stared at the place where the lights in the windows of the towers should have been. I think up until that moment I'd been wanting to avoid it as a way of moving on. But, in that moment, I got it. Not so much in my head, but more instinctively. Part of resetting your life is accepting where you are in your life right now.

'Russell. Are you still there?'

'Yes. I'm still here. Are *you* still there?'

It was a silly question, I know. I think I'd halfway said it to make her laugh. And she did. Just a little.

'I'm sorry I didn't call sooner.'

'Are you OK?'

'Mostly so. I will be, I guess.'

'Where are you?'

'It would not make you happy to know that.'

I leaned my shoulder against the bare window. Felt the coldness of the world through my sleeve. I didn't know what to say. So I said nothing.

'I still can't really use my hands,' she said.

My heart fell to about my knees. 'I didn't know it was that bad.'

'Well, I've had to have some skin grafts. And afterwards I need to be very careful with them. I

358

had to figure out how to push the numbers on the phone with the eraser end of a pencil. I held it between my wrists.'

'Does it hurt a lot? Are you in a lot of pain? Will you tell me about how it was for you, how it is? I haven't known, and I've been going crazy.'

'I will. But maybe not right now, if that's OK.'

'Does it hurt to hold the phone now?'

'I have it on speaker.'

'Oh. Good. So . . . ' I wasn't sure how to say what I wanted to say next. 'So you did have my phone number the whole time?'

'Yes.'

Long pause. It had to be said, though. 'So is that really the only reason you didn't call? Or is there more?'

Silence.

I was not about to fill it.

'Well. There was also the fact that I was not alone. My father gets someone always to stay with me. Because there's so much I can't do on my own. And there were other problems. I had to get a neighbor to buy me a pre-paid phone card. So my father wouldn't see this on the phone charges. But to be truthful . . . '

Here it comes, I thought. My gut turned to concrete and steel, preparing for the hit. I thought again about — or maybe just *felt* about — that phone call I'd finally made to Kerry. My silence had already told her everything she needed to know. The call was just to confirm. I steeled myself for the assault I felt coming.

' . . . actually, there were two times I was alone. But not for long. And it was near the beginning. I was on a lot of painkillers. I felt like I couldn't think clearly. I knew you'd ask me if we would ever see each other again. I didn't know what I would say. I needed more time.'

'Will we ever see each other again?' I felt disinclined to prolong my misery.

'See? I was right about that.'

She waited, probably to see if she'd made me laugh. Even a little bit. But I wasn't in a laughing mood.

'Well,' she said. 'This is why I'm calling. This is what we have before us to be discussed.'

A great rush of excitement came up through my pathetic, useless armor.

'You mean we might?'

'Well, of course we *might*. Might is easy. The hard part is knowing what you really will do. For sure.'

'Where are you? Go ahead and tell me.'

'I am in Kafr Dawar.'

Her words reverberated inside me, as if I were entirely hollow. As if I were a cave in which she could set off an echo.

'You're in Egypt?'

'Yes. My father took the insurance money and flew us back.'

'I could send you a plane ticket.'

'And how would you afford this? They're not cheap.'

'I'm selling my mom's house. When the sale goes through, I'll be all set again. Plus I just had a good job interview. I might be working again soon. But I'll buy you a ticket right now if you want. I'll put it on a credit card. I'll be paying them off soon enough, anyway.'

'I can't go back to that place. That awful little town with those awful little people. I couldn't live there after what happened.'

'Well, you're in luck. Because I'm back in New York.'

'But . . . Russell . . . '

'What?'

'It was easier when we lived in the same town, and we could just go on getting to know each other. Let's say I fly there. And . . . what? We are then living together? After knowing each other for how long?'

In the silence that followed, I breathed in and out about three times. I purposely made the breaths deep and slow. I closed my eyes and wished for the right words. Not the words most likely to manipulate her into doing what I wanted. The right ones.

'Here's what I always tell myself in situations like this. I'll give you the same advice I'd give myself. Picture yourself looking back on the decision ten or twenty years down the road. Let's say you try it, and it doesn't work out. How much will you regret it? Now let's say you don't try it, so you never know. Then how much regret?'

I'd guess it was about thirty seconds that I sat there. Looking at the empty spot on the skyline. Watching snow swirl weakly outside my window. Wondering when she would speak.

'I miss you,' she said. 'I have to think about this. I'll call again.'

'I can't call you?'

'No. You can't call me. I'll have to call again. When I can. I don't know when that will be.'

'Can I ask you a question?'

'Sure,' she said. But she sounded unsure.

'Do you think war is always pointless?'

'That's a strange question. That's not what I thought you were going to ask.'

I wanted to explain, but my thoughts were too much of a jumble. Nothing came out.

'I don't know if war is always pointless,' she said. 'I know it's always tragic.'

'OK,' I said. Feeling a little better. 'I can live better with that.'

'What was — Oh. My father is home. I have to go.' And then the click.

I sat there on the floor by the window until after three in the morning. Not really even thinking. I can't recall thinking much of anything. Just echoing. Reverberating. Like an empty vessel. Maybe that was the good news. Maybe emptying out was the first solid step toward a genuine reset.

16 December 2001

The phone woke me at the crack of 11 a.m.

I grabbed it up before it could finish its first ring.

'Is that you?' I asked desperately.

'Hmm,' a male voice said. 'Yes and no. I *am* me. But I have a funny feeling I'm not the me you were hoping for. Officer Nick Michelevsky. From your lovely hometown. The thriving metropolis of Norville.'

'Oh,' I said. What else could I say on such short notice?

Note to self: Just say hello. Don't assume it *is* Anat.

'You sound asleep.'

'I was.'

'Isn't it *later* where you are?'

'I was up most of the night.'

'Right. Well. All sleeping habits aside. You'll never guess who turned up on my doorstep this morning. Seven o'clock sharp. With his full entourage. I bet you'll never guess.'

'I bet I won't even try.'

'Chris Kerricker. Plus controlling dad, crying mom, and nervous attorney. All of a sudden he has a new version of events. All of a sudden it turns out he just might have been in attendance

363

that night, after all.'

'That's . . . bizarre,' I said. 'I tried everything to make him admit that.'

'So we all noticed.'

'What changed?'

'Two things. According to him. Time. I guess you can bear the weight of a thing like that for a while, but it gets heavier as time goes on. But I don't think that was the main thing. I think the main thing that got under his skin was this article in the paper about your mutual friend Vince Buck.'

'Right. I know. I read it.'

'I think it confused him. He told me they were calling that night 'Make a Muslim Pay Night'. That was their cute little felonious nickname for it. Figuring somebody had to pay for what happened to Vince. Now it turns out they should've been taking it out on some blond-haired, blue-eyed American family. Apparently Vince's death at the hands of the enemy was the one thing he could really hold on to in all this. Made him feel justified.'

'Maybe it's not confusion. Maybe he really gets it now. That it's not all so black and white.'

Michelevsky snorted laughter. 'I wouldn't go that far. Kerricker's a pretty basic thinker. I looked into his eyes a couple times and didn't see anything quite so nuanced. Anyway. Now we got a situation on our hands. Because his statement this morning is pretty much exculpatory for a certain blood-relative of yours we all know and love. Wouldn't be for somebody else. But for someone with Ben's . . . capacity . . . '

'What did Chris tell you?'

'He still claims he wasn't a key player, but at least he admits Ben wasn't, either. He says he stayed pretty far back — him, Chris, not him, Ben — too far back to hear most of what was said, but he saw Jespers pour the gasoline, and he wasn't liking the turn of events so well by then. I think he didn't know the night was about to go in quite that heavy a direction. So he was just about to take off. But then he saw what happened. He says Ben didn't exactly *throw* the match. He said it was more like Ben *dropped* the match. Jespers hands it to him, and keeps badgering him to do it, but Ben isn't doing it, so then Jespers kind of . . . you know . . . barks at Ben. And it makes Ben nervous, and when Ben gets nervous he gets clumsy. You know that as well as anyone.'

'Oh, my God,' I said. 'That *so* totally sounds like Ben.'

Finally. Finally a version of events that made sense.

'That's what we all thought. So now we have a bit of a problem. This could spring your brother.'

'*Could?* Why *could?* Why not *will?*'

'Well. I think it's still up to the doctor in charge. I could actually be wrong about this, because I haven't run it all by them, yet. And this is the first we ever had one of these around here. This could take some looking into. But I think somebody at the hospital would still have to certify that he's no danger to himself or others. Granted, this was the only thing we had on paper to say he was. So let's just say if the doctors and the hospital employees haven't seen anything to suggest otherwise . . . I can't say for a fact it'll go this way. Like I say. It'll take some looking into. A little legal sorting. But, now, let's just say he gets sprung, which could happen. Here's the problem. What the hell are we supposed to do with him?'

'That's not a problem. I'll come get him.'

I swung my feet over the edge of the bed. Looked around for my shoes. Then I realized it would take days to tie up the paperwork. And that Ben was in Kansas, not down in the lobby.

'Ben in New York? That'll be some kind of transition. That, I'd like to see.'

'I bet he'll like it better than where he is now.'

'I'm just glad it's you making the transition with him, and not me. That's all I've got to say.'

20 December 2001

The woman behind the desk at the state hospital got talky with me all of a sudden. Which was odd. She never had before. Maybe it made a difference that my status had just changed. I was no longer next of kin to one of the dangerous loonies she helped incarcerate. My next of kin had proven well short of dangerous. And besides, he'd been officially released. We were just waiting for him to be brought out.

'So, did you fly out here?'

'No!' I said. As if she'd asked me if I'd just jumped off a tall building or through a ring of fire.

'I don't blame you. Nobody wants to fly now. My friend in LA took a plane. She's cavalier. She says they're watching airports more than any place, so it's safer than most other things. But you know what she told me? They have soldiers in uniform at the LA airport. Standing by the security checkpoints, holding AK-47s. Soldiers. Like a GD war zone. That would freak me out way too much. So how did you get here?'

'I drove my mom's old car again. I have no idea how many more miles it's got in it, but I took it for a checkup and a service, and it seems OK. I really hated to drive all this way again. I just drove home a few days ago. But I didn't like my chances of getting Ben on a plane anyway. I can think of a dozen parts of the experience that could freak him out. Besides, I don't even know if he has a picture ID.'

'Oooh. I never thought of that.'

The big door buzzed, then popped open. Ben emerged, accompanied by a psych tech I'd never seen before.

'Hey, Buddy,' I said.

In typical Ben fashion, he raised his head to look at me, but missed by a mile.

'Did you come to take me home?'

So here was my moment. I'd had more than two full days on the road to negatively anticipate this moment.

Now I had to tell him that the only house he ever remembered living in was being sold. That all of his belongings were gone. Because I'd allowed them to be sold or disposed of. I had to tell him he was going with me to a new place, and would never again see the town he'd lived in all his life. That every routine he'd ever clung to was gone. That every moment of his life would be unfamiliar from here on out. My only mitigating factor was the hope that all of this would be better than where he'd just been. Still, this was going to be one hell of a tantrum.

I remembered Michelevsky saying he was glad it was me making this transition with Ben, not him. Just for a split second I wished I was Nick Michelevsky.

'Here's the thing, Buddy. I am and I'm not. I'm here to take you out of this place. But we're not going to the home you know. We're going to *my* home. It'll be a new home to you.'

Then I waited for it.

'Will you be there, Buddy?'

'Yeah. I will.'

'That's fine,' he said. 'Let's go.'

★ ★ ★

We were on Interstate Route 35 toward Kansas City. Looking to pick up the 70 into Missouri. In other words, we'd been on the road a while.

Ben had been silent. Absolutely silent. Just looking out the window, but not aimlessly. Really looking. In whatever direction there was something to be seen.

Finally he said, 'I didn't know all this was here.'

'What, the world?'

'All this.'

He looked around some more. For a couple more miles.

'Is it a good thing to be seeing it now?'

'It's fine.'

'You seem different.'

He looked in my direction. His gaze made it about as far as the gauges on the dashboard.

'Different how?'

'You seem quiet.'

'It was too noisy in the hospital. I hate that. I like it quiet.'

Then he went back to looking out the window.

★ ★ ★

369

Ben fell asleep somewhere in Missouri. Slept most of the way into Kentucky. I'd purposely struck a southern route because the interstate was snowy and slick in places.

Somewhere on the home side of Louisville, I needed sleep, too. So I took an exit with four lodging signs, and cruised around until I saw the word 'vacancy'. I parked in their lot and shook Ben by the shoulder.

'Come on, Buddy. Let's get us a room.'

But it was absolutely impossible to wake him. No matter how many times I shook him, he kept snoring lightly.

I got out and walked around to the passenger's side, and opened his door. I let his seat down. All the way back. Nearly flat. So he'd be more comfortable. Then I got back in on the driver's side and did the same with my own.

What could I do? I couldn't leave him in the parking lot by himself.

I think I dozed for about an hour before my cell phone rang, snapping me awake again.

I shook the sleep out of my head, and answered on the second ring.

'Hello?'

I learn.

'Oh, good,' my favorite voice said. 'You're there.'

'Well,' I said. 'I'm somewhere.'

'Where are you?'

'Kentucky.'

'What are you doing in Kentucky?'

'I have to tell you something.'

370

Something that could ruin everything. Something that probably *would* ruin everything. I kept hearing Chris Kerricker saying, 'She sure as hell won't want to spend her life with the guy who set her business on fire. Right under her hands and knees.' I'd been hearing that a lot lately. Ever since I offered to take Ben back.

'All right. Tell me.'

'I have Ben with me again.'

'Oh! You got him out of jail. That's wonderful. How did you do it?'

'Well . . . ' Needless to say, I was thrown by her reaction. 'Turns out it never really was any of his doing.'

'Of course. I knew that. Didn't you know that?'

But that proved a difficult question to answer.

It was cold in the car. I wondered if Ben was warm enough. Maybe we'd have to drive again. Just to run the heater and stay warm. I breathed out and watched my breath turn into an icy cloud.

'So you might still come back?'

'Are you still willing to pay for a ticket?'

'You know I am. I won't be home for another day. At least. But then I'll check the prices.'

'From Cairo,' she said. 'I'll travel by ground to Cairo.'

'I could just wire you enough money.'

'You could wire it to the American Express office nearest the Cairo airport.'

'When will you come?'

'That's the part I don't know.'

'Will he try to stop you?'

'Not physically. He knows I'm a legal adult. But he will try to talk me out of it. And I'll need someone to help me. I can't even pack for myself, not to mention carry heavy bags. He will try to prevent anyone from helping, but that's probably all. But all the same, I'll go when he's not around. It will break his heart. That's the biggest thing I needed to think about. If I was willing to break his heart. But then I decided . . . I decided your father raises you, and then he needs to let you go to start a family of your own. Your father is the past. Your partner is the future. It's nice to keep a good relationship with your father, but for that to happen he must tolerate the partner you choose. It's just the way life is. So I hope I can have some contact with my father. But that will be up to him.'

That stopped the conversation for a moment. I lay still in the frozen air, watching the clouds of my breath.

'I hear you say you really are coming. But I'm having trouble letting myself believe it. It feels too good to be true.'

'You know I never stopped loving you, Russell.'

'I wish I could honestly say I always knew that.'

'How did you think those feelings could go? Where did you think they would disappear to?'

I pulled a deep breath. And said it. 'I had an experience. With a woman I guess I thought I loved. Something bad happened, and she was associated with it in my head. I couldn't get the two untangled again. It did kind of seem like the feelings went away. And to answer your question, I don't know where they disappeared to. I only know they disappeared.'

'Let me ask you this, then. You say you guess you thought you loved her. That's not a very strong endorsement. Were the feelings you had for her as clear and strong as what we've felt?'

'Not even close.'

'There's your answer, then.'

'I thought you wouldn't come home if I had Ben. I let you go all over again in my head, because I thought when I told you he was here, that would be that. I thought I had to decide between the two of you if I went through with picking him up. But what else could I do? No one else will take care of him. How could I leave him in that hospital when I know he doesn't deserve to be there?'

'If you did,' she said, 'if you would, then you would not be the person I thought you were. And then I would not come back, because why try to make a life with a person who would do such a thing as that?'

'I wish I could be more like you. He's been acting weird. I can't understand it. He's been really quiet. And agreeable. He says everything's fine. At first I thought they broke his spirit. But I've been watching him. And he doesn't seem broken. He seems kind of . . . satisfied. I don't know what to make of it at all.'

'Maybe he's learned that the things he used to throw tantrums over were not as big as he thought.'

'Maybe. I was even thinking maybe he threw

tantrums because they worked on Mom. And they worked on me. But maybe when you're in with a bunch of insane criminals it takes more than just pacing and crying to get attention. Maybe he figured out he's not the center of the universe.'

'If you don't mind my saying so, you're overthinking it. Be grateful. Hope it lasts. I really hate to say this. I would talk to you all night. But I need to save some minutes on my calling card. I'll need to let you know . . . '

I wanted to ask, Are you really coming? But I knew better. She couldn't promise such a thing. She would if she could. It was better than what I'd thought I had before she called.

After we said our goodbyes, I drove for several more hours. To stay warm. And because I knew I wouldn't get back to sleep anyway.

21 December 2001

It was nearly dark again by the time we neared home.

Ben powered down the window and stuck his head out, craning his neck to see the tall buildings towering above the car.

'I never saw buildings that tall,' he said, with a slight push of volume to be heard over the wind.

I was thinking, Wait till you see Manhattan. But I wanted to spring it on him a little at a time.

'What do you think of them?'

'They're fine. Why ask them to be shorter?'

* * *

I opened the three locks on my door, and we stepped into the apartment.

'This is home now. What do you think?'

Ben was already headed for the Christmas village.

He stood in front of it with his mouth open. I locked the door. Walked around him and plugged in the power cord. I heard him suck in his breath when the lights came on in the windows of the little houses.

'Makes me think of Mom,' he said.

'Yeah. Me, too.'

'I'm sleepy. Where do I sleep?'

'I'll show you your room. I cleaned out my office for you. I hope it's OK.'

'Do I have to share it with anybody?'

'No. It's all yours.'

'Then it's fine.'

'I really have to apologize for the fact that I don't have any of your stuff. We'll just have to start buying stuff. We'll buy clothes and whatever else you need. But, here. Let me show you what you've got to work with for now.'

I led him into his new bedroom, the second bedroom that used to be my tiny home office. My office was now even tinier, shoved in the corner of my bedroom.

'Right now it's just an air mattress on the floor, but we'll get you a proper bed.'

He reached a hand down to it. Pushed it, then let it spring back.

'It's fine,' he said.

'You have this little half-bathroom of your own, and I got you soap and a toothbrush. And I put a washcloth and a hand towel in there for you. When you want to take a shower you'll have to use the big bathroom off the hall.'

'That's fine,' he said.

He pulled off his jeans and shirt and climbed into the little bed I'd made him. In his jockey shorts and undershirt. His feet hung off the end.

'Goodnight, Buddy,' he said.

'Hope you sleep well.'

'It's really quiet. I like quiet.'

Actually, it's no more quiet in Jersey City than

it is in Manhattan. You can hear the voices of people on the street all night long. You can hear the bass of car radios as they low-ride by. Car doors slamming. Car alarms going off.

But Ben was snoring a few seconds after I flipped off the lights. Before I even stopped staring and let myself out of his room.

22 December 2001

It was the following day. I woke up to find Ben sitting at my kitchen table eating breakfast cereal. As if he'd lived here all his life.

'Morning, Buddy,' he said.

I decided it was time to have a little talk. I'd put it off way too long.

'I want us to think about a memorial for Mom.'

'Memorial?'

'How do I explain a memorial? It's like a celebration. But a sad celebration. For somebody who died.'

'Is it like a funeral? Because I don't like the guns.'

'No. Nothing like that. We have a box of ashes for Mom. And we have to think about where to put them.'

'Ashes.'

'It's what's left of somebody after they die.'

'Where do *you* want to put them?'

'Well. Sometimes people sprinkle them on a place they think the person who died would like. Or did like. Sometimes people take a boat a couple miles out to sea and sprinkle them on the ocean.'

'Oh, no. I don't want Mom out there. It's too cold and wet.'

'Where do you think she should be?'

'My room.'

'Really? You want to keep Mom's ashes in your room?'

'I think so. Can I see what they're like?'

'Sure.'

I brought the box in from my room. I'd received her ashes in a heavy wooden box, vertical, about the size of a gift box for a big bottle of whiskey. Despite my not liking that analogy. It had a top that lifted off. I hadn't lifted it.

I set it on the table in front of Ben.

'Can I open it?'

'I guess.'

He worked for a moment or two on the snug-fitting lid while I wondered if this would prove to be a mistake. Then it popped off. Inside was a heavy plastic bag with a twist tie at the top. You could see the ashes clearly through the plastic. Ben looked in for a moment or two.

'That's all that's left when somebody dies?'

'Um. No. Not really. She left us the Christmas village. You said yourself it makes you think of her.'

'Anything else?'

'Yeah. Actually. You want to come see?'

He left his breakfast cereal to get soggy and followed me to the hall closet, where we took down the boxes marked BEN and RUSTY and carried them into his room.

I told him these were all the parts of us she'd saved, all our lives, and that by saving them and collecting them like this, it was almost like her love for us was all in one place, where we could still see it.

379

Right, I know. Sounds like a bad greeting card. But it seemed like a good way to present it to Ben.

'Can I open mine?'

'Sure.'

So we both started digging around in all that stuff.

It took me about an hour to realize that this was our memorial. Plowing through the ridiculous minutiae she'd treasured, observing, each at our own level, how much she must have loved us to have hung on to all that worthless crap.

23 December 2001

Anat called me at about ten in the evening, New York time.

'I almost missed my plane,' she said. 'Waiting for him to go. But I didn't. I'm on it now. But I have to talk fast. They're about to close the door, and then I'll have to hang up. 10.44 a.m. Egypt Air. LaGuardia. I'm sorry. I know Newark is better, but I couldn't get Newark. Not at the right time. Is it OK? Is it a problem?'

'It's fine. LaGuardia is fine.' I sounded like Ben. Everything is fine.

'So you'll be there. What would I do if you weren't there?'

'You sound really scared.'

'I have to go. They're closing the door.'

Then she hung up.

★ ★ ★

I sat up all night. I didn't even try to sleep. I didn't even bother to lie down. I never even closed my eyes.

24 December 2001

'This is a long . . . thing,' Ben said. 'What is this?'

'This is the Holland Tunnel.'

'Tunnel,' he said. 'Like underground?'

'Actually, it's underwater.'

Silence.

He rolled down his window and looked straight up. At the roof of the Holland Tunnel. Then he pulled his head back in again.

He said, 'I don't see any water up there.'

I said, 'Here's hoping you never do, Buddy.'

He rolled up the window, and turned to me, leveling me with a spontaneous grin. 'I can't wait to see Anat,' he said.

And something broke through in me. For days I had been watching Ben as if he were about to shatter like a china cup. Listening to him say he was fine, but unable to fathom how he could be. And so assuming he was not.

But I looked into his grinning face, and he was. I could tell.

'So you're really fine?' I asked.

'I've told you that like a million times.'

'I guess I didn't believe it.'

'Why?'

'I don't know. I guess because nothing's been fine for so long.'

'I know!' Ben said. 'Everything was so not fine in the hospital. So that's why when I got out it really was. And now with Anat coming, I'm really happy.'

'Happy,' I said. 'That's even better than fine.'

'OK. Then I won't say I'm fine any more. I'll say I'm happy.'

Which, according to my career goals, is all anybody ever really needs to be.

★   ★   ★

We were six or seven miles outside the airport. Snared up in the inevitable traffic. But it didn't matter. Because we were so early it was ridiculous.

My cell phone rang.

My heart jumped into my throat. Not literally, of course, but there's a reason behind that expression. I just hadn't known it until now.

I thought, She changed her mind. I thought, Part of me knew she would.

I looked at the incoming number. It wasn't Anat. It was someone who had never called me before. I swallowed my heart and answered.

'Hello?'

'Russell?' A man.

'Yeah. This is Russell.'

'Russell. Greg Wasserman. So, listen, Russ . . . I called to offer you that position. Unless you've already accepted something else.'

'I haven't. I accept. Happily.'

'Good. Welcome to Wasserman & Tate. I won't lie. You got a lot of points for being Hatcher,

Swift & Dallaire. Not to say you weren't a good applicant. But we all talked it over and we felt like, since God knows we can't do anything for the rest of your people . . . '

'I'll try to make it seem like a good decision.'

'We're not worried. Stan Harbaugh speaks highly of you. I'm sure you'll work out fine. I put a stack of paperwork in the mail to you. Any questions, let me know. Otherwise first business day of the new year. Nine a.m. sharp.'

'I'll be there. Thanks.'

And we clicked off the call.

'Who was that?' Ben asked.

'My new boss.'

'You didn't tell me you had a new boss.'

'I didn't know. Until just now. Until he called.'

'Is that good?'

'That's very good. We're about to have a lot more money. Maybe we could move into Manhattan. Maybe we could hire a full-time housekeeper to be your new buddy. What would you think about that?'

'That would be fine,' Ben said. 'I mean, I'd be happy if we did that.'

★   ★   ★

It was the first time I'd met anybody at the airport post-9/11.

You didn't get to meet them at the gate any more. And probably we'd never get that back again. Life just rolls on, adjusting to whatever was subtracted.

Ben and I staked out a spot at the edge of the

384

baggage claim area, right on the front lines, where limo drivers held up their signs, flagging people by their printed names.

I paced. Ben held still.

'Why are you so nervous?' he asked. 'A minute ago you were happy.'

I opened my mouth to explain. And saw her. I saw her moving with the crowd. Scanning with her eyes. Until she locked on to me.

She was dressed more traditionally than I'd ever seen her, in a long skirt and something that looked like several wrapped layers on top. Her hands were too white, and too thick. I couldn't tell if they were bandaged, or if she was wearing protective gloves. Or if they just looked like that. She was still too far away.

I knew a lot of things at once. Too many things, really. They stretched the inside of my chest until it hurt.

I knew it might be a shock when I saw the extent of her burns. I also knew it would ultimately change nothing. However she was now would be however she was, and we would deal with it. I knew she might not get along with Ben at close range. Or they might be instant family. I knew she might not get along with *me* at close range. Or we might get married, have two children and live happily ever after. I knew Nazir might come around and come for a visit, or he might never speak to us again. He might even reject his own grandchildren in his rage.

And I knew that my only way through this mass of simultaneous future outcomes was to hold tight to the idea that it was possible to get to OK from where we were now. Not assured. Just possible.

She walked up to me — us — and stood face to face with me, our noses about six inches apart. We looked into each other's eyes, unsure half-smiles on both of our faces.

'There he is,' she said.

We do hope that you have enjoyed reading this large print book.

Did you know that all of our titles are available for purchase?

We publish a wide range of high quality large print books including:
Romances, Mysteries, Classics
General Fiction
Non Fiction and Westerns

Special interest titles available in large print are:
The Little Oxford Dictionary
Music Book
Song Book
Hymn Book
Service Book

Also available from us courtesy of Oxford University Press:
Young Readers' Dictionary
(large print edition)
Young Readers' Thesaurus
(large print edition)

For further information or a free brochure, please contact us at:
Ulverscroft Large Print Books Ltd.,
The Green, Bradgate Road, Anstey,
Leicester, LE7 7FU, England.
Tel: (00 44) 0116 236 4325
Fax: (00 44) 0116 234 0205

Other titles published by
The House of Ulverscroft:

DON'T LET ME GO

Catherine Ryan Hyde

Ten-year-old Grace knows that her mom loves her, but her mom loves drugs too. There's only so long Grace can fend off the 'woman from the county' who is threatening to put her into care. Her only hope is Billy. Grown man Billy Shine hasn't left his apartment for years. People scare him. And so day in, day out, he lives a perfectly orchestrated, silent life within his four walls. Until now . . . Grace bursts into Billy's life with a loud voice and a plan to get her mom clean. But it won't be easy, because they will have to take away the one thing her mom needs most . . .

SECOND HAND HEART

Catherine Ryan Hyde

Vida is nineteen, very ill, and has spent her short life preparing for her death. But a new chance brings its own story, because for Vida to live, someone has to die. Meanwhile, Richard has just lost his beloved wife in a car accident. He hasn't even begun to address his grief, but feels compelled to meet the girl who inherited his wife's heart. Then, in hospital, Vida sees Richard and immediately falls in love. Of course he dismisses her as a foolish child. But is she? Can two people be bound by a *Second Hand Heart*?

WHEN I FOUND YOU

Catherine Ryan Hyde

When Nathan McCann discovers a newborn baby boy half-buried in the woods, he assumes he's found a tiny dead body. But then the baby moves and, in one remarkable moment, Nathan's life is changed forever. The baby is sent to grow up with his grandmother, but Nathan is compelled to pay her a visit. He asks for one simple promise — that one day she will introduce the boy to Nathan and tell him, 'This is the man who found you in the woods.' Years pass and Nathan assumes that the old lady has not kept her promise, until one day an angry, troubled boy arrives on his doorstep with a suitcase . . .

THE SNOW CHILD

Eowyn Ivey

November, 1920. Jack and Mabel have staked everything on making a fresh start in a homestead 'at the world's edge' in the Alaskan wilderness. But as the days grow shorter, Jack is losing his battle to clear the land, and Mabel can no longer contain her grief for the baby she lost years before. The evening the first snow falls, their mood unaccountably changes. In a moment of tenderness, the two build a snowman — or rather a snow girl — together. Next morning, all trace of her has disappeared . . . yet there, in dawn's light, running through the spruce trees — Jack can't shake the notion that he glimpsed — a child? And how to explain the little but very human tracks Mabel finds at the edge of their property?

SECRET OF THE SANDS

Sara Sheridan

It is 1833 and the British Navy is engaged in surveying the coastline of the Arabian Peninsula. Young and ambitious, Lieutenant James Wellsted is determined that his Navy career will be a path to glory. His plans go awry when two of his shipmates go missing while gathering intelligence and Wellsted must mount a daring rescue. Slavery is still rife throughout Arabia. Zena, a headstrong Abyssinian beauty, torn from her village, is now being offered for sale in the market of Muscat. However, her fortunes change when she finds herself the property of the Lieutenant. She must accompany him on his hazardous mission, little knowing the fate that awaits them. Each will be forced to make a choice — one that will change their lives forever.